GREAT BRITISH HORROR VI

ARS GRATIA SANGUIS

Great British Horror VI
Ars Gratia Sanguis

Edited by
Steve J Shaw

**BLACK
SHUCK
BOOKS**

First published in Great Britain in 2021 by
Black Shuck Books
Kent, UK

Set in Caslon by WHITEspace
www.white-space.uk

Cover design and interior layout © WHITEspace, 2021

978-1-913038-71-7

In remembrance of the thousands.
Family, friends and strangers.

Untitled (Cloud of Blood)

Brian Evenson

In late December, after the suicide of my father, without consulting my mother who, long institutionalized, could not be counted on to give rational counsel, I made the decision to sell every painting in my father's house, all the art he had acquired over the last half century. I made this decision despite there being, in truth, only one painting for which I felt I absolutely must acquire a new owner before I began to think of myself as that new owner. Yet it was better, so I reasoned, to sell them all. That way, the painting would not realize it was being singled out.

The painting in question had always hung above the mantel in the formal dining hall of Sallowe, the drafty dwelling that had formerly served as our country house and was now all that remained of the family estate. I have no knowledge as to when or where my father purchased the painting. Indeed, I do not even know if he purchased the painting at all. Perhaps he received it as a gift or even won it playing cards. As far as I could remember it had always been there, an anomaly in the house, resembling, as it hung above our mantel, nothing so much as a great cloud of blood.

It was my father's favorite painting – though perhaps *favorite* is the wrong word. Shall we say, rather, it was the painting my father was most drawn to, the one with which he had the deepest relationship? Indeed, if I came down from my bedroom late at night, I would often find my father in the dining hall, stationed as if frozen on the meticulously shining parquet floor, staring deeply into the painting. Sometimes, too, he would speak to it, and then pause, seemingly awaiting an answer – though he would immediately stop this activity whenever he noticed my presence.

It was a large squarish painting, nearly as tall as a man and equally wide. The painting had no title, none that I knew anyway. When the removal service arrived to pack and wrap it for shipment to the gallerist in Birmingham, I obliged them to be the ones to lift the painting off the wall – I did not care to touch it. I had, after all, seen what it had done to my mother, and had noticed, too, that in all the years I had watched my father in apparent communion with it, I had never seen him touch it until the night just before his suicide. I did insist the workmen wear gloves, ostensibly so as to limit damage to the painting or its frame, but in actuality as a safeguard for the workmen themselves.

Before they wrapped the painting, I required them to hold it upright while I stationed myself behind it. Stooped slightly, careful not to touch the painting proper, I slit the brittle kraft paper backing the frame then cut portions of it away with my razor knife. *With all respect, sir, you don't want to be doing that,* grumbled the removals foreman. *Lessens the value.* When I ignored him, he shrugged, muttered something under his breath, and gave up. Beneath, the reverse of the painting proved rather messy: the canvas had been haphazardly and irregularly fastened to its stretchers with tacks of all sizes and of every variety. The mist-like spray that covered the front of the painting continued around onto the canvas tacked to the stretchers and, surprisingly, was on the reverse of the canvas as well, as if the painter had for some reason chosen to paint even the side of the canvas never meant to be seen. Upon this back of the canvas, among the mist there, the artist seemed to have tested his brushes: a series of firm regular lines, in deep red, six lines in all, stood in the upper left quadrant. They had almost the appearance of tally marks.

"Very good," I said, and straightened. "You may continue."

They did so, the foreman still mumbling under his breath. I stepped slowly away, gradually drifting to the far side of the hall where I waited in abeyance until the removers had wrapped the painting thoroughly, heaved it up, and carried it out of the house. I watched from the hall windows as they loaded it and the other paintings into their truck. I was still watching when, at last, they drove away.

The last time I had seen the reverse of the painting – the only other time I had seen it – had been when I was very young indeed. A decision had been made to repaper the walls of the formal dining hall. I do not know for certain who it was who made this decision, my mother or my father, though I suspect the former. Indeed, at least in my memory, I seem to remember my father anxiously hovering, a kind of panic threatening to rise and take possession of his face, as the papering commenced. On that occasion, I watched the proceedings from just behind the baize door that hid the passage running most directly to the kitchen, holding the door ajar just a crack. Just as I would do with the removers three decades later, my father insisted the paperers be the ones to lift the painting off the wall. Under his direction, they leaned it against the dining room table, leaving its reverse exposed.

Then, once the workers were back on their ladders and distracted with scoring and soaking the old wallpaper, I watched my father slit the paper backing crosswise, then vertically. With a spare pair of driving gloves he extracted from his jacket pocket, he pulled back the upper left quadrant of paper, staring long and hard at what lay underneath.

But then, abruptly, agitatedly, he fled the room.

The workmen, busy with the walls, were paying him little mind. After a moment's hesitation, I came out from behind the shelter of the baize door and made for the painting.

It was but the work of a moment for me to lift what remained of the backing paper myself and see what it was that had so interested my father. I saw, simply, the back of the canvas, colored just as the front with the exception of the series of firm, regular lines, four in all, deep red, that had been marked in the upper left quadrant. I could not see why my father had felt the need to stare at them for so long.

A moment later, I heard the clearing of a throat behind me. I turned to find my father standing there, a roll of kraft paper in his arms. I stepped back. As was my father's way, he did not scold me; indeed, he did little beyond that initial clearing of the throat to acknowledge I was even there. Soon, he had a workman down from his ladder and had convinced the man to tear off what remained of the old cut backing, measure and cut a piece of kraft paper to replace it, and then use wallpaper glue to affix it to the sides of the frame.

Here is what I cannot be sure of: was the backing I slit years later the same backing that I saw applied that day? I believe it was – there was an irregular corner that I seem to remember in the backing I had seen applied that day and that I could still see years later. And yet I must concede that there was ample opportunity in the thirty years that followed for my father to have replaced it. Or, say, in the first decade of those thirty years: the paper I slit was sufficiently brittle and discolored that I could not believe it to have been applied more recently than that.

And yet, every time I turn it over in my mind, I remain thoroughly convinced that it was the same backing I had seen applied when I was a boy. Which makes it all the more disturbing that when I slit the backing myself I now found not four red hashmarks, not even five. There were six.

I received a letter from the gallerist, as he preferred to be called, acknowledging receipt of my paintings. He expressed excitement at the prospect of selling them, along with barely concealed surprise I had not chosen a dealer based in London. There seemed little point in sending a reply to this. A few days later, a second letter arrived from him in which he enclosed a potential price list for the paintings, detailed the gallery's commission and fees, and proposed as well that I drive down to Birmingham for the day so we could discuss details of the hanging and formulate copy for a catalog. I wrote back asking him to lower the prices by 20% to facilitate rapid sale and indicated I would leave the matter of cataloging entirely to him: he should feel no need to consult me about any of these minor details.

I believed that to be the end of the matter, and indeed for all the paintings except for one it was. But about this painting he wrote me a third letter. *Was it true*, he asked, *that there was in fact no title for* – and here he proceeded to describe what could only be the painting I have characterized as resembling a cloud of blood – *or was it simply that I did not know the title? And how curious that it was painted on both sides!*

I chose to send no reply.

A few weeks later he wrote yet again to ask if the untitled painting might not be, was it at all possible, a late, admittedly minor, Turner? There was a certain similarity in the way the light of the setting sun was conveyed, he claimed. If there was some way of tracing provenance, it would mean the painting was worth a great deal more than he had initially estimated. It would not be unheard of, he claimed, for a painting of similar quality to have been kept sequestered for years within the walls of a West Midlands family house only to suddenly reappear. Would I please examine my father's papers to see if there was anything to be found?

To this letter I did write back. *I will not*, I said, *examine my father's papers, since the idea that that painting is by Turner is ludicrous. Furthermore, it is clear to me that what you perceive to be a hazy sunset is in fact a cloud of blood, resembling nothing so much as the spatter my father left on the wall above his bed in the aftermath of his suicide. You shall oblige me by listing the painting for the price previously discussed, without any allusion to Turner in the catalog copy. If you cannot see your way to following my wishes in this, trust that I shall secure another representative.*

Perhaps not surprisingly, I did not hear back from him again.

I did, however, eventually, weeks later, receive a letter from someone claiming to be his wife, a letter which included a not-insubstantial cheque. She apologized for not writing sooner about my father's paintings, and expressed concern that she had had no inquiries from me about them in the meantime. She would perhaps have been surprised to know that I had thought of her and her husband's gallery, and of my father's paintings sojourning therein, not at all. I had no need of money, and I had no interest in the paintings once they had been sold: I only wanted that one untitled painting out of the house.

I imagine you are curious as to how successful the gallery has been in placing your paintings, she wrote. I was not, in fact, curious at all. *You may be curious, too, as to why it is I, rather than my husband, who writes to you.* Well, yes, admittedly, I was slightly curious about that, but only slightly: had she herself not raised the issue I would simply have assumed that her husband was the public face of the gallery while she was the person behind the scenes who handled the bookkeeping and the dispersal of cheques. But despite this slight curiosity, the last thing I expected was for her to continue on in her letter to reveal to me that her husband was, in fact, suddenly, unexpectedly, dead.

I came very close to telephoning this woman I had never met to quiz her down on the circumstances of her husband's death, but, in the end, propriety stayed my hand. Instead, I called the office of the *Birmingham Mail* and allowed myself to be shuttled from underling to underling until I was foisted upon someone who was able and, more importantly, willing to look up the gallerist's obituary and read it to me over the telephone.

It wasn't that the obituary said anything specific about the gallerist's death. Rather, it was all that it very deliberately chose *not* to say that convinced me that the gallerist, like my father, had committed suicide.

But I am getting ahead of myself. This telephone call came later, after I had finished reading the letter from the gallerist's wife. The only thing that truly interested me about the letter, the fact that her husband was unexpectedly dead, had been mentioned almost in passing, and nearly immediately she was on to other things. *The shop, unfortunately, is to be shuttered: it was always more my husband's passion than my own.* Still, she was *pleased to inform you that between the two of us before his passing we managed to place your paintings. Or nearly so: one remains unsold, despite my husband having an especial fondness for it and holding it in the highest regard. This painting I have had returned to you.*

Early that evening the crate containing the unsold painting arrived at Sallowe. There was no doubt in my mind as to which painting it was, but I still felt compelled to make sure. I pried at the crate until the top was off and I had revealed that familiar rendering of a great cloud of blood.

I had begun to close the crate again when a thought struck me. I went to the other side of the crate and, careful to touch only the frame, began to lift the painting free. I lifted it until the jagged edge of the torn paper backing was revealed, then lifted it further still, until I could clearly see the row of hashmarks. They were just as I remembered them – or so I initially thought. After a moment I felt less certain. Though my arms began to shake from holding the painting suspended by its frame, I began to count them. One. Two. Three. Four. Five. Six. Seven.

That night, I dreamt of how the gallerist died. I had never met the fellow, never seen him, which perhaps explains why in this dream he did not possess a face. But being able to give a reason for the blank surface that existed there instead made it no less unsettling.

This faceless man, this art dealer who called himself a *gallerist* and who had perhaps enjoyed a few years in one of the outer boroughs of London before again being exiled to his hometown of Birmingham, was in his gallery, which I had never seen and which was, perhaps as a result, a windowless, expressionless white cube. I do not know where his wife was: only he chose to appear in my dream, perhaps because he was the only one of the pair of them that was dead. He was alone.

Or, rather, not alone exactly, but not with someone either. He was in his blank gallery, his head devoid of a face yet somehow still staring at a painting on the wall, a painting which resembled nothing so much as a great cloud of blood.

Yet he wasn't merely staring. He had positioned his hands lightly just above the surface of the canvas itself and was moving them slowly back and forth as if caressing the air just above the painting's surface. And then, as I watched, he dropped his hands and moved his absent face closer and closer to the canvas until, finally, his head pushed through the surface and disappeared inside. And then, headless, smoothly and bloodlessly terminated at the neck, his body collapsed to the floor.

I woke up late, feeling groggy. I slowly dressed and went down to the kitchen, foraged in the larder for the remains of a loaf of bread. I cut the last slivers of ham off the bone suspended from the hook in the ceiling. I reheated yesterday's insipid tea, an act which, as it turned out, made it even less sipid.

I sat at Cook's table and ate, ruminating, staring at the place where Cook had sat for so many years. There were slightly shinier patches on the table's surface where she had rested her elbows year after year, until, like my father, she was gone. And yet I could still see her there, and not, all at once.

I thought of the other rooms of the house, of the absent bodies I associated with them. Of the gardener and the way he used to reluctantly amble to the kitchen door, hat gripped anxiously before him with both hands, and wait to be invited in. Of my mother, tall and glittering as a jewel, coming to perch elegantly on the edge of my childhood bed to bid me goodnight. Of my father standing in the dining room, open-mouthed, staring at that great cloud of blood that would eventually take him. Not ghosts exactly, but presences nonetheless.

All dead now. Except for my mother, that is, who, though not dead, was hardly functional, not likely ever to leave the facility to which she had been confined. *I should visit her*, I told myself, and knew that this was true, that I should, but also that it was not likely I ever would.

Did I blame my father for my mother's condition? No. Instead, I blamed the same thing for her institutionalization that I blamed for his death. I knew it was not my father who had grabbed her hand and forced her delicate fingers to touch that cloud of blood – even though, yes, in another sense it had been. But my father had not been himself at the time. He was only doing the bidding of that great cloud of blood.

I dumped my leavings in the rubbish bin and left the kitchen, departing a different way than I had come, down the narrow and darkened and unadorned passageway that I knew by heart. I would sell the house, I told myself as I walked. It was, after all, far too big for a solitary individual such as myself. I did not belong here. And then I came to the green baize door. Cracking it open, I peered out into the formal dining hall.

Shall I tell you what I expected to see? For a brief moment I felt I was in the past, a young child in short pants again, and that I was about to come upon my father staring at the painting. But this moment passed very quickly. Did part of me expect to see the painting hanging in its usual place over the mantel? Well, yes, in fact. After all, for decades, until very recently, it had always hung there. And so, just for a moment, I was not surprised to see it hanging there. Until I remembered that, now, it should not be, that I had never lifted it out of its crate.

But it *was* hanging there, shimmering slightly, so that, as I stared, it began to appear that the cloud of blood was not on the canvas at all but hovering slightly before it. I was, I confess, tempted to reach out and brush my fingers against it, just to assure myself the cloud was still affixed to the canvas, but I resisted. I was tempted, too, to cry out, but I mastered myself with sufficient rapidity that I do not believe the painting noticed.

I have no clear notion of how the painting was returned to the wall. I was, and still am, the only one in the house. I suppose it is possible, just, that I did it myself, in my sleep, or awake but somehow apart from myself: when I am desperate enough, anyway, I can briefly convince myself that this might have been the case. But most of the time I am convinced that the painting achieved this by its own means, that it sorted a way to work fully free of its crate and across the floor, and crawled back up the wall to regain what it considered its proper place.

What did I do? At first, nothing. I tried above all to show no fear, as one does whenever encountering a hostile dog. I tried to do nothing that would alarm the painting. I simply stared at it open-mouthed, just as I had seen my father do. Or rather, stared into it, for it felt as though I were entering into some sort of compact with it. As I stared, I could feel myself falling deeper and deeper into the painting, and the cloud expanding, leaving the canvas to stain the entire room. The painting had, I realized, decided on its new owner, and that new owner was me.

With a great exertion of will, I broke the painting's gaze and turned away. Then, as nonchalantly as possible, I began to lay the fireplace for a fire. I had to strike a dozen matches before I managed to get one that would stay alight. It had almost burned to my fingers before the kindling feebly began to glow, but at last it caught. Once the blaze was finally roaring, with eyes closed I reached up, grabbed hold of the painting and threw it into the fire. This was, I was convinced, the only way that I could save myself.

But I had made a mistake, an irreparable one. I should never have believed that I could destroy the cloud of blood. I began to cough. By burning the painting, I had merely managed to transmute it from one form to another, to a form more ethereal and less fixed, less subject to restraint. For in burning the painting I breathed its smoke in, and by doing so brought the painting inside of me.

Now I am coughing up blood. For the moment it comes in darkened clots, great thickened gouts of it, and then I am given a respite and it comes not at all. But I know soon the clots will smooth and diminish in size and disperse. There will come a day when there will be no respite, when with every breath I shall breathe a cloud of blood, propagating the painting within my flesh and spreading it upon every surface that surrounds me.

I have nearly finished all that I have to tell. Once I do, I can see no choice but to follow in the footsteps of my father. I will finish this account then I will screw the cap onto my pen, climb the stairs to my father's bedroom, remove his pistol from the drawer of the nightstand, and make an end to myself. Will that stop the cloud? I do not know. I hope so, but I cannot be certain. If I am being honest, I doubt it.

I leave these words as a warning to whoever finds me, as a caution. Do not, whatever else you do, touch my corpse. Treat it as you would the most precious of paintings. Handle it with kid gloves, with care, and then, once your respirator is firmly affixed, burn it until nothing whatsoever remains.

From Life

Muriel Gray

She'd worried that the lights in the studio would make him go off on one. In fact, Kim had bitten her thumb nail down to the quick with worry and it had bled.

But when they got there Darren hadn't bothered about the lights. He hadn't screamed. He hadn't curled into a ball, fallen to the floor and kicked, or hidden his face in her breasts. He'd just stared at the handsome boy with tufty hair, wearing a shiny suit, who was standing across the other side of the studio waiting to do the weather.

When they'd sat down, he'd waved cheerfully across at Darren and Darren just stared back. The weather boy pretended to be busy as he waited for his turn. Most people gave up on Darren after one try.

The couch was hard foam. Not soft and comfy. It smelt of cleaning fluid. They started filming without mentioning it.

"Now, it's true," said the lovely girl presenter who'd welcomed them in, "that he'd never seen Kelvingrove art gallery? Not even once?"

The presenter was beautiful to Kim. She was round, like a peach. Not fat. Just all health and plumpness, with shiny hair and perfect skin, but with so much make up on you could scratch your name in it with a matchstick.

"No. We were just passing. On the bus. Just the once."

The presenter nodded. Smiling. Encouraging Kim to say more.

"Upstairs. He likes up the stairs. He just keeked over it at. Like I say. Just the once."

The presenter turned to the camera.

"Well let's have a look at the absolutely amazing drawing Darren did when he got home that day."

The screen behind them filled with his work.

There it was. In pencil. An almost unbroken, confident line following the bewildering complexity and undulations of the huge red sandstone, Hispanic-baroque edifice that dominated the heart of Glasgow. Ornate towers were rendered in perfect perspective. Every carved detail, every pillar and architrave, every etched window arch and loftily perched statuary, all captured by masterly draughtsmanship. Not a line had been altered. No hesitation or smudging. Perfect.

Darren had started to moan a little. Begun to rock gently. Kim stretched a hand out to him but knew better than to touch. The peach presenter looked nervous.

"Now this is Darren Lynch, the young artist behind this wonderful drawing."

Her smiling face morphed seamlessly into a chat show mask of sympathy. Head cocked to the side.

"Kim. Darren has severe learning difficulties, is that right?"

Kim stroked her son in the air, inches from his skin.

"Yes. Darren has very high spectrum autism. And… some other difficulties." As the presenter's eyes began to betray that acidic broth mix of pity and disgust that Kim knew so well, she added:

"But he loves his drawing. Loves it."

"Well that really is the most amazing thing. And you're sure he does it all from memory, or did you maybe have pictures of the building at home?"

"No. He looks at something the once and that's it. Then he just…"

Darren's whine was getting louder.

"…he just remembers it. All of it."

"So Darren. You're ten years old now. When did you first start to draw?"

Then the presenter had made the mistake. She leant

right forward towards him, hands clasped, very close. The smile was all wrong for a start. Far too many teeth.

They got another taxi to take them home. On account. A real treat since the television studios were three bus rides away. The driver was very understanding about what was happening, told them several times he had the contract back in the day to carry 'the disabled kids' but Kim glanced back when they got to their block and watched him get out of his cab and go to check the back to see if it needed cleaning.

Darren couldn't handle being in lifts and Kim had given up asking the council to move them, but the nine flights of stairs weren't so bad when you didn't have shopping bags. Happily, the McCredies weren't sitting on the stair landing at floor six, looking for trouble. That was always difficult. The wee shites.

After she'd got him settled, given him his medicine, his sketchbook and pencils, put his headphones on and found *The Aristocats* on his iPad, she opened a family size packet of crisps and went online, to speak to the only people she really knew.

Marnie P asked her how it had gone, and she said fine. Though Kim said she wished now she hadn't posted the picture of Kelvingrove that had led to the interview on Facebook, because Darren had kicked off. But then there had been the taxi rides and a day out of sorts. She thought their bit would go out on tonight's news. On the Scottish news, after the big news. The girl who had got them the taxi told her it might not though, if anything else happened that was more important.

Marnie P said she'd look out for it. Then there was a lot of talk about a famous person's daughter who'd killed herself, but Kim didn't know who she was so she went to look on Ebay to see if anyone had bought her handbag. Nobody had.

Darren had made a drawing. Of course, it wasn't the weather boy in the suit he'd been staring at. It was the inside and outside of the taxi. Every perfect detail, even though he'd spent most of both journeys with his head buried in Kim's lap, kicking and thrashing. There in pencil was the drivers' taxi licence card and photo hanging on the dashboard. It has his number and name. Thomas Calder. The back of his head showed he was going a little bald and the label of his jumper was sticking out his collar. There was a piece of litter on the floor. A receipt. £4.50 from a coffee shop somewhere.

Darren had finished, so Kim lifted the page off the floor where he'd dropped it and put it with the others. He'd been a very good boy. She kissed his head, his sweet, sweet head, and told him how much she loved him.

She held his face in her hands. His front teeth were crooked and broken, never fixed after a bad fall aged five. The rest had grown round the cracks like coral, shaping his overly wide mouth into a gaping maw instead of the smile she knew he was always trying to make. One eye stared forever to the left and the other darted as though following an invisible moth. This was the face she loved and had loved ever since his broken little body came into her world ten years ago. It was her fault that Darren was in the world. It was also her joy. He was all she had. To Kim he was perfect.

Darren rocked and hugged himself. She went to microwave their dinner.

She knew what going viral meant, but it was still a shock. She hadn't been able to watch TV last night because Darren had a fit and she had to hold him down until it passed and give him his medicine in the way he hated. Kim was used to sleeping where and when she could, which was only when Darren was asleep. He'd stayed awake moaning and hitting himself until 4.30 am and then she managed a few hours, still in her clothes, lying beside his bed on the floor.

Nobody texted her or phoned her, because Kim and Darren didn't know anyone here except the social worker and their GP. They were the only two contacts on her list. But when she went online while Darren was having his lemon cake and eggs her pulse started thumping in her throat. Everyone was talking about them. Everyone. People in America even. It was all mostly nice but some of it was the worst things she'd ever seen. Calling Darren names even the McCredies hadn't come up with.

She switched off her phone and went back to sleep with her head on the table while Darren hit her gently on the arm with the last bread roll.

Later, when her phone started to ring and ping and make noises she'd never heard before, she guessed that the lady from the TV studio, who'd had her number in case the taxi didn't come, must have given it out.

She answered the first one, a young woman from London who wanted them in her newspaper. Then another from a man at an Australian radio station. She didn't answer the phone again. Then people came to the door. Horrible people. Men in puffer jackets with cameras, and young women in sculpted woollen coats, all asking to see Darren, and trying to make Kim say something.

She closed the curtains and didn't answer anything again.

Marnie P said not to worry, because these things didn't last very long. That people trend for a very short time and it would be ok.

She was right. By the end of the week nobody talking about Darren and how amazing he was at drawing, because someone in the government had stolen some money and been caught, and a homemade bomb had been found on a cross channel ferry.

Kim checked Ebay again to see if anyone had bought her handbag, but nobody had, and the auction was over.

She wondered what else she could sell but couldn't think of anything. They were going to have to go to the shops soon to buy food, so she had to make the preparations for going out with Darren, and that would take over an hour.

It was more than six weeks since the viral thing had come and gone when the doorbell rang again. Kim hoped it wasn't the newspaper people again. Maybe someone from the council. They sometimes came unannounced, and she enjoyed it because it was company, even though it was usually bad news about the damp, the housing waiting list or something the McCredies had done and blamed Darren.

It wasn't the council. It was an elderly woman and a tall young man. Neither were remotely like the newspaper or media people who'd come calling before. They were beautifully dressed and smelt like an expensive perfumed candle. The man had a slim briefcase, and the woman carried an exquisite leather handbag. Kim wondered how much that would fetch on Ebay and understood why hers hadn't sold. So unexpected and unusual was their appearance that when they confirmed they'd come to see her and asked if they could come in Kim said yes.

Darren was in the bedroom, so she could give them tea. Kim had water because there were only two matching mugs, and she was embarrassed in front of such well turned-out guests.

"Mrs Lynch" began the man whose accent was like one of those rich foreign footballers.

"No. I'm no married. It's just…Kim."

He nodded. "Ms Lynch" he continued, and she melted a little inside a little at how polite he was. "My name is Jaques Theodor Kocher and this is my mother, Sofia Kocher."

"Hello" said Kim because she couldn't think of anything else to say.

"We have come to ask your son to draw something for us."

Kim was disappointed. She thought the viral thing had gone away. She felt foolish for being so lonely she'd let anyone in. Her tone became defensive.

"Darren doesn't do that. I'm sorry. He doesn't. That TV thing? All of it. It was a mistake."

"I understand."

"He won't draw what you tell him. He just draws… things. Things he wants to draw."

The man nodded again. The elderly lady took a sip of the tea and quickly put down the mug. She took a small silk handkerchief from her sleeve and dabbed delicately at her lips as though she had narrowly avoided poison.

"I told everyone. All the people wanted him to draw. But I told them no. He doesn't."

The man took the tea and drank it all. He gave his mother a side glance of reproach.

"This is your home Ms Lynch?"

Kim nodded, eyes down.

"Aye. For now. It's difficult to get moved. You know."

She sipped her water.

"This is actually quite a nice block" she lied.

The man looked out of the grimy window, two bars across it, to the dismal view beyond, then back at Kim and smiled. His elegance and handsomeness were having an effect on her she hadn't felt for years. It was not unpleasant.

"We are not here for a photograph of your son. Or for a small piece of news to put in a newspaper. What we are here to offer you is a future for your son. And yourself."

Kim felt tears well. The man's voice and his words, despite their bluntness, contained such authentic sympathy that something slipped beneath the wall she carefully guarded against sentiment of any kind.

"I'm sure your son would prefer a house perhaps? A garden? Somewhere safe and quiet."

She was confused now. A little frightened. She sipped more water and blinked.

"May we meet him?" said the woman. Her voice sounded a great deal older than her elegant exterior.

There was a high whining noise from the bedroom. It made Kim strong again. No longer uncomfortable. She stood. Weighed her guests up and waited a beat.

"Aye. Ok. But he's a wee bit wary of strangers."

"As are we, Ms Lynch."

Darren didn't kick off too badly. He just lay down on the floor and hit the sides of his head with his palms. But he didn't bite or hurt himself.

All three adults watched him for a few minutes.

"Does…Darren…" said the man hesitantly "…have speech?"

Kim shook her head.

"I always know how he is though. What he needs. How he's feeling. You know?" She looked at the woman.

"A mother can always tell, can't she?"

The older woman remained silent.

"Is it possible to see Darren's work?" asked the man.

Kim lit up. Proud.

"There's plenty." She got up.

"Can you just mind him a minute?"

When she returned a few moments later, the man was sitting on the floor beside Darren talking gently to him in a foreign language. German or something. She didn't know. Darren was pulling his hair and staring at the floor, but he was fine. Just fine.

The woman flicked through Darren's sketches, expressionless, and then handed them back to Kim.

"Thank you."

She nodded at the man. He stood up.

"Ms Lynch. I am going to leave this with you. It contains an offer and we'd ask you to consider it carefully."

He opened his case and handed her a large brown envelope.

The woman stood up, smoothed the skirt of her suit and shook Kim's hand.

And then they were gone. Kim washed the cups. The woman's lipstick marks on one were so lovely, with little bits of glitter in it, she felt she should leave it on. But she liked the kitchen tidy. It was something to do. She wiped the table round the brown envelope and then sat down. She would have a cup of tea now. And then she might open it.

Kim asked Jaques if she could post pictures, but he'd said no and asked if she would give him her phone to keep while they were staying.

She was disappointed. She'd only been abroad once in her 27-year-old life, and that was Spain over ten years ago, although she couldn't tell you where. It was a laugh with her friends in a hotel by the beach. Before Darren. Happy and free.

But she had never been anywhere like this. Wherever it was.

Their room had a vaulted, wood beamed ceiling and bow windows, with the prettiest window seat. It was scattered with fringed cushions sewn with pictures of harts and stags and the view from it was of a manicured garden, full of tall flowers and fruiting trees, all within an ancient wall backed by distant high snow-capped mountains.

At the corner of the garden was The Chapel. Jaques said that was where the thing to be drawn was. It looked so very old. Much older than the house, and the house was already the oldest building she'd ever seen. There were old buildings in Glasgow, but none were like this. This was like a fairytale. Odd little windows, tall chimneys and sloping roofs. Wooden lintels and ancient crooked steps leading to outbuildings where she could hear, but not see, lowing cattle, their bells tinkling. Sometimes chickens wandered across the garden and she felt she could watch them for hours.

The Chapel was built of a different stone from the house. Like stone that had been used somewhere else first and then used again. It was squat and grey, a little ugly. Its walls looked as thick as a fort and perhaps they had to be, to hold granite roof tiles the size of pavement flagstones. There were hardly any windows, but what few did exist were no more than slits. Over the last three days since they'd been here, she'd watched people coming and going through the wrought iron gate in the garden wall, back and forth from The Chapel. Sometimes they carried flowers. Sometimes baskets of food. Once a man and his daughter led a small screaming piglet across the garden and through the small ancient wooden door in the chapel. It didn't come back with them and she wondered where it had gone.

She and Darren were to stay in their room until drawing day. That was the arrangement.

It was fine by Kim. Darren wouldn't go out anyway. The journey had been traumatic, and he liked to lie beside a huge unlit fireplace under the beams and watch the light play on the ceiling, making shapes that the sun supplied by shining through the thick diamonds of old glass in the windows.

Delicious food was brought to them on a tray by a sweet silent girl who spoke no English. Even the strange things that Darren liked, and she was afraid they wouldn't be able to give him. There was a huge bathroom with a shower you could walk right under and a bath with curly legs standing on its own in the middle of a slate floor.

Kim didn't ever want to go home again. Looking out at the picture book view was more interesting than anything on her phone, and she liked seeing the people who visited and spent the day watching the light changing on the peaks of the far away mountains.

On the day after they arrived Mrs Kocher had come to see them.

She sat down on the large tapestry armchair at the end of the bed and looked at Darren, who was lying on his back playing with a baby's plastic teething ring that was his favourite toy.

"Are you both comfortable Ms Lynch?"

"Oh aye. Really comfy. This is great. Thanks again."

"Has Darren drawn since he's arrived?"

Kim laughed.

"Are you kidding? He never stops."

"May I?" Mrs Kocher gestured to the pile of paper she could see lying on the floor by Darren's bed.

Kim gathered it up and passed it over.

There were no pictures of the beautiful garden or the mountains. Not even a chicken, and she'd seen him glance at one as it pecked around under their window. They were intricate drawings of machines at the airport where they'd been taken to board the small private plane. The little trucks that drove about with steps on them. A detailed drawing of a trolley full of suitcases, the names visible on labels. And one of a woman in a side office of the airport portacabin they'd left from, who'd had a dog bed under her desk with husky puppies in it. That was Kim's favourite. She was going to keep that.

The last one was of Mrs Kocher herself. A perfect portrait. Her impassive face looking out from the car window that was parked on the runway to pick them up from their plane journey. It was not flattering. It was startlingly accurate. She looked at them all without expression then handed them back.

"His talent is fierce."

"Aye, well it's no from me" laughed Kim. "I can't draw a bath."

Mrs Kocher looked out of the pretty window and sighed through her nose.

"This is not my wish Ms Lynch. I have no desire for your son to attempt to draw what we take care of here."

Kim wiped at her nose and glanced at Darren. She was never certain if he could understand what was being said or not. He was head down, humming. Mrs Kocher, a woman with a posture as rigid as a soldier on guard, seemed to hunch a little.

"I'm sure Jacques has told you it has not been possible to capture it by photographic means?"

Kim nodded.

"Aye. The light or something?"

"But you should also know that there is great risk in capturing its image at all."

"I know Jaques told me not to ask. But is it like one of those old things you hear about in museums that crumble when you bring them into the daylight?"

Mrs Kocher looked very seriously at Kim, searching her face like a doctor trying to diagnose. Then for the very fist time since they'd met, she laughed. The woman looked about ten years younger. Her smile was radiant, and the laugh was deep, mirthful and genuine.

"No Ms Lynch. Were that so we, and all those that have gone before us, would have let the light in many, many years ago."

"I don't understand."

"If your son succeeds then what Jaques will possess is something I wish no part of. I am the last guardian, and I am tired. But please believe me when I tell you I am so very sorry you are here."

She stood up and looked across at Darren.

"You love him very much indeed."

Kim felt tears come again.

"He's the best boy there is."

"Then I pray he succeeds, survives and flourishes. And you should know that you are the mother I wish I had been."

She left quietly and Kim was alone, trying not to cry because it upset Darren. She failed.

Today was the drawing day. Soon they would be back in Glasgow, and this would seem like a dream. Kim was nervous, but she wanted to cherish it.

Jaques came for them in the afternoon just before it started to get dark. He was wearing a long coat, heavily embroidered with beautiful flowers and animals.

"That's lovely, that is" said Kim.

"Thank you" said Jaques and held his hand out to her. "It's been in the family a very long time. Many hands have repaired it."

It took her half an hour to get Darren out of the room and into the garden. She held his sketch book and pencils and he clung onto her waist and hid his face in her cardigan.

Mrs Kocher was waiting for them at the door of the chapel. She too had on a long dark coat, but hers was without embellishment. She looked like a priest.

She had been told what would happen, but Kim was still unsure. Panic rose in her chest.

"I'm not sure he'll go. There's a real chance he won't go. And if that happens, he really won't. Not without me. I'm so sorry."

"We can try Ms Lynch" said Jaques in his lovely voice, and her heart melted again.

"I can assure you Darren will be gone for no more than three minutes. Two of those will be his entrance and exit, for which you will be present."

Mrs Kocher took the paper and pencils from Kim without meeting her eye and opened the door to the chapel. Jaques held his hands out to Darren, and to Kim's surprise he took them. He turned Darren around, held him against his body, and together they backed into the darkness beyond the wooden door, like skydivers, falling.

Kim and Darren had so many new friends here. The house was small but charming. A newly-built two-bedroomed bungalow on an estate to the north west of Glasgow. It was the first time in her life she'd had her own bedroom and the neighbours were so kind, not minding when Darren made a noise and always saying hello to him in the garden.

There was the lady with a dog called Pippin on one side that Darren loved and made his gleeful wide-mouthed howling smile at whenever he saw it, and so she would bring it close so he could touch its fur and let it lick his face.

Nobody minded them at all, which to Kim was a miracle.

All these delights helped it become easier to forget about those first, almost unbearable months. It wasn't the move, the upheaval of their life. It wasn't the fact that she'd seen a glimpse of a world that was new and exciting and now had returned to the prison of her city and the eternal routine of caring. It wasn't even the loneliness that hit hard when she had given up her phone and any online communication in case she made a mistake, said a stupid thing to some stranger that would break the arrangement and put everything they had in peril. None of that.

Taking Darren's paper and pencils away had been the hardest thing she'd done.

The days and nights of his screaming, of holding him tight and calming him and trying to keep him from harming himself had made her feel a hundred years old. Those were the darkest of days when she'd wished they were back in the tower block making the best of the tiny life they had, a life that was safe and familiar. Wished she had never met the Kochers. Never made the promise that Darren would not lift a pencil to paper as long as he lived, and that Kim would never ever tell anyone about that promise. A promise that had brought from her a hollow laugh. As if she had anyone to tell.

She cried in the night, cursing herself for having shown

his drawing on the internet. Blaming herself once again for ruining their lives. Trading her son's only pleasure for the selfishness of a new house and a life away from the torment, hardness and misery that Darren had been oblivious to when he had a pencil in his hand, and a way to communicate to the world.

But as he began to calm, and their life grew a measure of routine and balance, she realised that at last she was happy. Darren was happy. Look at what they had. Neighbours, maybe someday friends. A leafy place to live where people washed their cars at the weekend. A little group of elegant shops only five minutes' walk, where people knew them and said hello. What else did you need to live your life, simply thankful for every day the sun would rise and set and that all was well?

Kim watched Darren beside her in the garden, lying on the newly laid grass, staring at the sky, and decided that life was good.

Once the summer grew hot Kim began gardening. She started with lupins and wild geraniums that the people next door had given her, and there was joy in choosing where they would go and in watching them grow.

Darren had kicked off at first when she hadn't paid enough attention to him while she was busy with plants, so once she knew he wasn't going to hurt himself she started letting him have a trowel, and together they would dig about in the neat beds.

Kim began, for the first time in her life, to make plans. Maybe someone could come in now and again and look after Darren and she could be alone to do things she wanted. A job. Perhaps she could even learn to drive, and they might get a car.

On sunny days Kim could sit even on the steps by the back door and watch Darren play without having to be by his side. It was heaven. She's given him his own little square patch of garden, made a little wooden sign with his name on it and stuck it in the ground. His smile had been so wide he soaked her top with drool as he hugged her and her heart felt twice its size.

They tried planting in it, but Darren always pulled the plants out and threw them away. No matter. She was just glad he enjoyed being there so much.

And on this, the sunniest of days, standing at the kitchen sink washing some dainty cups she'd found at the supermarket, with hearts on them like the cushions she'd liked, Darren digging away at his patch made her smile.

He had his back to her, working away. Busy as a bee. Something about his posture made Kim put down the cup. His trowel was lying in the middle of the lawn. He was still. Quiet. Hunched. Bent over the way he used to be when she knew exactly what he was doing.

Kim felt a panic ripple in her gut. She opened the back door and walked slowly down the steps. Darren turned his head slightly at the noise of her steps, then turned back to his task and hunched lower. Her walk turned to a trot.

There was no time. She was too late. Darren's garden patch was nothing but a square of parched earth. Earth he'd made into a canvas.

He was holding a stick, and Darren was drawing.

Kim's legs buckled and she slumped down beside him. She gently took the stick from the tight fist of his hand and looked into his face.

His eyes were full of tears, his face contorted in pain, but there was peace in it.

And as she let her gaze shift from the beautiful face she loved so much to the obscenity before them on the ground, the world she knew fell away from her.

Nothing was as it seemed anymore.

If anything so hideous, so filthy and unholy, so inarticulable and dark could exist in the same universe as something as beautiful as the boy who had gazed upon it and had survived to remake its image in the dry soil, then there was no God she knew, and no life worth living for any creature that would ever inhabit the earth.

What abyss could ever be deep enough to hold the horror that was now outlined by shadow in a square of scratched earth in a small garden of a Glasgow suburb?

Her bellow, that cut through the hot evening air as she clawed and scratched out the hideous lines on the soil with fingernails breaking and bleeding, was not the same animal howl she had made when Darren's life had been laid out for her by the doctors 11 years ago.

This was a grief and sorrow for the hollow promise that the world made sense. A roar of agony at this truth laid out to be seen by all mankind, revealing their world was a sham. That they skimmed on the surface of an ancient and indestructible darkness like water boatmen on a fetid pond.

It was Pippin's barking that made the neighbours call the paramedics, by which time the thick dark blood that had run like tears from Kim Lynch's eyes had dried to a crust on her cold face, and her son, hunched over her with his head in her lap, had screamed himself hoarse.

Jo Levington finished off the meeting of health professionals with a light smile and a bouquet of thankyous. Folders were closed and briefcases were filled. She was relieved. The embarrassment of how the client had slipped though their net was not going to be investigated. Kim Lynch had never presented with any major mental health issues. There was no record of her asking for help other than rehousing, but her fortunate inheritance that had bought the new house halted any questions that might have been asked about that. Conveniently that would also help pay for some of Darren's care, now he was safe.

The care home had everything he needed, and in the notes from their original social worker Jo had found that Darren had loved to draw. A brief Google had revealed that he'd been quite the celebrity only a year or so back.

Mistakes get made. They were sorry about his mother. It was often the ones who cope the best who crack the hardest, and lessons would be learned. That had been written on the whiteboard, and she was rather pleased with it as she wiped it clean in the emptied room.

She would make sure that Darren Lynch would have all he needed to find that pleasure again.

If she'd learned anything in this difficult and challenging job, it was that art is such a great healer.

Having a Benny

Sarah Lotz

They had to choose an artwork to talk about in class the next day, and because Robbie hadn't found a painting he liked yet and it was almost home time his fingers were making his worksheet wet and crinkly and his insides were going fluttery like they always did just before he had to puke.

Ms Amani clapped her hands and said, 'Five more minutes,' and then she told Jason off for running and Jason went 'Aw what? No fair Miss,' which was stupid because Ms Amani got extra strict whenever a kid answered her back. Robbie would have liked to watch Jason being told off some more, but he didn't because it was then that he saw it. Most of the paintings in the art museum were of olden day people doing things with rabbits and deer and stuff or splotches of paint that had no story to them, but Robbie could tell straightaway that this one had lots of story to it and as he walked up to it the pukey feeling went away.

The label on the wall said it was by someone called Cold War Steve which was a funny name for an artist but maybe Steve used to be in the army. Robbie knew from art class that it was called a collage as it was made up of cut out photographs of people and buildings and he recognised some of them which made him feel like the picture was meant just for him. There was Lady Lashurr who was a rapper Mum had liked and Malala Yousafzai who they'd learned about in school because Ms Amani said she was 'an inspiration to us all'. Behind the people was the Birmingham cathedral, the big mosque in town, and the Rotunda tower that everyone used to call the Smartie Tower before Smartie tubes stopped being tubes and became hexagonals. But the thing he liked most about it was a man's giant smiley head in a woolly beanie hat that was looking out from behind the Rotunda. The head made him feel warm inside and although it didn't have a body and was the size of Godzilla, instead of being freaked out by it the people in the picture looked happy, even Malala, who had lots of reasons to be freaked out because she'd been shot by some bad men who wanted her to stop saying that girls should be allowed to go to school and then she'd had to move to Birmingham.

'Like that one, do you?' a voice said, and Robbie looked away from the picture to see an old man with a shiny head standing next to him. He wasn't supposed to talk to strangers, but he thought it would be okay as the man was wearing a Birmingham Art Museum nametag that said "Jacob" which meant he was a guide and probably wasn't a pervert. To be safe he nodded instead of saying yes but the man didn't seem to mind or expect a proper answer which was good as Robbie wasn't used to people talking to him for no reason. He'd read in one of his books of animal facts that dogs could smell cancer in other dogs and "gave them a wide berth" and almost everyone treated him like he was a dog that had cancer. He didn't have cancer but when Mum had got sick with it a lot of her friends had given her a wide berth too.

But the man didn't move away which was good but also bad because he smelled of smoke like Auntie's best friend Nadia always did. 'The artist is from around here and it's a love letter to the city. Makes you proud to be a Brummie, doesn't it?'

Robbie said it did make him proud because it did in a way and then he asked the man if he knew who the head was.

'That's Benny Hawkins. He was a character in a soap opera called *Crossroads* that was filmed in the West

Midlands back in the sands of time. It was a shoddy old thing, although I reckon there are clips on YouTube if you're interested. That's why the piece is called "Benny's Babbies".'

Sometimes people's names matched their faces and this one matched the head because Benny was a kind name. And *babbies*. He liked that as well because Mum had called him her babby before she'd found out about his Imaginings and started giving him a wide berth too.

'The two artworks either side are by the same artist. These are more like his usual dark, satirically funny style.'

Robbie hadn't noticed them before because he'd been too busy looking at Benny's head. They were also collages, but they weren't as colourful as the babbies one and they *were* a bit funny but not in a ha ha happy way. One was of some politicians he knew from the Channel 4 news with their shirts off playing in a canal that had dead fish and an old shopping trolley in it. The other one was of the inside of a dirty old bus and the passengers were cut out olden day people from paintings except for one which was a photograph of Phil Mitchell out of *EastEnders* which Auntie watched sometimes if there was nothing on Netflix. But instead of being all angry and shouty like he usually was in *EastEnders*, Phil looked fed up as if the other people on the bus were too much to cope with.

'If you like these, there are loads more online. When you get home, you should ask your mum to help you Google them.'

'I can't ask my mum to do that because she's dead,' Robbie said.

The man blinked and he stopped smiling. People's faces always shut down whenever he talked about Mum being dead even though death was supposed to be natural. 'I'm sorry to hear that, son. Perhaps you could ask your dad, then.'

'I don't have one because I'm a sperm baby.'

The man made a harrumphing sound that sounded like

a mix between a cough and a laugh. 'Who's taking care of you then, son?'

'My Auntie Poll, but I won't need to ask her to help me Google them because she lets me use the laptop whenever I like as long as I promise not to chat to perverts.'

The man harrumphed again. 'I see. Right. You know, they sell copies of Benny's Babbies in the museum shop. You can get a poster of it for your room. Would you like that?'

Robbie almost said 'duh' because who wouldn't like that? but he didn't because that would be rude, so instead he told the man the truth, which was that he *would* like that, but he couldn't buy one because Auntie said he had to save his pocket money to replace his phone which he'd left on the bus after Nadia took him swimming at the old leisure centre that one time.

'*There* you are Robbie.' Ms Amani came clip-clopping towards them, looking as fed-up as Phil Mitchell on the bus. Then she said to the man, 'I hope he wasn't bothering you.'

'Not at all. Got yourself a right little art appreciator here.'

Ms Amani did that thing where she smiled with her mouth and not her eyes. 'Come on then, Robbie, let's go and find the others.'

The man gave him a wink and said he'd be welcome back anytime and Robbie had to run to keep up with Ms Amani because she was walking so fast.

Robbie didn't think he'd ever see the man again but when Ms Amani and the helpers were doing a head count, he came walking up to Robbie and handed him a rolled-up piece of paper. 'Here you go, son.'

'What is it?'

'Benny's Babbies of course. And don't worry, you won't have to use your phone money because it's on me. From one art appreciator to another.'

Robbie felt a bit like he was going to cry but then he remembered his manners and said thank you.

'You're welcome,' the man said and gave him another wink.

No one sat next to him on the bus so he could put the poster on the seat beside him where it would be safe. Feeling the tickle of eyes on his face he looked up to see Jason and Sammy looking at him and whispering. He looked back at them and thought how awesome it would be to Imagine a zombie sitting between them and gnashing its teeth. As if they sensed what he was thinking they stopped whispering and started fiddling with their phones. He looked out of the window to take his mind off Imagining because his Mum had made him promise never to use what she'd called His Gift in public and he'd only broken the promise once when he'd seen some Year 6 boys picking on a new kid because there were no teachers around to tell and the kid was crying and needed help badly. He'd Imagined the scariest thing he could think of which was this tall monster without a face called The Slender Man. The bullies and the kid had run off screaming and the police had come to school and after that Mr Patel did a special assembly about Stranger Danger.

The people on the streets outside all looked as sad and worn-down as Phil and it was the same on the walk home. Even though the council were building a new leisure centre at the end of the street no one looked happy, but that could be because there were lots of flowers in plastic wrappers against the railings opposite the SuperSaver, which meant that a kid had stabbed another kid again.

When he let himself in Auntie and Nadia were in the kitchen and he could tell from their extra loud voices that they'd been drinking what Auntie called her juice and even though the window was open he could smell the funny cigarettes Nadia liked to smoke.

'How was the school trip?' Auntie asked him and he said that it was fine although he could tell that she wasn't really interested.

'What you got there, kidder?' Nadia asked in the fake happy voice she put on whenever she spoke to him.

'It's a poster. A man gave it to me for free.'

Auntie frowned because she didn't trust men. 'Why'd he do that?'

'Because I like art.'

'Let's have a look at it then.' They moved the sauce bottles and Nadia's ashtray which was full of dead cigarettes that looked like squashed maggots and unrolled it on the table and Auntie used her juice glass to hold it down on one side which Robbie didn't like because he was worried that it would leave a ring.

'Wow,' Auntie said and then she laughed which she hardly ever did in a happy way. Mum used to say that Auntie Poll had a face like a smacked arse but when she laughed it wasn't like an arse, so he was glad that he'd shown it to them. They recognised lots of people in the picture but the thing they liked the most was a cut out of a takeaway called The Golden Egg and Nadia said, 'Me and your Auntie used to go there after we'd been clubbing, Robbie,' and then she and Auntie said some stuff about getting shit-faced and the letter E and God those were the days.

He pointed at the head. 'Do you know him?'

'Oh yeah,' Auntie said with a smile in her voice. 'That's Benny wotsit.'

'Wasn't Benny a bit… special?' Nadia looked at him when she said it because special was one of the words she used whenever he overheard her and Auntie talking about him, along with weird and odd and different and 'are you *sure* he isn't on the spectrum, Poll?'

'Can I have it back now?' he said.

'Alright,' Auntie said. 'Don't have a benny.'

Robbie didn't know what she meant by that but then Nadia said, 'It's a saying that means don't get in a strop. Auntie Poll was trying to be funny.'

'Oh.' He *wasn't* having a strop. He just wanted to go to his room because even though it was nice to see them happy for once he'd had enough of their juice breath.

'Go on then,' Auntie said. 'I'll call you when food's here.'

Nadia helped him roll up the poster and he was glad to see the glass hadn't left a ring. As he went upstairs, he could hear them laughing about the egg place again which made a change because they usually talked about him whenever he left a room.

He decided to put the poster on the wall opposite the bed even though it meant he'd have to take down his *Cobra Kai* one to make space. When he was sad and he was sure Auntie wouldn't come into his room he sometimes Imagined Danny LaRusso from *Cobra Kai* because Danny wasn't scared of anything and was a really, really good dad. Whispering sorry to Danny and the poster he pulled the Blu-tac off its back and used it to fix the babbies on the wall. He propped up his pillows and sat up in bed and looked at it for a while. Then he opened Mum's old laptop which still had a selfie of him and Mum as a screensaver that she'd taken at the West Midlands Safari Park when he was three. If you looked very hard you could see a giraffe in the background.

The kind man was right. There were lots of clips of Benny in *Crossroads* on YouTube and Robbie could tell it was an old series because it was obvious the people in it were faking except for Benny who seemed like a real person and always wore that woolly hat except for one time when he went to a funeral. People were always laughing at Benny or rolling their eyes behind his back but like Malala this didn't stop Benny being a good person.

Then he did what the man said and looked up Cold War Steve's other pictures on Google Images. Benny wasn't in any of them, but Phil from *EastEnders* was in loads and in almost all of them he looked like he was about to cry. One of the pictures was of a beach with pigs and skeletons with shields running around and it had giant cut-out heads in it too. Only these weren't happy like Benny's because the heads had the faces of snarly old men and were stuck onto huge slimy worm bodies that were coming up from the sand as if once upon a time they'd been buried there and had been waiting for the right time to strike. The Old Men Worm Monsters made him feel sick and also empty inside and he had to close the laptop and look at the babbies to push them out of his mind.

'Robbie!' Auntie shouted from downstairs. 'Food!'

Nadia sometimes stayed for tea and he was glad she hadn't tonight because they were having biryani from Golden Moments and she would have eaten all the best bits. They always ate in front of the flatscreen with their plates on their laps as Auntie liked to watch the Channel 4 news. She had a crush on Krishnan who was one of the presenters and her favourite thing to do in the world was to shout at the people Krishnan was interviewing as if they could hear her. He knew she'd had too much Auntie Juice because she wasn't watching what she said and called one of them a 'stupid fat bastard' and then she said, 'whoops, pardon my French.' After that there was a very sad thing about hundreds of dolphins who'd washed up on a beach somewhere because the ocean was full of poison. A scientist Krishnan was interviewing about the dead dolphins said that 'tragedies like this will keep happening unless people fundamentally change their behaviour.'

'It's enough to make you weep, isn't it?' Auntie said and although she'd said this to Krishnan Robbie nodded because it *was* enough to make you weep.

If only the world was like it was in Benny's Babbies and full of happy people in colourful clothes playing music on buildings and dancing and stuff. But it wasn't. It was more like Phil's from *EastEnders* where everyone was sad and stressed and there was rubbish and old cars everywhere and the Old Man Worm Monsters were waiting under the sand to strike. Everyone on *EastEnders* called Phil a hard man and even he was ground down by it all. When she was alive Mum was always going on marches and wearing t-shirts with slogans on them because she said everyone had to do their bit, but she also said that lots of people were selfish and didn't care enough to get off their fat arses and do the right thing. But maybe people couldn't get off their fat arses because they were all like Phil and were too sad to think about anyone but themselves. It was true that there were brave kids like Malala who after being shot refused to die or shut up and wrote a book and won a big prize, but there weren't enough Malalas. If there were, they wouldn't be called "exceptional" and there wouldn't be enough prizes to go around.

And then he had a thought that was like when you shake up a can of Coke because it fizzed and overflowed in his brain and it must have shown on his face because Auntie gave him a look and said, 'what's up with you?' and he said 'nothing' which wasn't true because something *was* up because what if he could be like Malala instead of Phil? What if he Imagined Benny's head appearing like Godzilla over Birmingham and beaming down his happiness onto the city and cheering everyone up like the babbies in the picture?

The Benny head was much, much bigger than anything he'd Imagined before but he thought he could do it if he tried very hard but that would mean he'd have to break his promise to Mum again and she'd said that if he didn't stop using His Gift then 'bad things will happen'. But he *had* stopped except in his room and that one time when he'd Imagined Slender Man but that didn't count as it was an emergency, and bad things had still happened and what was the point of having a gift if you couldn't use it?

Should he do a whole Benny or just a head? Just a head looking out from the Rotunda was good enough for the babbies so he thought it would be good enough for normal people too. He knew how to get to the Rotunda because Mum used to work in the Bullring but not even Auntie would let him take the bus into town by himself, so he'd have to come up with a plan. Sometimes in *Cobra Kai* the Miyagi-do kids had to tell lies to make their plans work so when he helped Auntie clean up the plates, he told a lie too and said that he would be late home from school tomorrow because he had to do drama. Auntie said, 'shouldn't you have a note about that?' and he lied again and said he'd lost it and Auntie rolled her eyes and said that was typical.

The next morning, he couldn't have eaten his cereal even if Auntie had remembered to buy any and when he got to school, he kept feeling like he needed to go to the bathroom even though he didn't. He'd forgotten that they had to talk about a painting they liked from the museum, but time ran out before Ms Amani got to him which was good because he was jumpy from the plan and bad because he would have liked to talk about Benny's Babbies being a love letter to Birmingham. After maths, instead of walking home he ran to the bus stop outside the mosque and no one not even the bus driver asked what a little kid like him was doing out and about without an adult.

It was busy in the forecourt outside the Bullring Shopping Centre, so he stood next to a bin which was out of the way of all the people walking back and forth and stared up at the Rotunda. He had to look inwards instead of outwards to Imagine and it made his head scratchy and tired if he did it for too long, but it also felt *right* as if his brain was normally like a jigsaw puzzle with all the pieces jumbled up and Imagining made the puzzle whole again so that you could see what the picture was. He put his fingers in his ears to block out the sirens and the traffic and looked inside at the black part and pictured the Benny head as hard as he could. He felt his mind pieces shaking and then they clicked together and *bam*, there Benny was. It made him say oh out loud because he hadn't expected it to be this easy. He made him a bit bigger, even bigger than the head looked in the picture, which Ms Amani said was called perspective, and moved it up and down until he thought it was in the best position. In real life the head looked weirder without a body holding it up, but he thought if Ms Amani was marking it, she'd give him a "very good" or even an "excellent keep it up!".

It took longer than he expected for people to notice because they were all on their phones, but then one shouted, 'What the hell is that?' and then everyone around him looked up and started filming it. Lots of people were saying the F word like Auntie did and a man was asking if it was a projection like a movie or a hologram or a giant balloon or something. A woman selling Big Issues who'd been sad before because everyone was ignoring her kept shaking her head and laughing.

'Who's it supposed to be?' some teenagers in hoodies kept asking and then an old woman in a headscarf said it was Benny from *Crossroads* and because the teenagers went 'wot?' she said some more about who he was although she used a bad word beginning with R to describe him when she should have said learning difficulties.

He had to stop after a few minutes as he could feel the inside pieces wanting to break apart and his head was hurting, and he also felt a bit floaty because he needed lots of food energy to Imagine and he hadn't had breakfast and only a bit of lunch because it was fish sticks. He sat down on a bench which was fine for a bit and then an old man sat down next to him and started talking at him and because this one did look like he might be a pervert Robbie got up and walked very fast to the bus stop.

When he got in Auntie wasn't in the kitchen and because the house didn't smell like smoke, he knew that Nadia hadn't been over. The toilet flushed from upstairs and then Auntie came in and she jumped when she saw him and said, 'Jesus, Rob, you almost gave me a bloody heart attack'. Then she gave him a funny look and did something on her phone and said, 'Here. Look at this'. On it was a video of the head taken from a long way away and with lots of people in the background saying 'what the fuck is that?' and laughing. 'It's like from that picture you showed us yesterday. How's that for a coincidence?'

Robbie didn't know what to say to that, so he did what

Jason always did whenever Ms Amani called on him in class and shrugged.

Auntie said lots of people had made the connection to the babbies picture and thought it must be Cold War Steve or the Birmingham Art Museum doing a stunt for publicity and projecting the image onto the Rotunda. 'They said it isn't them though, so it's a mystery.'

'Is it making people happy?'

'What? Why would you ask that?'

'Is it?'

'I suppose it is, yeah. It's certainly going viral.'

Viral was a good thing unless it was in a pandemic, so Mum had been wrong about bad things happening if he used his gift. His head was still a bit achy and he was getting really hungry so he asked Auntie if he could take a peanut butter sandwich up to his room and Auntie sighed and got up to make it.

The sandwich made him feel less floaty and he lay on the bed and stared at Benny's Babbies and pretended that Malala said 'nice work, mate' to him, and then he Imagined Danny la Russo and made him do the crane kick and a thumbs up.

The next day was Saturday so there was no school. He didn't feel like going to the Rotunda and he wouldn't be able to do that anyway without lying to Auntie again, so he decided to see if he could Imagine Benny from his room even though he'd never Imagined something from such a long way away before. He looked at the poster and tried and it *felt* like it had worked and because there were no distractions like sirens or people shouting 'oy bruv' or perverts, the pieces seemed to stay together for longer. He rested for a bit until his brain felt like it was juiced up again, and then he Imagined Benny some more. To see if it *had* actually worked, he opened Mum's laptop and looked on social media even though Mum said that social media made people stupider and poisoned their brains and she was right because Sammy and Jason were always on

Snapchat and Tik Tok and they were stupid. But he didn't need to go on it for long because wherever he looked there were videos of the head tagged with WTF and LOLLLL and smiley emojis and *#BennyTheHead* was trending.

When Auntie called him for his tea and Channel 4 that evening, Krishnan was doing a bit about it on the news. Krishnan normally looked angry-stern which Auntie said wasn't surprising because he spent his life interviewing wankers, but when he spoke about Benny's Head his eyes went soft. Krishnan interviewed the real Benny, who was an actor who looked much older than the head and spoke posh and he said he thought Benny would have liked being 'the face of Birmingham'. Then Cold War Steve also did a Zoom with Krishnan. Robbie had expected Cold War Steve to look like one of those gun men who used to be on the news when it was always about Trump, but he actually looked like someone's kind dad and it turned out his name wasn't actually Steve but Christopher which suited him more. Christopher said he had no idea who was doing it and something good had come from it as the Birmingham Art Museum had sold out of all the posters which meant they might survive the next round of council arts cuts.

Krishnan then said they were going live to Gary Gibbon who was Robbie's favourite reporter because of his name. Gary was standing outside the Rotunda and interviewing lots of people about the head and everyone said they thought it was funny except for a grumpy old man from the council who said that there were permits needed for this type of thing and that they were 'investigating the matter further', and a woman who lived in one of the posh Rotunda flats complained that Benny's eye had filled her whole window and she'd felt like someone was peeping at her. Auntie snorted and said, 'that's gentrification for you. You spend three hundred K on a flat and end up living next to the world's largest pervert.'

'Benny isn't a pervert,' Robbie said but Auntie just laughed and then she went serious because Krishnan was interviewing a tech expert who was saying that she 'couldn't give a definitive answer' to Krishnan's questions about who was doing the head and how they were doing it.

Krishnan got annoyed at this and said, 'But you must have some idea surely.'

The expert said something about it being 'tech we haven't seen before,' and looked a bit scared.

'Ugh,' Auntie said. 'Creepy.' Then her phone beeped, and she said that Nadia wanted them to go into town tomorrow to be at ground zero in case the head reappeared, and Robbie would have to come with them as it was too short notice to get a baby-sitter and the man from the social would have an eppy if she left him alone all day again.

They were a bit late to meet Nadia the next morning because Auntie had forgotten to buy milk again and she'd had to run to the shop and back so that he could have breakfast, but Nadia didn't care as she was smoking one of her funny cigarettes. All of the buses were full, so they had to take an Uber that smelled like old sick and bubble-gum and the driver said the traffic was terrible because it seemed like the whole bloody city was heading for the Rotunda. They had to get out on Broad Street and walk down and there were so many people that they had to squeeze through them, and a girl's backpack hit him on the side of the head. He didn't really mind because everyone was excited and laughing and there were stalls everywhere selling woolly Benny hats and hotdogs and T-shirts reading "Take Us to Your Leader Benny!" or "Oo Miss Diane" which Nadia said was one of the things Benny used to say in *Crossroads*. Robbie didn't know if he'd be able to Imagine Benny properly with all the noise and distractions, but everyone was looking up at the Rotunda and waiting and it didn't seem fair to disappoint them. He looked inside and shut his eyes and when he heard a huge cheer, he knew he'd been able to do it. Even Auntie was smiling, and Nadia was jumping up and down and laughing like one of the babbies and this gave him extra strength.

Auntie bought him a hotdog and Nadia bought a Benny hat and she and Auntie had a dance in front of a busker who was playing "Shake It Off" by Taylor Swift on his guitar and it was like a party. He could feel the pieces wanting to pull apart and his mind was starting to hurt but he didn't want to stop because everyone seemed happy and for once Auntie was being nice to him.

Then someone shouted 'Look!' and everyone looked up to where three little people were lowering themselves from ropes from the roof of the Rotunda and down towards Benny's head. Robbie thought that was silly because although Benny *looked* solid like a photograph or a human, if they touched him they wouldn't feel anything but air. Sometimes he thought he could make his Imaginings solid and real and make them move a bit more if he practiced but he'd never tried that before because it might make his head hurt too much. Robbie concentrated very hard and made Benny's eyes look upwards, but he was too tired to do it properly and one eye went in the wrong direction. A child screamed and started crying but mostly people laughed, and Nadia shouted 'You've gone all cack-eyed, Benny!'

A piece of his mind broke free and it ached too much to put it back, so he had to stop Imagining. When Benny disappeared everyone went 'Awwwwwwwwww' and then the police came and asked everyone to move back because of health and safety. Some men who were drinking out of plastic bottles said the F word at the police and Auntie decided they should leave in case things got out of hand.

On the walk to the bus stop Auntie mussed his hair and asked him if he'd had a nice time and he said that he had even though his head was still hurting and then Nadia said they should get Chinese for tea which was his favourite. When it arrived Nadia let him have one of her barbecue ribs and they all did fortune cookies and Auntie's said "You have a secret admirer" and Robbie said 'maybe it's Krishnan' which made Auntie laugh so hard she spilled her juice and then they all sat on the couch and watched a movie with Dwayne Johnson in it and he fell asleep on Nadia's shoulder and when he woke up Auntie was carrying him upstairs and he pretended to be still asleep as she took off his trainers and tucked him in.

At school the next day, lots of the kids were talking about Benny and when Ms Amani came in instead of telling people off for being on their phones like she usually did she said that they could talk about the head until everyone had got it out of their systems.

Ms Amani told them who Benny was in *Crossroads* which was a handyman and how the head was similar to the one in Cold War Steve's picture and that Cold War Steve was a political artist and that the picture was in the Birmingham Art Museum and 'some of you might remember seeing it there', but Robbie could tell that no one but him did. Then she asked how the head made everyone feel and lots of kids said they thought Benny was funny, but Adi said he thought the head was scary, which made Robbie feel a bit angry at him even though he would have liked to be Adi's friend but couldn't because Adi gave him a wide berth.

Then she asked them to think about what the head might 'symbolise', and Laura put up her hand and said that Benny was the face of the city, and Ms Amani said that she thought it was funny that they'd choose the head of a white man for that seeing as Birmingham was so multi-cultural and whoever was doing it should 'make their message clearer'.

Robbie was about to put up his hand up to say that Benny was there to make people feel happy and wasn't that obvious? but then Ms Amani said that was enough chit-chat and they should get on and learn about colonialism now. Robbie found it hard to listen properly because he kept thinking about what Ms Amani said about making the message clearer and he didn't know how to do that unless he made Benny say something, but he'd never tried to make an Imagining talk before, and he didn't know if he could. At break he ate all of his school dinner even though it was vegetable lasagne which tasted like the Uber had smelled because if he was going to try and do a voice, he'd need lots of food energy. Then he went to the staff car park which was out of bounds but was quieter than the quad and sat against a car wheel. He Imagined Benny at the Rotunda and then he looked deep inside and into the blackest part of his brain and pictured Benny's mouth moving and saying 'Be Happy' and just after that the pieces shook and seemed to snap together tighter than they had before. He had to stop almost straight away because it made bright spots dance in front of his eyes. He knew it must have worked because after break everyone was on their phones again and he asked Adi if he could see his and Adi said okay and showed Robbie a video of the head saying, 'Be Happy' and although the voice sounded more like Danny LaRusso's than Benny's no one seemed to notice.

'Be happy,' Sammy said, and then he pushed out his bottom lip with his tongue and said it again in a funny voice and everyone laughed, and Robbie did too even though it was wrong to laugh at people who had learning difficulties.

Every day after that Robbie made Benny say 'Be Happy' at break and soon he was able to Imagine Benny for longer without his head hurting but he had to be careful about it too because if he got too tired then Benny's smile became fake and he looked as if he was screaming inside and people complained that he gave them nightmares. Outside the SuperSaver someone had put up a banner reading, 'Birmingham, Home of Benny the Head!' and Benny hats were becoming a craze and Mr Patel had to have a special assembly to tell everyone that they couldn't wear them at school because they went against the dress code and Jason got double detention for wearing his in art. Every night there was something on the Channel 4 news about Benny and it was mostly good things as the people in the Rotunda weren't complaining anymore because they could rent out their flats for lots of money on Airbnb to Benny-lovers and a queen from DragRace made a song about Benny called *How's Your Head?* which went to number one on iTunes.

On Thursday night Nadia came over for tea which was scrambled eggs and toast because it was the end of the month and although he didn't like it as much as Deliveroo he ate it anyway because he was hungry. Krishnan was having a day off from the news, so Fatima Manji was there instead, and she interviewed another tech expert who was from America this time and he said they were 'analysing the molecules in the air in and around the head, but we're no closer to discovering the source of the phenomenon', which Auntie said was a fancy nerd word for 'we don't have a fucking clue'. Then Fatima went live to Gary Gibbon who was outside the Rotunda and talking to some people in Benny hats who were saying that they thought Benny was a miracle like Jesus or God because there was no other explanation and Gary asked them if in years to come 'our ancestors might end up worshipping a character from a soap opera?'

Auntie laughed at this and said, 'Stupid fuckers,' and then she nudged Nadia and said that if Nadia kept wearing her hat people would think she was one of them.

Nadia said that she didn't mind because she liked Benny's Be Happy message because it was nice to be positive for a change and then Auntie snorted and said, 'He should bloody well tell them to reverse Brexit and get rid of the Tories and do some proper good'.

That night in bed Robbie had a long think about what Auntie had said. Making people happy *was* proper good, wasn't it? But maybe she was right because there was still bad stuff on the news like wars and stabbings and forests burning and animals dying and even though Benny had made people happy and some people thought he was a miracle like Jesus they hadn't *fundamentally changed their behaviour* like the dolphin scientist said they should.

The next day at break he made Benny say, 'Reverse Brexit. Get rid of the Tories' and then he also made him say some of the other proper good things that Mum had gone on marches for and that were written on her t-shirts like Black Lives Matter and Trans Rights are Human Rights and Stop HS2 and This is What a Feminist Looks Like and Sounds Gay I'm In and For Fox Sake Stop Hunting. On his way back to class he heard Mr Patel saying to Ms Rogers that 'whoever was behind the head was finally showing their true colours' which sounded like a good thing.

Auntie wasn't in the kitchen when he got home but he could hear her speaking in the lounge. He didn't go all the way in because she was on the phone and was walking back and forth and had her smacked arse face on, so he stayed by the door and waited for her to see him. 'Yeah, I know that Nads, but it's doing my head in because I was saying that exact thing last night… yeah I know that fucking head said other stuff too… I don't know what I think. It's just… Look, can you come over?… Oh right. But do me a favour and don't wear that bloody hat… because someone on Twitter was saying that a bunch of fucktards are going around abusing anyone wearing them, that's why.'

Then Auntie spotted him and she jumped as if he'd scared her even though he was only standing there, and as she walked towards him he could see that the corners of her mouth were black which happened when she'd had lots of juice which wasn't really juice but wine out of a box. Without saying 'hello Robbie how was school' she closed the door on him, so he went into the kitchen and made himself a sandwich with spready cheese because the peanut butter was finished and then he went up to his room.

He did his maths homework and because he felt like he wanted to cry he looked at the babbies and then watched some *Cobra Kai* on the laptop and it was only when his tummy grumbled that he realised it was dark outside and Auntie hadn't called him for Channel 4 news and tea.

Downstairs, Auntie was lying on the couch and sleeping with her mouth open which she also sometimes did when she'd had too much juice. He shook her shoulder but she batted him away and mumbled something and then went back to sleep. There was a bag of McDonalds on the kitchen counter and he was so hungry he didn't take the gherkins out of his junior cheeseburger and he ate the fries too even though they were cold. Then he went back into the lounge and sat on the corner chair that used to be Mum's and turned on the telly. Channel 4 news had already started, and Krishnan was talking on Zoom to a man in a suit with a red angry face and asking him about the 'Impact of Benny's message' and the angry man said that whoever was behind 'the stunt' had 'played a blinder' because the head had become 'the focus of global attention' and 'was becoming a divisive political tool' and Krishnan seemed to agree which was strange because Krishnan hardly ever agreed with anyone who wore a suit. Then they went live to Gary Gibbon who was at the Rotunda again and behind him were lots of people shouting and holding placards that said things like NOT MY BENNY and CANCEL BENNY NOW and Gary was saying that the police 'were close to declaring a major incident'.

Everyone looked angry even Gary who never looked angry and Robbie's insides went tight and then fluttery and he burped and tasted gherkin. He didn't know what to do except turn off the telly and put a blanket over Auntie and go to bed. Robbie hadn't made Benny say anything bad, but Jason got angry in school for no reason all the time so maybe the people at the Rotunda were like Jason and needed a time out. But because he still felt like he'd made a mistake, he Imagined Benny and made him say 'Be Happy' again because although that hadn't made people change, it hadn't made them angry either and it was a clear message like Ms Amani said to do. Then he brushed his teeth and went to bed because Mum used to say that everything looked better in the morning.

When he woke up the house felt empty and quieter than it usually did although there were lots of sirens coming from outside. Auntie wasn't in her room which used to be Mum's room only now it had a different duvet cover and was loads messier and she wasn't downstairs either. He was hungry but there wasn't any bread so perhaps she'd gone to the SuperSaver. He was brushing his teeth when he heard the front door banging open and when he came down Nadia was sitting at the kitchen table and Auntie was leaning over her and pressing a cloth to Nadia's mouth and when she took it away, he saw that there was blood on it. Auntie said, 'I *told* you not to wear that hat,' and Nadia said, 'Nice. Victim blaming,' and then they both saw him, and Nadia said, 'It's alright, kidder, I'm okay,' and Auntie looked straight at him and said in a strict voice: 'It's not alright. Whoever's behind that fucking head should bloody well stop because—'

Then there was a banging sound that sounded far away but also wrong and dangerous and Auntie shouted, 'What the fuck was that?' and ran into the lounge and then Nadia got up and went after her and Robbie did that too because he didn't know what else to do.

Auntie was flicking through the channels and stopped on one that had "BREAKING NEWS: Unconfirmed reports of bomb blast at Birmingham Rotunda" at the bottom of the screen. Nadia kept scrolling through her phone and going 'oh God, oh God,' and Auntie changed channels again and there was a wobbly video of the Rotunda covered in dust and smoke taken from a long way away and with lots of screams in the background.

Auntie turned to look at him and said, 'Go to your room, Robbie,' in a cold dead voice and then he realised she had the same scared look in her eyes that Mum had got when she saw the first thing that he'd ever Imagined which was the Cat in the Hat. Ms Amani said that when they were worried about something, they should talk to a trusted adult but the only trusted adult he could think of was the kind man at the museum who'd given him the poster and he couldn't go there because there was a bomb, and he couldn't talk to Auntie because she was angry-scared of him now.

He took the poster down, rolled it up and slid it under his bed and then curled into a ball on top of the covers and shut his eyes tight. Mum, he wanted Mum. He'd never dared to Imagine her before in case it made him feel too sad, but he didn't think he could feel any sadder than he did now, so it seemed silly not to try.

There were lots of Mums he could choose to Imagine but he picked the Mum from the screensaver picture only he Imagined her sitting on the edge of his bed and wearing her favourite pjs with the flowers on them.

'I'm sorry, Mum.'

'It's okay, bab,' Mum said in a voice that sounded a bit like Auntie's when she was being nice because he couldn't remember Mum's real voice. He knew she was saying what his inside voice was thinking because it *wasn't* okay, and the real Mum would have said I told you so and that she wished he'd bloody well try harder to be a normal kid. 'Come here,' Mum said. 'Give me a hug.'

'I can't because you're just an Imagining.'

'Try it.'

He went and sat next to her and she *was* just air but then he looked inside his head and remembered what it had felt like when he was her babby and she'd stroked his hair and then the mind pieces shook and then they jumped together with such a loud CLICK that he could hear it outside his head and it made him cry out because it *hurt* and then the pain passed and when it was over he sort of knew that the pieces would never come apart again and then he felt the weight of something on his head and he realised it was Mum's hand. He opened his eyes and fell against her and she was real and solid, and he could smell her smell which was of Mum and fabric softener and feel her warmth.

'At least you got off your fat arse and tried to do something, Bab,' Mum said. 'Don't give up. Never give up.'

Because Benny hadn't given up when people had been mean to him. Neither had Malala. Neither had Danny LaRusso out of *Cobra Kai* when he was the karate kid and the bullies went after him.

'What should I do now, Mum?'

'You know what to do, bab.'

And he *did* know even though he knew Malala wouldn't approve of it because she was all about being peaceful and going high when mean people went low. Making people happy hadn't worked but when he'd imagined Slender Man that one time the bullies had *fundamentally changed their behaviour* straight away.

'I think,' Robbie said, 'that it's time to send in the Old Man Worm Monsters.'

'Yes,' Mum said. 'That should sort the stupid fuckers out.'

Then Robbie closed his eyes and Imagined harder than he'd ever Imagined before.

—Inspired by Benny's Babbies *by Cold War Steve*

Our Lady of Flies

Teika Marija Smits

Saturday night was film night, a nod to those first dates at the cinema when Abby and Krzysztof cared nothing for the film except that it gave them a reason to sit close and share popcorn; the thrilling sensation of the nearness of the other's skin robbing the giant screen of its flashy, bombastic power. But now that they were virtually "an old married couple", as Abby's friends kept telling her, they spent an ever-increasing amount of time arguing over which video to watch.

Krzysztof, as befitted a young man who'd grown up in the 1980s, liked action, westerns, horror and sci-fi. Abby, though she never considered herself a girly girl, had to admit to preferring romantic comedies. Sometimes they found a happy compromise; sometimes they went for weeks taking turns. This Saturday night happened to be Krzysztof's night to choose. He couldn't decide between *Alien* or *The Fly* and asked Abby which she'd prefer. Abby thought them both stupid but plumped for the latter, because at least it starred Jeff Goldblum.

Snug in the corner of the sofa, with her legs across the seat cushions, her feet in Krzysztof's lap and a crochet blanket across them both, Abby thought that they must look like a right old pair. As the strangely colourful opening credits flickered across the screen, lighting up their pitch-black lounge with spots of reds and purples and greens, Abby sighed and took another sip of white wine. How had her life come to this? She was twenty-four, for God's sake, not sixty-four. And what if the world really was going to end in five months' time, when 1999 gave way to the new millennium? Shouldn't they be at some wild party, getting drunk, or, at the very least, clubbing with Linda and the girls? For all Abby knew, she and Krzysztof might be dead by the end of the year.

"D'you want some popcorn?" asked Krzysztof, reaching for the family-sized tub of Butterkist on the coffee table.

"No," Abby said. "I'm trying to diet, remember?"

"Oh," he said, shrugging. "I forgot. Besides," he went on, in between munches, "you don't need to diet. You're fine as you are."

Abby gave him a playful kick.

"Hey! Look, can we just watch the film?"

"All right," she said, smiling to herself in the darkness. Whatever Krzysztof's other faults, he *had* always liked her body just as it was. Besides, she thought as she considered Geena Davis's figure, *she* had some curves to her, so maybe being stick-thin was overrated.

An hour into the film, their Siamese, Li Li, came rattling through the cat flap in the kitchen's exterior door and round into the lounge. She leapt up onto Abby's legs and dropped the something she'd been carrying in her mouth – a half-dead mouse. Abby cried out in disgust and yanked her feet off Krzysztof's lap, sending the tub of popcorn, blanket, cat and bloody mouse flying.

"Abby!" said Krzysztof as he got off the sofa and went to turn on the light switch. "It was only the cat."

"And whatever she had in her mouth," Abby retorted, blinking in the harsh white light as she tried to see where the mouse had gone.

Krzysztof, too, had his eyes on the floor, and whatever it was that Li Li was now stalking.

"Oh great, it's still alive," he said as a thin, dun-coloured tail disappeared beneath the opposite sofa.

Abby hit 'pause' on the remote, leaving Jeff's decomposing face looming large on the telly, and then picked the blanket up and pulled it over her drawn-up knees. She absentmindedly grazed on the popcorn as she watched Krzysztof's attempts at catching the still-lively mouse.

There was a sudden mad dash as cat and man chased after the mouse which had made a break for the hallway.

"Oh, for fuck's sake!" Abby heard Krzysztof say as she continued to crunch on popcorn.

"Um, Abby, a little help here please," he called. "It's gone into the spare bedroom. Under the wardrobe. So we're gonna have to move it."

Abby sighed as she got off the sofa. Clever mouse that, she thought – going into the room of horrors. It was so stuffed full of Krzysztof's mum's ugly, heavy furniture that even skinny Li Li wouldn't be able to catch it in there.

Half an hour later, they decided to give up the hunt. Between the two of them they could only move the ancient wardrobe a couple of inches away from the wall before its side scraped against the bed's footboard. And getting the queen size sleigh bed to move was tricky because before they could do that the chest of drawers beside it would need to be moved, and its passage was blocked by a couple of stacks of boxes of old books. The whole room was like one of those sliding tile puzzles (only with antique, mahogany furniture for tiles), and presiding over it all was the only piece of art in the whole house – a golden icon of the Madonna and Child.

"I'll get it out when it's dead," Krzysztof said, shooing Li Li from the room and shutting the door behind them. "It'll be easier."

"And how long will that take?" asked Abby, suddenly feeling sorry for the mouse.

"God knows. But if it continues to stay under that wardrobe that's all we can do for the time being. We could always clear out the room tomorrow. I'll ask Rob over to help me lift the wardrobe."

"What a hassle," Abby said, sighing, as she trudged

back to the lounge and resettled herself on the sofa. "Li Li's a menace."

"No she's not. She's just doing what cats do. Isn't that right?" Krzysztof asked of Li Li in his "baby" voice as he crouched and rubbed her furry cheeks with both hands. Li Li stood on her hind legs and shoved her face into his chin.

Abby stuffed another handful of popcorn into her mouth and tried not to hate herself for being so envious of them both – Li Li for having Krzysztof's full, and very affectionate, attention, and Krzysztof for being so loved by "their" cat, although it was clear that, having been Krzysztof's cat since he was fifteen, Li Li loved only him. "Look, are we gonna watch the film, or what?"

"Yeah, sure," said Krzysztof after a pause. He gave Li Li one last kiss then stood and went to turn off the light, but the moment he reached for the switch the phone in the hallway began to ring.

"That'll be your mum," said Abby, her voice flat. With a sigh, she reached for the copy of *Now* on the coffee table as Krzysztof went to answer the phone.

Sure enough, the sound of Krzysztof speaking in Polish confirmed Abby's prediction. It was the third time that his mum had called today, and Abby had a feeling that this was going to be a long one. Looking for an article, an interview – anything that she hadn't already read – she flicked through the magazine and found herself reading a snippet of gossip. *Check out these photos of gorgeous, curvy Kate! Could she be pregnant again? Let's hope so! After her last miscarriage it would be the news she and hunky hubby Tim – and us – are waiting for!*

Abby quickly turned the page, willing herself to unsee the word 'miscarriage', to blank Kate and her perfect husband and their happy news from her brain. Instead, she engrossed herself in an article entitled 'Your Perfect Diet' while eating the last of the popcorn.

When Abby woke the next morning, the events of the previous night were distant, forgotten. It was only when she emerged from their bedroom and saw Li Li scratching at the shut door of the spare room that she remembered the mouse.

"Shoo!" she said, half-heartedly. "You can't go in there, you stupid cat. Go on, go and bother Krzysztof instead."

Li Li paused to lick her paw and glared at Abby.

Abby, who didn't appreciate being scrutinized by a cat, went to the kitchen, her pink and fluffy too-big slippers causing her to shuffle along the wooden floor like an old woman. "God, I really am turning into an old fogie," she muttered as she turned on the kettle and wrapped her baggy dressing gown about herself. Looking down at the slippers that her mum had bought her ages ago – before she'd buggered off to Spain with her new boyfriend – she told herself that she really ought to buy a pair that fit. Along with some new clothes. Everything of hers was old, like the nightdress she was currently wearing, or too big. That was the downside to buying everything from catalogues.

Still, she thought with a shiver, it was better than the alternative – standing in front of one of those nasty, circus-like mirrors in a shop's changing room whilst trying on clothes that couldn't fail to look crap on her. There was something about those places – the harsh fluorescent light, the confined space, the stale, somewhat sweaty air, not to mention the flimsy curtain, her sole protector of modesty – that turned her into a panicky, breathless wreck. Even now, the thought of all that pasty white flesh, the fat rolling and puckering beneath her skin, made her feel sick. God no; the catalogue clothes would have to do.

A sudden 'click' broke into her thoughts. And then the sound of Li Li meowing. She went to the hallway and saw that the door of the spare room was open – Li Li must've somehow managed to open it. The thought of the mouse escaping into the rest of the house propelled Abby into action – she rushed into the room and closed the door behind her firmly. She really didn't want the mouse to reach their bedroom, or the kitchen.

"Stupid door," she muttered. She'd have to get Krzysztof to do something about it. She'd been on at him for a while now about fixing all the door handles, which were loose and prone to opening at random times. That was the other thing she disliked about this isolated 1970s bungalow – the landlord had, apparently, "done it up" before her and Krzysztof had begun to rent it, but what that had really meant was that he'd given the walls a lick of paint, put in some cheap laminate flooring and replaced the old internal doors with untreated pine ones which had tacky frosted window panels. And although she knew nothing about carpentry, it was obvious that the doors had been fitted badly. Worse still, the slimeball landlord was spectacularly good at sidestepping their requests for repairs.

"And stupid cat," she said, as she watched Li Li prowl about the cluttered room, sniffing at the floor, and then at the wardrobe, her nose shoved as far as it could go beneath it.

Abby, who had just now begun to think that shutting herself in with Li Li and the mouse wasn't the best of ideas, suddenly felt a strange, creeping sensation on her left shin. Her head jerked downwards and she saw the cause of her tingling skin – a bluebottle.

"Ah!" she cried, instantly lifting her foot. "Get off me!"

The bluebottle, unperturbed by its shifting perch, clung on.

Abby swiped at it and, eventually, lazily, it left her leg to fly about the room, finally coming to rest on the shoulder of the Madonna in the golden icon on the wall.

"What's the matter?" said Krzysztof, letting himself into the room and closing the door behind him.

"Oh, nothing," she said, her eyes still on the bluebottle that was slowly creeping towards Mary's mouth. "Well, it was a fly."

"I thought that maybe you were mouse hunting."

"Not likely."

Krzysztof, spotting Li Li by the wardrobe, crouched beside her and asked her what she could see.

"She's not going to tell you, is she?" said Abby. "She's obviously after that bloody mouse."

Krzysztof sniffed and then made a face. "Smells pretty bad down there."

Li Li then took a cautious step backwards, as though something revolting was making its way out from beneath the wardrobe. Another fly. Li Li whacked it with her paw and then, after giving the crushed insect a couple of prods, ate it.

"Oh God!" cried Abby, as Li Li crunched it down with relish, "that's just gross."

Yet another fly emerged from beneath the wardrobe, but this one managed to evade Li Li's paws, and instead buzzed upwards, to circle the room. It too made its way to the shimmering icon.

"Well," said Krzysztof, turning to Abby as two more flies flew into the air, "looks like that mouse is dead."

"Urgh, poor thing. Eaten alive by flies. Can't stand the noisy shitbags."

"Abby," said Krzysztof, standing and getting onto the bed so that he could draw the curtains and let the bluebottles out of the window, "it's not the flies that killed it."

"I know! It's that murderous cat of yours that killed it! But still… just the thought of a fly laying its eggs on a dead body…" Abby couldn't help but shiver with horror, "…it's just disgusting."

"You know," began Krzysztof, in his 'I'm going to tell you an interesting historical fact' voice, while wrestling with the sticky window fastening, "the Greeks used to think that flies spontaneously generated from rotting food. And other decaying matter."

Yes, thought Abby (though she didn't voice it), *you've told me this a hundred times.*

She continued to watch her boyfriend, whom she was sure she knew inside out, as he did his best to wave the flies out of the window.

"But you can see why that idea stuck, can't you? I mean, last night, we shut the door on a room that's got a dying mouse in it. Next morning the place is crawling with flies."

"God I hate them!" she reiterated, her eyes on the golden icon, which seemed to be attracting the flies. "They're so dumb. I mean, you've got the window wide open, and they're just..." she flung her hand towards the painting, "...sitting there."

"Give them a moment! They'll make their way towards the light when they're less dopey. They're freshly hatched. Like newborns, really."

Abby shuddered, the word 'newborn' driving a spike of pain into her chest. She turned towards the door. "Well, I'm not hanging around to watch a bunch of shitty flies. I'm going to make a cup of tea." She left the room just as the flies, sensing the sunlight, flew out of the window.

All throughout the following day, Abby found herself ruminating on what Krzysztof had said about the flies. Between teaching her mostly disinterested pupils about glaciers and rainfall and CBDs she could think of nothing else. He'd been so... nice to them. And what he said about them being newborns... well, that had just been cruel. Hadn't he realised what day it was? Or had he realised, but didn't care? She didn't know which one was worse.

On the drive back from school she was quiet, distracted; her unseeing eyes on the gently sloping Suffolk fields, the lush greens and golds of summer.

"You all right?" asked Krzysztof after a while, taking his left hand off the steering wheel for a moment so that he could give her thigh a quick squeeze.

"Yeah," she said, after a moment. Should she mention the date? The hurt she felt at his words yesterday? "Oh,

I don't know," she said, suddenly crossing her arms and pressing them hard into her chest – the place in which she always felt a stab of pain whenever she thought about their lost baby. The foetus, as Krzysztof always called it, which her body had cut loose and ejected with a rush of blood and pain and sorrow.

"Hard day? Was Clive being a twat again?"

"Oh, you know. Just the usual. He wants to check over my reports before they get sent out. Because, obviously, I can't be trusted to do a good job. But it was Alicia who was really doing my head in. I'm sure she was making fun of me in the last lesson, but I couldn't catch her doing it."

"Tell me about it. That girl's a nightmare."

"Yeah, but she fancies you, so it's not quite as bad as being called Miss Piggy every time I turn my back."

"But Abbs, if I were to do, or say, anything that could be viewed as even slightly inappropriate, I'd lose my job. Look at what happened to Rob."

"Rob's an idiot."

"Yeah, but he didn't *actually* do anything wrong."

Abby sighed. Yet another conversation in which they failed to communicate with each other. It was getting boring.

"Listen, Abbs, there's only another week to go. Less, in fact. Four days. And the last Friday of term will be a breeze. I'm just going to let them watch videos." Krzysztof suddenly broke into a grin. "Maybe I'll show my sixth formers *The Fly*. Say it's educational, and that it'll teach them everything they'll ever need to know about science."

"Yeah," she said, with a wry smile, "the Head will love that."

"Come on, Abby, cheer up! We're only four days away from freedom. And in a month and a bit we'll be in Spain. On the beach."

A picture of her flamboyant mum – all oiled, bronzed flesh and bingo wings – greeting them at Alicante airport, flashed across Abby's mind. The heat, like a mugger, would clobber them as they left the cool of the air-conditioned terminal. Her mum would start to criticise her appearance. She didn't think it much to look forward to.

"Oh, and I hope you don't mind, but I promised Mum I'd help her put a shelf up tonight. So, I'll drop you off first, and then go on to hers, okay?"

Abby exhaled deeply, a stream of bitter air leaving her lungs. "Yeah, whatever." What Krzysztof didn't seem to understand was that not only was he allowing himself to be treated like a doormat by his mother, but that he was saddling her with the same kind of treatment.

"Look, I know she's always asking me to do stuff, but it's coming up to the anniversary of Dad's death, and she's finding it hard. Especially with her sister being ill and everything."

"But what about your brother? Why can't he do any of this stuff?"

"Abby! He's in Bristol. Is he really supposed to drive halfway across the country to put up a shelf?"

Abby shrugged. In her opinion, Krzysztof's brother had made a smart move when he'd taken that job at Bristol uni. That way he didn't need to be at the beck and call of their ever-needy mother.

"I don't know, it's just…" she turned her head away from Krzysztof, her eyes now on the reflection of herself in the passenger window. From this angle, she looked elfin-like, ghostly. Almost pretty. "…well, we don't seem to have much time to ourselves anymore, do we? I mean, as a couple." She was sure he'd know what she meant. Since the miscarriage three months ago they'd barely even kissed.

Abby glanced at Krzysztof, suddenly fearful of his response to this alarmingly frank statement that had vomited out of her mouth. Seconds of silence went by as Krzysztof concentrated on overtaking an annoyingly slow tractor ahead of them.

"Yeah, I know," he conceded as he accelerated the car away from the tractor. "You're right. But listen," there was that grin again, "come Friday afternoon we'll have all the time in the world, right? We'll be able to sleep in, talk. Do stuff, you know."

Abby considered her silent reflection. This was the moment – the last good opportunity she'd get that day to mention the date. The miscarriage. Her grief. "Do stuff. Yeah. That'll be nice."

"Four days!" Krzysztof reiterated, oblivious to her lack of enthusiasm. He suddenly turned the stereo on. "Mind if we listen to the radio?"

"Fine," she said. And as the sound of Prince singing '1999' washed over her, she – or was it her reflection? – quickly wiped away the tear that had slid down her left cheek.

After Krzysztof had dropped her off, Abby found herself besieged by Mrs Motherwell, their one and only next door neighbour, who pressed upon her a plate of biscuits. "They're coconut crunch. I know your Christopher loves them."

Abby gave her a weak smile. Her "Christopher", as the old woman always called him, didn't love coconut crunch. But he was too polite to say so.

"Thanks," she said, as she stepped onto her porch and started unlocking the front door – surely a sign for the old biddy to return home? – "that's really kind of you."

When the old woman continued to remain rooted to the spot, Abby added, "I'd invite you in but I've got a ton of reports to write. You know?"

"Oh, of course!" she said. "But don't you go overdoing it. You two, you're always working so hard. It's not right how much they make you do at that school of yours. And make sure to treat yourself to a cuppa and a biscuit. You're all skin and bones."

Abby gritted her teeth, trying not to grimace. *That* was a bit rich coming from a woman who was, basically, just a sack of wrinkles.

"I will, I promise," she said, before going into the house and quickly shutting the door behind her.

Skin and bones! As if. "Christ!" she hissed. Why did their closest neighbour in this godforsaken hamlet have to be such a judgemental busybody?

She went to the kitchen and put the plate of biscuits on the counter. She considered throwing them straight in the bin – after all, Krzysztof wouldn't want them, and then she'd find herself eating the horrible things – but instead she put the kettle on and got herself a mug.

A sudden noise – as though something big had come crashing to the floor – made her freeze.

Abby, her heart pounding, instantly thought: *burglar.*

As quietly as she was able to, she slid open the cutlery drawer and then extracted their sharpest, and largest, knife. Slowly, she tiptoed to the source of the noise – the hallway – and wondered at her bravado. But if there was someone in their house, would she actually have the nerve to use the knife in her hand?

And then a forlorn "mew" came from behind the closed door of the spare room.

"Oh, Li Li!" Abby cried in relief, as she opened the door and the cat shot past her legs in a blur of beige and brown. "Well," she said, on seeing the knocked-over box of books, "I guess that explains the noise."

She suddenly laughed, relief coursing through her, and put the knife down on the chest of drawers. "A burglar," she muttered, as she put right the box of Polish books. "Yeah, right. Like we've got anything worth stealing."

Instinctively, she turned to look at the golden icon on the wall. She had no idea of its worth (she guessed it wasn't very much), but it might look appealing to a burglar. Quite apart from the gold paint – or was it gold leaf? – there was something inexplicably alluring, powerful, about the ochre-coloured image, the Madonna and Child. There was that sharp, urgent ache in her chest again. *Mother Mary. Perfect Mary. Virginal Mary.* Ha! What a joke.

An image of Krzysztof's mum thrusting the icon into his hands, insisting that he put it up in their bungalow, flashed across Abby's mind. Later that same day, when he'd gone against the landlord's wishes and put a nail in the wall for the picture, she'd asked him why it was so important to his mum. He'd mumbled something about it being a blessing to their house. To their relationship. To the bringing forth of children. She'd laughed at the time; thought it a load of old nonsense.

Now, Abby had a sudden desire to pick up the knife and thrust it into Mary's stupid orange head; to see the destruction she could cause as she carved her anger into that beatific and unnaturally narrow face – a face that was so unlike her own.

But instead, she turned away from the icon and sat on the bed, hugging herself tight. She found herself sobbing, her face suddenly streaming with tears and snot. She felt so empty. Alone.

After a while, her tears subsided and she felt calmer. Better.

As she wiped her left sleeve across her nose, she felt a tingle on her right hand, like the tiniest of caresses. A fly. Abby, for once, wasn't instantly repelled by the bluebottle, which must've been a straggler – one of the last to be hatched from the mouse's body before Krzysztof had removed it. She considered its fat, jewel-like body, its lacey black wings and huge, domed eyes, and thought it curiously beautiful.

Then a litany of names of bacteria, straight from Krzysztof's A-level biology worksheets, scrolled across her mind: *Salmonella, Shigella, Campylobacter, Enterococcus.*

"Urggh," she said, suddenly waving the fly away and getting off the bed. She left the room and closed the door behind her. She would leave the little shitbag in there. Krzysztof could deal with it later.

That Friday afternoon, when the summer term was finally at an end, Krzysztof drove them down to The Vixen – the nearest pub to the school and, as it happened, the one most popular with Haverhill's underage drinkers. They'd only planned to stay for a beer or two, since Krzysztof was driving, but when most of their older colleagues had drifted away and a couple of Krzysztof's friends arrived they decided to make a night of it. They could always kip on a friend's couch. Or get a taxi back.

Abby, who'd been knocking back the wine since Rob had plonked himself down on their table in the beer garden and begun to witter on about his new business, tried to extricate herself from the dull-as-shit conversation by asking Krzysztof if he'd play pool with her.

"Maybe later," he said, failing to pick up on Abby's desire to escape.

"Fine," she said, standing. "I'll play by myself then." It had to be better than listening to egghead Rob, who kept referring to himself as an entrepreneur. Ha! As if a twenty-four-year-old man with that little hair on his head could ever be a successful businessman.

But when she got to the pool room, a couple of guys were already there. She was about to turn around and leave when one of them called out to her. "Miss Pallant!"

It took her a moment to realize that this tall, gorgeous guy was the same spotty sixteen-year-old whom she'd taught a couple of years ago. "Ricky! Wow! Fancy seeing you here."

"Likewise." He picked up a cube of chalk and thrust his cue into it. "Wanna game?" he asked loudly, over the noise of the music coming from the crackly speakers.

"Um, well… I don't want to interrupt."

"Nah, no worries. I was just about to whip Darren's arse." He bent over the pool table and then lined up his shot. *Smack!* He potted a red. Then another. Finally, the black. "See?"

"Nicely done," said Abby, her eyes flicking over to

where Darren was standing, wondering how he'd react. He simply shrugged.

"Cheers. Say, Daz, will you get me and Miss…"

"Abby. You can call me Abby."

Ricky grinned and then pulled a wallet from his back pocket. It was stuffed full of notes. "All right then, can you get *Abby* and me some drinks." He passed a couple of fivers to Darren. "Payday," he said, by way of explanation.

Darren took the money without hesitation (as though waiting on Ricky was an everyday occurrence), asked Abby what she wanted and then left to get them their drinks.

"So what's brought you to The Vixen?" asked Ricky, as he fed a 50p into the coin slot of the pool table. "There's no oxbow lakes or other features of geographical significance 'round here."

"Oh ha, ha. Very funny." She then raised her voice as the balls were released and came clattering down the chute. "End of term." Should she mention Krzysztof? "I'm here with… friends."

Ricky nodded; began to rack up.

Abby, her heart racing as her not-quite-truthful words faintly buzzed around the pool room, went to pick up a cue.

"Ladies first," said Ricky, giving Abby the chance to smash the cue ball into the pack, splitting open the holy triangle with sudden force.

When Darren came back with their drinks, Abby had potted most of the yellows. He gave a snort of laughter. "Now whose arse is being whipped?"

Ricky laughed off the comment and took a swig from his pint of lager. "You gotta play nice with the ladies, eh, Daz?" he said with a wink.

Darren nodded, gave Ricky a sly smile. "All right then. Well, I'll leave you two love birds to it."

Before Abby could protest, Darren had left the room and the wooden door had banged shut behind him. To hide her embarrassment, Abby bent over the table and lined up her next shot. She tried her best to squash the thought *he likes me!* by considering the trajectory of the cue ball. *Smash!* In went another yellow. Now there was just the black to pot. And it was an easy-enough shot to make. *Smash!*

Ricky clapped his congratulations and then passed Abby her glass of white wine, his eyes moving upwards from her cleavage. "How d'you learn to play like that?"

"I suppose it's called a squandered youth," she said with a laugh. "No, it's just that my mum used to work at a pub. Well, her bloke ran the pub, and so I kept myself busy playing pool."

Ricky nodded. "Cool."

"Listen," said Abby, swallowing hard, "what did Darren mean about lovebirds and stuff?"

"Oh," said Ricky, surprised, as though he'd completely forgotten about Darren's earlier words. "He knew that I fancied you, when I was at school, like, so I guess he figures this is my chance to impress you."

As Abby felt her cheeks redden, her hand automatically lifted the wine glass to her lips and she found herself draining it.

"Want another?" asked Ricky.

"Um, yeah," she said, nodding vehemently, "but I'll get it. I need to go to the loo first anyway. D'you want me to get you another pint while I'm at the bar?"

"Sure. Stella."

"Okay. I'll be back in a sec. Oh, and rack them up again, will you? I want to give you another chance to see me beat you."

Ricky grinned. "You wish."

The ladies toilets were full of not-quite-eighteen-year-olds checking their make-up and gossiping. Abby did her best to keep her head down, to ignore them. But as she walked through the crowded bar area she couldn't help but notice

Alicia, all dolled up, and with a few of her friends, heading for the door to the beer garden. As Alicia opened the door, a square of dusky sky showing Abby that it was later than she thought, Abby overhead her say something about Krzysztof. "Mr Dabrowski? 'Course I'm going to talk to him. I know he fancies me. Good job the pig isn't with him tonight."

Abby felt herself swelling with anger and shame. God how she hated that little slut! Well, Krzysztof was welcome to her.

When she finally got the barman's attention, she ordered herself a bottle of wine. A pint of Stella for Ricky.

She smiled to herself as she took the drinks to the hidden-away pool room. To Ricky. ...*I fancied you...* Although he'd used the past tense. But the way he'd looked at her now... his eyes on her breasts... surely he still liked her?

Two more pool games later, when the wine had begun to make Abby's usually precise shots anything but, she was sure that Ricky still liked her. She'd just made a pretty good break – a red had shot into one of the corner pockets – and was bent over the table, cueing up, when Ricky had sidled up to her. He'd tried to put her off her next shot. Teasingly, he'd nudged her hip.

"Oi!" she'd said with a laugh. "That's not allowed!"

"Oh, isn't it?"

He'd tickled her waist, making her tingle with pleasure, desire, and she'd stood upright to find herself only inches away from his face, his body tight against hers. And from the hard mound she could feel in his jeans she really, *properly*, knew that he liked her.

'1999', by Prince, suddenly blared out of the speakers.

"So what d'you reckon?" he said. "Will the world come to an end in 2000? Maybe we should live like it's going to? I know how I'd spend my last ever evening."

Hours later, when the creeping daylight showed Abby the full horror of her actions, she would identify this moment as the turning point. She should've pushed him off her, told him that she had a boyfriend who was practically her fiancé. Instead, she thrilled to Ricky's touch as he stroked her cheek with his index finger.

"I always wanted you," he said quietly, the fingers of his other hand brushing through her loose, blonde curls.

Abby's groin pulsed with heat, and her already-moist knickers became slick with desire. He then put his mouth to her ear. "I'd fantasise about you. Imagine us fucking on one of the tables in the geography room. How about a pool table instead?"

"Ricky, I—"

But it was impossible to say no. She simply responded to his urgent kiss, drinking deep of his saliva, the smell of him, the intoxicating taboo of what they were doing.

Then his hand was up her skirt, inside her knickers, his fingers probing her flesh and *poking, poking, poking*, making her groan with pleasure. Then he was lifting her onto the table, and she was lying on the green baize, her legs splayed, reaching for him as he tore off her knickers and thrust his cock inside her.

This was not a good moment for Krzysztof to find her. And yet, that was what happened. Abby froze. Ricky, too intent on his own needs to notice their white-faced, round-eyed spectator, continued to fuck Abby for a few moments more until he came.

Abby simply looked at Krzysztof, her eyes suddenly filling with tears. "Krzysztof, I—" But what was there to say?

Krzysztof shook his head urgently, as though his mind might be able to convince him that what his eyes had seen was false. But of course it was no good. The scene before him was too graphic. Too abhorrent. He turned and fled, the door slamming shut behind him.

Ricky, finally noticing Abby's distress, asked her what was wrong.

"Didn't you see, you arsehole?" she said. "It was my boyfriend."

"Mr D.?" said Ricky, pulling away from her and rapidly doing up his jeans. "You still with him?"

"Yes." She got off the table as quickly as her reeling head allowed her, and then pulled down her skirt. "But probably not anymore, thanks to you."

"Me? So it's my fault?"

But Abby wasn't listening, she was already running after Krzysztof.

Of course he wasn't in the pub any longer. And as soon as she entered the parking area she saw their car – his car – speeding down the road, into the darkness. She raced after it, shouting and waving, but had to stop as a stitch pulled her up short. Bent over, panting, her hand on the pain in her abdomen, she glanced up to see the car's red tail-lights disappear around a corner. A sudden image of Krzysztof in a mangled car, blood running down his chin, sent another stab of pain into her gut, and with only a moment to realise what was happening to her, she vomited.

"Jesus!" she said, looking down at the splat of semi-digested pork scratchings and peanuts that had been her dinner. Desperate to rid her mouth of its acidic coating, she longed to go back to the pub for some water. But she couldn't face seeing anyone who might know what had just happened. She spat out as much of the grossness as she could and then forced herself onwards. She'd just have to walk home. All eleven miles of it. It would give her a chance to sober up. To figure out what to say to Krzysztof. But as she recalled the look on his face when he'd seen her on that pool table – God, what must she have looked like? – a sudden, excruciating twist of guilt wrung at her insides. Surely there was no coming back from an act that terrible?

Mostly, Abby stuck to the fields. She felt safer there, surrounded by the moonlit wheat, the forgiving darkness that didn't show her what she really looked like, but what she imagined she looked like. She was simply a girl that had made a mistake. A really awful mistake, but one that could be rectified in time. Krzysztof would see her – barefoot and dishevelled, emerging from the silver crops, looking for all the world like a woodland nymph – and he would take her into his arms and forgive her. But as the sick-encrusted stilettos in her right hand bumped against her knee, and the tatters of her knickers rubbed between her sticky thighs, her feet dusty and sore from the parched earth beneath her, she couldn't quite convince herself that that was what Krzysztof *would* see.

It was only when Abby got home in the early hours of the morning, when the dawn light was beginning to dust the ground, that the full force of the previous night's events hit her. There was no car in the driveway. Had Krzysztof been in an accident, as she'd feared? But he hadn't been drinking that much. Still, driving while angry, upset, a couple of pints inside him…

No, she suddenly realised, shame rushing through her, of course he wouldn't be here. He'd be at his mum's, crying on her shoulder. And his mum would be gabbling away in Polish, telling him that he was too good for that Abby. That she always knew that they weren't right for each other.

Abby took the key out of her purse and let herself in, flinging the stilettos down the hallway. Their bungalow was unchanged, as it had always been, but now, with another gut-wrenching pang, she realised that it might not be "theirs" for much longer. As she went through the lounge to the kitchen, she felt the furniture glaring at her. The oversized sofa was Krzysztof's mum's. The coffee table had been made by Krzysztof during his brief interest in carpentry. The rug had been Krzysztof's dad's. The videos and most of the books declared themselves as belonging to Krzysztof. When she poured herself a pint of water, the glassware and crockery and cutlery all declared: *Krzysztof's, Krzysztof's, Krzysztof's.*

There was virtually nothing that belonged solely to her.

When they came to dividing their belongings it would be an easy enough task.

But no, she told herself, downing the water in one go. She couldn't be thinking like that. What she needed to do was focus. First, she had to eat something. She grabbed the first thing to hand – a couple of Mrs Motherwell's coconut biscuits that were still on a plate on the counter. Then she'd get out of these disgusting clothes. Shower. Go to bed. Things would look better after she'd had a sleep.

Abby woke in the middle of the afternoon. For a few glorious moments the horror of what had happened the night before was forgotten. Then it all came back in a nauseating flood – Ricky fucking her on the pool table; the shock on Krzysztof's face as he'd seen her, legs akimbo, her hands on Ricky's naked arse; the long walk back home when she'd naively thought that Krzysztof would forgive her. She curled herself into a ball, her arms around her knees, and sobbed, digging her nails into her legs. *I hate you!* she screamed into her chest, tearing at her own flesh. *I hate you, I hate you!* She longed to strip away her skin, to gouge away the flesh that Ricky had made dirty with his lust. Her lust. But it was no good. She wasn't strong enough to do much damage.

A sudden noise made her stop. A scrabbling at the closed bedroom door. And then a mew. *Li Li!*

Abby leapt out of bed and opened the door, for a fleeting moment thinking that maybe Krzysztof was back. But no, as she stepped into the hallway, she could see that there was no Krzysztof. Just Li Li crying for food. But there *was* an envelope poking through the letterbox. And was that the sound of a car leaving their driveway? She rushed to the front door and flung it open, Li Li bolting out, but the car was already gone. It was then that she noticed her rucksack sitting on the porch. She'd put it in Krzysztof's car yesterday, at the end of school. It contained a couple of folders of teaching materials, some end-of-year thank you cards and chocolates from pupils who actually gave a shit. She picked up the bag, shut the door, and then dumped it in the hallway. It was yet another reminder of her life pre-last night. She pulled the envelope from the letterbox and quickly opened it. Inside was a brief note from Krzysztof. It simply said: *Staying at mum's. Look after Li Li – she wouldn't like it in the flat. I'll pick her up in the last week of August (along with all my stuff) when the rental agreement comes to an end.*

Abby clutched the letter to her chest, swaying on the spot. She leant against the wall for support, but her legs crumpled beneath her and her back slid down the wall as her body heaved with sobs, tears streaming down her face. So that was it then. Krzysztof had left her.

Abby wasn't sure how long she'd been sitting on the hallway floor – minutes? Hours maybe? But it had become reassuringly dark now and the insistent ache of hunger was pulling at her stomach. She slowly got up and went to the kitchen. On opening the fridge door she considered what to eat. There actually wasn't much in there. They'd usually go food shopping on a Saturday, but of course that wouldn't ever be happening again. Abby felt the heat of yet more tears at her still-burning eyes, and she did her best to hold them back. It was no good crying anymore. It wouldn't bring Krzysztof back. She pulled out a half-empty packet of ham, a tub of margarine, a jar of pickle, and from the couple of slices of bread left in the bread bin she made herself a sandwich.

"It's not all bad," she said, the false reassurance at her lips. "At least I can watch whatever film I want." She opened the freezer door. Seeing the two lone tubs of Häagen-Dazs within the freezer, she added, "And the ice cream's all mine."

But as she got herself settled on the sofa – ready to watch *Pretty Woman*, a plate of sandwiches and crisps on her lap – the sound of the phone ringing in the hallway made her heart leap. She immediately went to the phone and was about to pick up the receiver when she stopped herself. What if it wasn't Krzysztof? She couldn't handle speaking to her mum. Worse still, it could be Krzysztof's mum ringing to give her a piece of her mind. She hovered in the hallway, unsure what to do, until the answer machine clunked into action and she heard her own voice saying that she and Krzysztof were busy right now, but could they leave a message?

Giggles erupted from the speaker. It was Linda and the girls. "Listen, Abbs. We're off into Cambridge tonight. To that new club, you know. If you and Krzysztof want to come call us back. Like right now. We're going in fifteen minutes. We can get the taxi driver to pick you guys up. Love ya!"

As the answer machine became silent again, Abby sighed with relief. She had zero interest in going to a club. Just the thought of alcohol, a dance floor filled with sweaty bodies, the girls screaming in mock horror as she recounted the events of last night – *You did what? With one of your old pupils? Ooh, you tart! But what was he like? Was it any good?* – was enough to make her feel nauseous again.

She returned to the sofa and pressed 'play' on the remote control. She was desperately hungry, but she wasn't sure she'd be able to eat the sandwich she'd just now prepared. She ignored it until she got to her favourite scene in the movie – when Julia Roberts, gorgeous in her new clothes, told the previously snooty shop women that they'd made a big mistake in not serving her – and then scoffed the lot, along with a tub of Häagen-Dazs.

The food made her feel a little better; the sweet creaminess of the ice cream coating her insides with love, self-worth, validation; the feeling of satedness dulling the still bitter recriminations needling at her mind. *You can get through this*, she told herself. That was the kind of thing the advice columns in the trashy magazines she read would say. It was what her friends would tell her.

An image of Linda and the girls popped into her mind – they'd be at the club now, ordering shots of tequila. Would they be talking about her? Saying that she was a boring fart for not coming out with them? If only they knew how *not-boring* she had been last night. But then she saw Linda, round-eyed, whispering, *Did he wear a condom? No?! So what if you're, you know…? And what about, you know, diseases…?*

Abby's stomach did a flip and she suddenly retched. Her mouth became slick with saliva and she could hear Krzysztof, in his teaching voice, saying, *That's your body's way of protecting your teeth from the stomach acid about to flow through your mouth.*

And as she ran to the bathroom and vomited into the toilet bowl she could hear Krzysztof's roll call of STDs: *syphilis, chlamydia, gonorrhoea, herpes, crabs, hepatitis B, HIV.*

She clutched hold of the toilet bowl, desperately wishing she could go back in time and rewrite the past.

By the middle of the following week Abby had fallen into a new daily routine. She'd spend most of the day sleeping, wake in the afternoon, then move to the sofa in the lounge – her now crumb-coated dining area-cum-movie theatre. She'd stay there until the early hours of the morning, watching romantic comedies and grazing on whatever food was left in the cupboards. Eventually, she'd drag herself back to bed again.

But by the end of the week the cupboards were pretty much empty. Still, at least her period had started, so that was one less thing to worry about. She knew she needed to go shopping, but she couldn't face a trip into Newmarket. She'd be all right for another week or two – there was a packet of rice which would keep her going for ages, a tin of beans which she could make last for a few days. There were the chocolates too, in her rucksack, and the windfalls from Mrs Motherwell's apple tree that always dumped its fruit on their back lawn.

An urgent problem was the fact that Li Li had no more cat food, and she was refusing to eat the little Whiskas left in her bowl. Abby had tried making the foul, desiccating food look more appealing by moving it about with a fork, muttering to herself that the little shit didn't deserve any more food until she'd finished everything in her bowl, but when maggots had begun to writhe about in it, Abby had to concede that Li Li was right to not finish it. She flung the lot in the bin.

Li Li, who didn't look any thinner for the lack of regular feeding, rewarded Abby one afternoon by bringing in a mouse and letting it go in the spare room where, of course, it ran straight beneath the wardrobe. Incensed by the stupid cat's antics, she picked her up and flung her out the front door. Abby then spent the next half hour trying to catch the creature, but with no success. Exhausted by her efforts to move the furniture about and to get at the mouse, she ended up sitting on the bed and gazing up at the picture of the Madonna and Child. Though Mary held her son in both hands, her eyes were on Abby.

She thought the woman looked sad. Disappointed. It was as if she was searching for some scrap of goodness in Abby's soul, but had found her utterly lacking. It made her squirm with embarrassment. Shame. Guilt.

But that was what women like her mum, and Mary, did to girls like her. They made them feel ugly. Inadequate. Impure.

Suddenly, she stood and glared at the icon. Well, she would show her. She would become the most beautiful of them all. And no one would ever again look upon her and judge her to be unworthy. And Krzysztof would beg her to come back to him. It would take work, of course. She'd need to diet, *properly*, buy some new make-up and clothes. She'd even suffer the horrendous changing rooms if it meant she could look all glam. But it would be worth it. She'd start today.

❖

Calorie restriction was the way to go, obviously. As Krzysztof always said, the formula for losing weight was straightforward enough: reduce calories in, increase calories out. But as she wasn't a jogger, or into aerobics, the calories out bit wasn't going to happen. She just had to make sure she ate less. A lot less.

The hunger pangs were, at times, excruciating, but Abby suffered the pain by telling herself they were merely messages from her body, telling her that the beautifying process was working. She imagined herself an incomplete statue, emerging from a block of marble. And with every ache of hunger, more fat would be carved away from her flesh, revealing the perfect body beneath. She was like a sculptor, only she wasn't using a chisel or a mallet – she was wielding the scalpel of self-denial.

But the greater the decrease in her weight, the greater the number of flies in the spare bedroom. Li Li, no doubt pissed off about the lack of food – or was she leaving gifts of dead mice for Krzysztof in the hope that they'd make him return? – was adding daily to the pile of rotting rodents accumulating beneath the antique wardrobe. Abby, unable to move the furniture about to get at the mice, left them there, pulling the door shut on the fly-infested room. When she was in Newmarket, she'd buy some fly spray. That would sort the problem. She'd go in a day or two, when she had a bit more energy. Besides, Li Li didn't seem to be starving.

Four weeks into the summer holidays, Abby finally summoned the strength to go into Newmarket. She caught the bus on its afternoon circuit of the villages and spent most of the slow and halting journey staring out the window.

Eventually, they got to their destination. But as soon as Abby got off the bus, her legs unsteady beneath her, and began to walk up the high street, she saw something that made her freeze. Up ahead were Krzysztof and Rob, with a couple of young women. They were going into The Golden Lion. One of the young women, who had long, black hair and cheekbones to die for, was hanging off Krzysztof's arm as though she were a shiny new handbag.

Abby, her heart pounding, immediately turned into the nearest shop. It was a newsagent-cum-bookshop and she strode towards the fiction section with real purpose, as though she couldn't wait to get her hands on the latest Dan Brown. But when she got to the bookcases she merely stood there, trembling, wondering what on earth she was going to do. But she couldn't just stand there, looking like a plum. She grabbed a book, and with unseeing eyes looked down at its cover, which bore an image of a pig's head on a stick, flies buzzing round it. Who *was* that girl? And how could Krzysztof be with someone else, so soon? It was horrible. Insulting. Abby, suddenly aware of the pig leering up at her, the blood dripping from its mouth and eyes, began to feel lightheaded. And what was going on with her legs?

Thud. The book fell from her hand and she followed after it as the bookshop spun about her and everything blurred into black. *Thud.*

According to the white-haired shop assistant who'd thrust a cup of milky tea into her hand, Abby had only lost consciousness for a few seconds. But to Abby, it had felt like a lifetime. As she tentatively reached for the side of her head, which was throbbing like a bastard, she discovered a hot, fast-growing lump where her head had collided with the floor.

"Go on, drink some tea. It'll do you good. And you'll be wanting a chocolate bourbon. Cure for any ill, they are. Go on," the old dear insisted, practically putting the cup to Abby's lips.

Reluctantly, Abby took a sip of the calorie-laden tea.

"That's it, you'll be right as rain soon enough. I'm

not surprised you fainted. It's this heat, isn't it? And you probably skipped lunch."

Abby nodded, keen to accept the woman's ready-made excuse. When *was* the last time she'd eaten? She couldn't remember. She had a memory of tipping the last of the rice into a pan of boiling water, but when had that been? Yesterday? The day before? Last week? Her stomach, unused to the sweet milkiness of the tea, contracted in displeasure.

"Thank you," said Abby, attempting to raise herself off the chair. "But I'll be all right. Really."

She gripped the back of the chair as she felt herself swaying.

"There's no rush, really," said the shop assistant. "Take your time. You sit there whilst I get you that chocolate bourbon. All right?"

Abby sat back down again and gave the woman a weak smile. "Thank you."

Abby wasn't quite sure how she managed to get back home, but somehow she did. Having abandoned the idea of doing any shopping, she'd left the bookshop and walked all the way home, stopping to rest frequently. A walk that should have taken an hour and a half took her over three hours, and there were many times that she cursed herself for not getting the bus, or a taxi. But that would've involved hanging around in Newmarket for a while longer, and she couldn't risk being seen by Krzysztof. Not yet. She returned home about an hour or so before dusk.

On entering their bungalow, the phone rang. Abby let the answerphone get it and with a sinking heart heard her mum's voice. "It's me, darling. I just wanted to check what flight you and Chris will be on tomorrow. Give me a call when you get a moment. Me and Terry are going out now, but you can leave a message."

Fuck! She'd completely forgotten about their trip to Spain. What was she going to say to her mum?

Exhausted, she slumped down beside the small table which bore the telephone and idled away a half hour by examining her sore feet. They were so painful that she was sure they must be bleeding. But no, they were the same as ever: misshapen oblongs, the stubby toes like fat chipolatas. The bathroom scales might be telling her that she'd lost weight, and a lot of it, but they were lying to her. She looked as she always had – her round face was no thinner, and her thighs and arms were as chunky as before. No, if she were to ever get Krzysztof back, she had to step up her dieting. Of course! There were probably some calories in the herbal teas she'd been drinking – she'd have to stop drinking those. And there'd be no more nibbling on the last of the Weetabix. Or taking nasty chocolate bourbons from stupid shop assistants who had no real concept of what "being on a diet" meant. What she really wanted was sleep. But first, she had to phone her mum.

With a shaky hand she picked up the handset and dialled the long Spanish number. Thankfully, after a couple of rings it went to the answerphone and Abby recited her prepared lie: "Hi Mum, sorry about the late notice, but we can't make it anymore. Krzysztof's mum's not good, you know, so he's got to stay with her. I'm fine, just busy with the girls. Don't bother ringing back, I'm pretty much out all the time. So… yeah. Bye."

She dropped the handset into its cradle and then took herself off to bed, doing her best to ignore the continual buzzing that was coming from the spare room.

Abby was woken by the sound of someone knocking on the front door. As she stumbled down the hallway she recognised the bent-backed shape of her neighbour through the frosted glass panels. *Jesus!* What time was it? She couldn't face being seen by Mrs Motherwell but, equally, the old hag would think it odd if she didn't answer.

Abby crouched at the letterbox and lifted the flap so that she could speak through it. "Is that you, Mrs Motherwell?"

"Yes, dear. I'm sorry, have I caught you at a bad time?"

"Um, yeah, I've just now stepped out of the shower, and I'm not properly dressed or anything."

"Oh dear, I am sorry. I'll come back later."

"No! I mean, I can talk for a minute."

"Well, dear, I just wanted you to know that I've left you some cake on your doorstep. I haven't seen you for ever so long. I guessed you were already on holiday, and that I'd got the dates for looking after your cat all mixed up. And that you'd forgotten about giving me your keys. But then I saw you going out yesterday. So I hope you don't mind, but I've been feeding her. She's ever such a sweet thing, isn't she?"

"That's fine. And thank you. But, yeah, I've been busy lesson planning. And Krzysztof's with his mum. Helping her out, you know."

"Oh yes. He's a good man, he is, looking out for his mum."

"Yeah, well, I'd better go now."

"Of course, dear. But don't work too hard!"

Abby let the letter box flap fall back down and then sat with her back against the front door. She waited for a few minutes before opening the door a fraction so that she could bring in the cake. There were two thick slices of Victoria sponge on a willow-patterned plate, and her mouth began to water the moment she saw them. Slamming the front door shut she fought the urge to gobble them down right then and there. No, she couldn't. The cake was a test. A test of her love for Krzysztof. If she didn't eat the cake he would come back to her. And the very act of throwing the vile thing into the bin would be the final flourish of her scalpel of self-denial. The moment the cake was gone she'd be so hollow from within she'd be like living marble – her pale skin, free of fat, would be translucent and she'd glow with beauty, both inner and outer. And when Krzysztof next saw her he'd be astonished by her transformation. He'd want her back.

Quaking with hunger, her stomach a giant maw of want, she forced herself to the kitchen and dropped the cake into the swing bin. As the lid swung backwards and forwards, releasing a cloud of flies, Abby had to restrain herself from plunging her hand into the bin to retrieve the cake. The flies buzzed their displeasure at being disturbed, and forced Abby to return to her bedroom, where she hid under the covers, hugging herself tight. She couldn't get the cake out of her head. How long would she have to stay in bed until the want, and the pain, went away? She dug her brittle nails into her skin and thought of Krzysztof, how, in a few days' time, he'd be here. She had to look her very best for him.

Abby drifted her way through the next few days. Too weak to shower, or brush her hair, or deal with the bloody flies that were all over the house, she kept to her bed and dozed. When the sunlight streaming through the thin curtains became too harsh, too probing, she took herself off to the lounge, closed the blinds and put on a romantic comedy. She knew her body was doing something remarkable – achieving perfection – it was just a shame that it took up so much energy. She had to get clean, put on something nice for Krzysztof, but it was all so exhausting.

One morning, though, she woke to the sound of someone calling her.

She stumbled out of bed, her vision hazy, dream-like. Was it Krzysztof? Was he here to pick up his stuff?

She thought she saw a figure moving within the spare room and so she opened the door and went inside. The room was abuzz with flies – the air was thick with them, their noise and erratic flight paths; their fat, blue bodies. She wanted to leave, to get out of there, but she was mesmerized by them, the way they seemed to be communicating something to her. They seemed agitated, angry somehow. Abby looked to the icon and suddenly understood their distress. They were all desperate to be near the Madonna and Child. Indeed, the picture was crawling with flies, as though it were a beacon of sunlight guiding them out of darkness. To freedom. Mary's eyes alone were uncovered. And she was looking straight at Abby.

Before, Abby had only seen a disappointed, or judgemental, look there, but today she saw something different. It was a look of approval. Of pride even. And as the flies, one by one, left the picture to settle on Abby's bare skin, she finally understood. Her own skin was glowing gold. And looking down at her feet, she could see that they were beginning to turn orange, the colour of Mary's skin. She *had* achieved perfection.

Abby, her head reeling – from depth of emotion or hunger, she didn't know – fell to her knees and pressed her palms together. "Thank you," she whispered. "Thank you."

And as her whole body slumped to the floor, her eyelids drooping, her heart beating out its final ellipsis, she knew that any minute now Krzysztof would come. And they'd be together again. For good.

But first, she had to slip away with the Holy Mother; to escape into a paradise in which her and Krzysztof's baby had grown and been born and lived. Just for a moment. It wouldn't take long.

The flies, covetous of their new icon, smothered Abby in hungry kisses.

Everybody's Always Losing Somebody

Sean Hogan

Like so many other stories, it began with a cottage on the edge of a forest.

The New Forest, to be exact. Alex had Googled several holiday homes in the area, intent on finding the perfect getaway for him and Charlotte, and finally settled upon a small 17th century thatched cottage, perched on a hillside on the periphery of the woods. The front of the building looked out over a gorgeous view of the surrounding Avon Valley countryside, while the back garden led directly onto a woodland trail, snaking deep into the heart of the forest. He envisioned them going for long morning walks, then returning to picnic on the front lawn, luxuriating in the bucolic vista stretching away before them.

Admittedly, Alex had a complete antipathy for the English countryside. No, make that *all* forms of countryside. Once, after he and Charlotte had first got together, and their affectionate teasing had not yet atrophied into rote contempt, he'd enjoyed piquing her by continually insisting that *countryside is just city waiting to happen*. In those days, the statement would have been met by a theatrically-shocked gasp, perhaps a playful slap, whereas now his pet jokes were habitually greeted by a look of bored disdain.

Still, he reminded himself that there hadn't been too many jokes of late anyway. Aware that whatever had previously kept their relationship buoyant was now slowly leaking away, like air from a slow puncture, Alex nevertheless found himself helpless to prevent it. He could hear the sly hiss of escaping gas, but could not manage to locate the leak or succeed in staunching it. If pressed,

Alex would probably have struggled to articulate what he wanted from his and Charlotte's partnership anymore, but he knew that what he did *not* want was to be alone. He had been single for six terrible, sexless years before they'd met on an online dating site, and he had absolutely no wish to return to that miserable state of affairs, especially not now that the inexorable march of middle-age was causing his greying hairline to recede at roughly the same inverse rate as his stomach expanded, i.e. well beyond the limits of his current trouser waist size.

So, in sheer desperation, he'd agreed to the one thing he'd always previously resisted, the one concession he'd always considered to be a deal breaker (even if he'd never *quite* articulated it in that fashion, knowing full well what the dire consequences of such candour would be): that he and Charlotte should have a baby together. While siring a baby to serve as some kind of relationship band-aid was doubtlessly an unforgivable thing to do to a child, he was nevertheless certain that Charlotte would make an excellent mother, and as for Alex, well, he would simply do the best he could. His own father had never given the slightest impression that he was particularly interested in any of his three children, and while Alex could not, in all honesty, argue that it had been an ideal childhood, neither did he think he'd turned out all that badly, considering. Above all, he counted upon feeling the sort of primal, uncontrollable love he'd always heard gripped new parents. But what if that love should fail to materialise? Well, Alex had always prided himself on possessing a certain sense of responsibility, and therefore vowed that, out of sheer principle, he'd make a better job of parenthood than his father, regardless of any private qualms he might hold about the situation.

It had taken some time – enough that Alex had begun to worry about his potency (had he left it too late?) – but eventually Charlotte had fallen pregnant, and for a time, the plan seemed to be working. Like rainfall restoring a wilting flower, his wife had blossomed anew; the colour returning to her cheeks, her demeanour visibly brightening. No longer did she loll brokenly around the flat they shared, her limbs lifeless stems. She had dedicated herself to turning their small spare room into a nursery, and as the room had painstakingly been transformed, so had Charlotte. At last, she could again look her husband in the eye, laugh at his little jokes and idiosyncrasies. The gnawing disquiet that had afflicted Alex for so many months gradually began to subside.

And then, disaster. Charlotte had lost the baby. Alex had returned from work one evening to find her locked in the bathroom, weeping bitterly. She did not emerge for hours, despite his entreaties and promises that they could try again. In the end, she had only vacated the bathroom after Alex had given up and gone to bed, and even then she simply took some spare bedding and slept on the floor of the nursery, where she'd remained ever since. For his part, Alex could barely bring himself to set foot in the room now. He had crept in there one afternoon while Charlotte was out with a friend, and marvelled at how the once-cheerful space now felt as cold and desolate as a morgue. All his hopes and dreams were entombed inside, as though they were stretched out lifelessly on a marble slab. Yet again, he could hear that insinuating hiss of escaping air, as the life he had made for himself slowly began to wither away.

So it was that they now found themselves on the road to rural Hampshire. When he'd first proposed the trip to Charlotte, she had given him a long, dull look and simply said, *Why?* It had taken him several weeks to talk her round, although it was probably more truthful to say he had simply worn her down. Even now, she sat silently in the passenger seat staring out at the passing countryside, her enervated expression suggesting nothing more than someone trapped in front of an endless loop of daytime television commercials, advertising payday loans and funeral insurance.

'Beautiful, isn't it?' Alex asked her.

'What?' The sort of curt one-word response he was becoming increasingly accustomed to.

Taking one hand off the steering wheel, he gestured vaguely. 'All this. The countryside.'

'Don't tell me *you* care,' she retorted, her eyes drifting up to the car roof, as if hoping it would suddenly peel away and allow her to ascend to a heavenly refuge.

His hands tightened around the steering wheel. Alex found himself seized by a sudden urge to twist it to the left and send them violently spinning off the road, to end it all in a gnarled tangle of shattered glass and twisted metal.

But instead, he remained silent for a moment, before saying, almost too quietly to be heard, 'Won't be much longer now.'

The cottage was as beautiful as the photographs on the website promised. They were met outside by the owner, a tall thin man in his sixties named William. To look at, he reminded Alex of a figure made out of pipe cleaners, impossibly skinny and angular.

Ignoring their host, Charlotte got out of the car and wandered off down the front garden to look at the view, leaving Alex to make small talk with the man.

'Gorgeous place you have here,' Alex told him. 'Do you live far away?'

'In town,' William replied. 'It's just a short drive. I can be here in fifteen minutes if you need anything.'

'Oh, I'm sure we'll be fine,' Alex assured him. 'I'm not planning on bothering you. I just wondered why you don't live here yourself.'

The older man grew pensive. 'I did, for a long time. My parents owned it before me. I grew up here. But when I got older…' He paused. 'Well, it just wasn't practical after a while.' He looked around with a faint sigh. 'I'll always love it up here, though.'

'And I'm sure we will too,' Alex said.

'Will you be going walking in the forest?' William enquired.

'Oh, I should think so. I'm not much of a rambler personally, but my wife likes a good walk.'

William's gaze moved to Charlotte, standing with her back to them at the edge of the garden. Something about the affect of her unmoving figure put Alex in mind of a widow who'd lost her husband at sea, and had spent every waking hour since on the shore, forlornly waiting for him to return.

William's soft voice jerked him from his melancholy reverie. 'Well, mind how you go on those forest trails. They can be tricksy. You can get all turned around and before you know it, you won't know where you are.'

Alex thought he knew precisely the feeling, but said nothing.

After William departed, Alex tried to tempt Charlotte out for a jaunt into the woods, but contrary to his earlier characterisation of her as a keen walker, she claimed to be too tired after their journey and instead took refuge in a hot bath with a large glass of wine.

Alex sat downstairs on his own for a short time, but knowing that his wife was lying there sulking right above his head made him jittery and uncomfortable, as though he were lingering under a storm cloud waiting to be struck by a bolt of lightning. So in the end, he decided to go for a walk by himself.

Grabbing a couple of cans of lager from the fridge and shoving them into a satchel, he called up the stairs to Charlotte. 'Just going for a walk. Won't be long!' He didn't wait around for a reply, and almost certainly didn't expect to receive one anyway.

As promised, the cottage's back garden bordered a woodland trail, and Alex duly set out into the forest, invigorated by a stubborn desire to enjoy himself and thus prove some kind of a point to Charlotte. It was shady and cool beneath the trees, and despite his avowed antipathy to all things rural, Alex soon found himself soothed by the quiet hush of his surroundings. Mulling his present situation over, he vowed that he would make the most of the weekend, even if he had to do it entirely alone. Let Charlotte wallow in her own misery if she so desired. There was only so much a man could do, after all. Why should he let himself be dragged down alongside her?

He hadn't been walking long before he started to grow short of breath. Ruefully, Alex was forced to concede that these gentle country strolls were harder work than they looked, at least for a sedentary type like himself. Never mind running, why *walk* before you can walk? Slumping down at the base of a nearby ash tree, he leant back against the silvery trunk and popped open a can of lager. Taking a long swallow, Alex then unleashed a hearty belch, and was immediately struck by the unbridled vulgarity of the gesture, here in this enchanted idyll. For an instant, he was seized by an irrational urge to apologise to the empty forest. He had always prided himself on being resolutely unimpressionable, but even Alex had to admit that there was something almost magical about his surroundings. He supposed it was the wash of emerald light suffusing the space around him that lent the forest a somewhat unearthly air. Whatever it was, he found himself growing wonderfully relaxed, despite the recent stresses and strains of his marriage. If the rest of the weekend turned out like this, perhaps he might even be forced to reconsider his long-held attitudes towards the countryside.

Closing his eyes, he took another mouthful of lager, taking care to sip it more delicately this time. Bliss. He began to think about simply remaining here for a couple of hours. In time, Charlotte might start to wonder exactly what had happened to him. *Worry*, even. It would do her good to have to think about someone other than herself for a change, Alex decided.

The next instant, he became aware of raised, excited voices nearby. It sounded like children playing. He opened his eyes and looked around in irritation. Typical. A whole bloody forest and he had to end up in exactly the same spot as a bunch of noisy kids. He silently prayed that their games would quickly take them elsewhere, or else he'd be forced to trudge defeatedly back to the cottage. Alex could easily imagine what Charlotte's quietly withering response would be. *You weren't gone very long. Get tired out, did you? Perhaps you should get yourself down the gym.*

There was a flash of movement amongst the trees, signalling the arrival of the children. Apprehension uncoiled in his belly like a serpent. He couldn't stand gangs of kids. They'd probably be lippy little bastards, looking to bolster their street cred by mouthing off to an adult. Alex had been bullied at school, and still suffered a helplessly Pavlovian response when confronted by groups of unruly children. He took a nervous gulp of lager, trying to reassure himself that they'd probably be made equally apprehensive by his presence in the woods. If he was lucky, the children would think he was a lurking paedophile and give him a wide berth.

A twig snapped sharply over to his left, putting Alex in mind of a fracturing bone. His head snapped around with a jolt to glimpse a boy of about ten years old peering at him from behind a tree trunk. To the rear of the boy, Alex could see more of the children, strung out in a line across the forest, as though they were participants in a search party.

'Hello, sir,' the boy said.

Sir. That was a reasonable start. 'Hello yourself,' Alex said, trying to conceal his can of lager in his crotch.

'We're looking for our friend. Have you seen her?' the boy asked him.

'Sorry, I haven't. Is she lost?'

The boy glanced at him cagily. 'I think she's hiding from us.'

'Are you playing a game?' Alex queried. 'It'd be cheating if I told you where she was, wouldn't it?'

A dark-haired girl of about the same age as the boy stepped forward. 'Tell him the truth, Mick. It isn't a game. We were mean to her.'

So they were bullies after all. Poor kid. 'Well, that wasn't very nice of you, was it?' Alex said reproachfully.

'We want to say sorry,' the girl said. 'But now we can't find her anywhere.'

'Well, I'm afraid I haven't seen her anywhere around here.' Alex said. But before he could continue, the boy Mick spoke up again. Pointing at the can nestled between Alex's thighs, he asked: 'Is that beer you're drinking?'

'Yes,' said Alex, taking the beer and offering it to him. 'Do you want a sip?'

Mick edged warily forward. 'Thanks.' He took the proffered can and took an wary sip, before pulling a demonstratively unimpressed face. 'Ugh.'

'You'll get used to the taste one day,' Alex said, accepting the can back from the boy. He looked over at the dark-haired girl. 'Well, if you made your friend run away, I think you should probably keep looking for her. It'll start to get dark soon.'

The girl nodded, and at once, the children collectively began to retreat back into the trees, becoming one with the forest once more. As he watched them disappear, Alex found himself niggled by an insistent sense that there was something indefinably odd about the group. But what? They'd been polite enough, certainly. He supposed he probably shouldn't have offered the boy alcohol, but nevertheless found himself strangely heartened that the kid had been innocent enough to accept.

Then it struck him: their clothes. He was by no means an expert on children's clothing, but hadn't everything they'd been wearing looked unfashionably out of date? And weren't kids these days obsessed with logos and labels? The children's clothing had all been stuffily functional, and cut in such a way that might have led you to believe it was decades old.

Dismissing the thought, Alex finished his beer and shoved the empty can back inside his satchel. This *was* the middle of nowhere, he told himself. He was used to city kids, with their expensively flash clothes and smart little mouths. Things were probably very different out here in the sticks. Alex could well imagine country folk having an abiding horror of waste. And doubtless there was still such a thing as the rural poor, even in this day and age. Those kids might have been wearing clothes handed down from their parents, or even their parents before them.

For a moment, he began to ponder that it might actually not be a bad way to raise his own child, before he remembered that there *was* no child, not anymore. And maybe not ever.

Charlotte had begun preparing dinner by the time Alex returned to the cottage, and this small act of domesticity led him to hope that the meal might signal a fresh start to the weekend; a chance for them to sit down together like a normal married couple, to companionably eat, drink, talk and reconnect. Whatever had been misplaced in their relationship could be found again, Alex was sure of it. He knew he needed to work a bit harder at things, and was perfectly willing to make that effort, just as long as Charlotte would only meet him halfway.

But when he poured them each a glass of wine and began to loiter around the kitchen, telling her all about his small epiphany in the forest earlier, she merely looked at him in irritation and sighed.

'Alex, I can't do anything with you in my way,' she muttered.

Stung, he told himself it was better not to retort. Instead, he grabbed the wine bottle and took it through to the dining room, where he sat gazing through the cottage's front window at the valley beyond. Everything looked so peaceful out there. Part of him envied people their lives here, the simple purity of it. Alex began to fantasise that he could just walk out the front door now, stride out into the verdant Hampshire countryside and simply keep on going. He was convinced that, before too long, he'd find another home more than willing to take him in; a cluster of friendly, welcoming faces to sit down with him at the dinner table and chat about the day's events over a hearty meal.

Despite this conviction, he finished his glass of wine and immediately poured himself another generous measure, without asking Charlotte if she'd like one too. She'd quite plainly said she didn't want to be bothered, after all.

So, by the time Charlotte brought their dinner to the table, Alex was well on his way to being agreeably drunk. Placing a plate of chicken curry in front of him, she peered at him suspiciously. 'Are you pissed?'

'Just enjoying myself,' Alex said, perhaps more forcefully than he'd intended. Not wanting to catch her eye and risk starting a fight, he instead stared down at his meal until she moved away to take her own seat at the table. While doing so, he couldn't help noticing that Charlotte had slopped some curry over the edge of his dinner plate while serving and hadn't bothered to wipe it away. Little things like this spoke volumes, he decided.

Still, he would rise above it. He ate a mouthful of the curry and murmured in audible appreciation. 'This is good,' he told Charlotte, in case the point hadn't been made loudly enough.

'Mmm-hmm,' she replied, without looking up.

He reached over and refilled her wine glass. 'It's really nice out in those woods,' he said.

'I'll bet.' Said through a mouthful of curry.

'We could go for a walk in the morning, if you like.'

Charlotte washed her food down with a swallow of wine and looked at him unwaveringly. 'Alex.'

'Yes?'

'You *made* me come here.'

'Oh, come on,' he snorted. 'I didn't exactly *force* you, Charlotte...'

'You made me come. After I told you I just wanted to be left alone for a while.'

Had she told him this? Alex didn't remember. It was impossible to hear what she was saying half the time anyway, with her face forever pressed into the fucking pillow.

She continued: 'So despite what I said, despite *everything*, we're here now, but I still want to be left alone. That hasn't changed. One bit. Do you understand?'

'Yes.'

Charlotte stared at him like an impatient schoolteacher. '*Do* you?'

'No, not really,' Alex finally admitted, his manner growing churlish.

'I didn't think so,' she said, her voice cutting into him.

Fuck this. It was *his* turn, he decided. 'I don't understand how this is meant to be helping us, Charlotte. There are two of us in this equation, aren't there? So why am *I* the only one making a fucking effort here?'

She gazed at him from the other side of the table, only a matter of inches away. If he were to lean over, Alex could easily have kissed her, slapped her, anything. But they might have been staring at each other across a vast expanse of desert for all that their proximity implied.

Finally, Charlotte responded, her voice low and emotionless. 'You have no idea how much of an effort I'm making.'

Alex said nothing. He could only sit and watch as his wife pushed her plate away, got up and stalked from the room. Despite possessing little remaining appetite, he forced himself to stay at the table and finish his meal, simply because he had absolutely no conception of what he might possibly do otherwise.

Charlotte did not emerge from the bedroom for the rest of the evening. Alex considered clearing the dinner table and washing up, but decided instead to plant himself on the living room couch and finish the beers in the fridge. It seemed like a low enough bar, all things considered. Still, he was only midway through his last can of lager when his head finally grew as heavy as the rest of him and he passed out.

By the time he woke up again, it was gone 2am and the moon was high and bright in the sky. His mouth tasted of stale lager, and he could feel the first black wisps of storm clouds gathering in his head. For some reason, the melody of a long-forgotten children's nursery rhyme was also whirling round his mind. *Peter, Peter, pumpkin eater.* God knows what he'd been dreaming of.

Heaving himself up from the couch, Alex shambled through to the kitchen and poured himself a glass of water. Thinking that it might not be a bad idea to add some fresh air to the restorative mix, he opened the kitchen door and stepped out into the back garden.

Outside, the night was cool and clear. The trees of the nearby forest loomed over the garden, their branches etched in silver moonlight. Alex sat himself down at the patio table and gazed ruminatively out at the expanse of woodland. His incipient hangover was not being helped by the thought of facing Charlotte again in the morning. This cosy weekend getaway was by now looking like one of his more legendarily foolish ideas. At least in London he could have escaped to the pub with a mate. Out here, he was completely trapped. There was nowhere to go, no one to see. All at once, he began to loathe the countryside again.

Then, his brooding was suddenly interrupted by a distant, imploring cry in the forest. 'Sally! Sally, where are you?'

It was a young girl's voice, rendered spectrally eerie by the darkness. Alex realised it must belong to one of the same children he had encountered earlier that afternoon. But what on earth were they doing out in the woods in the middle of the night? Did parents simply allow their kids to run rampant around here?

'Sally, we're sorry! Please come back!'

They were still looking for their missing friend, it appeared. Surely *she* couldn't still be out there too? Hopefully this girl Sally had simply given them the slip and was by now safely back at home, tucked up in bed. And if the others *were* bullies, it served them right being stuck out in the woods fruitlessly searching all night. Alex's mind flashed back to some of his own playground humiliations. He would have wished far worse fates on his erstwhile childhood tormentors, he knew that much.

'Sally!'

Bewildered, Alex got up from the table and took a few hesitant steps towards the edge of the forest. Despite himself, he still found he had an instinctive urge to be a grownup and chase after the kids, tell them they had no business being out this late and to get themselves straight home. Only the prospect of making an utter fool of himself stumbling around the darkened woods, possibly even getting hopelessly lost, prevented him. He stood there at the end of the garden, teetering between the desire to do the right thing and the far more appealing option of retreating inside the cottage and going back to sleep. Why wasn't Charlotte here with him? *She* would know what to do. Unable to make up his mind, Alex remained exactly where he was, locked in helpless stasis.

It took a glimpse of darting movement in the corner of his eye to finally prompt him into any sort of action. Glancing around, Alex caught sight of a pale, furtive figure lurking on the threshold of the woods. But as soon as he had registered it, the figure just as quickly concealed itself behind a tree.

Could this be the missing girl, he wondered?

'Hello?' Alex half-called out, half-hissed, suddenly

afraid he would wake Charlotte. 'Are you Sally? Do you need help?'

At the sound of Alex uttering the name, the figure peered out from its hiding place, allowing him to observe it clearly for the first time.

What he saw was a young girl, or at least what had once been one. She was quite naked, her pallid flesh mottled with mould and dirt, her skin streaked with dried blood. Alex could make out several deep wounds all over the girl's body, injuries that might have been inflicted with a small knife, or perhaps a sharpened tree branch. His hand flew to his mouth in horror, at the same instant his eyes met hers.

Or would have done, had her eyes not been empty pits in her face, as black and bottomless as the grave that had spawned her.

Alex stumbled backwards, struggling to maintain his balance. At the sight of his terror, the girl opened her mouth to giggle, and Alex saw that it was filled with grave earth. Moaning, he lurched crazily around, flapping his arms at the air in a frantic bid to remain upright. He crossed the lawn like a bad comedian overplaying a drunk routine, his eyes fixed desperately on the door to the kitchen. It was only a few short yards away, Alex told himself. But at any moment, he thought he might feel the girl's touch on his shoulder, the chill sensation of those small, clammy hands clasping tightly around his neck as she climbed upon Alex's back and rode him gleefully around the garden.

Because didn't she only want what all small children wanted? To play and play until it was time for them all to go home to bed?

The next moment he was inside the cottage, and turning to scrabble frantically at the lock. Alex dared not look up, lest he see the girl scurrying towards him across the lawn, like some unspeakable clockwork toy. As he attempted to turn it, the key jammed halfway, and hadn't William *told* him there was a trick to locking the back door? He let out an anguished, inarticulate cry of rage and fright, each inseparable from the other. Perhaps aided by his uncontrollably shaking hand, Alex at last managed to jiggle the key in the correct fashion to ease it on its way, and the door locked with a heavy click. Still without looking up, he blundered noisily across the kitchen and into the hallway, where he threw himself inside the downstairs toilet, locked its own door tightly against the terrors of the outside world, and spent the rest of the night there, sitting huddled on the toilet seat.

He emerged the next morning to find Charlotte eating breakfast in the kitchen. Bright sunshine streamed in through the window, bathing the room in a beatific glow. On the face of it, everything was idyllic, perfect. But Alex knew this was a lie. It was wrong, all of it. His marriage, this place, *everything*.

Munching on a salmon bagel, Charlotte gave him a sidelong glance, taking in his dishevelled hair, his dulled, scarlet eyes. 'What on earth were you doing in there?' she said contemptuously.

'Didn't feel well,' Alex replied, shuffling over to the coffee machine.

'Mmm,' Charlotte said, leaving him in no doubt as to what she diagnosed as the cause of his distress.

Alex poured himself a coffee and sat down at the kitchen table. He desperately wanted to tell his wife about what he'd seen, but how? She was barely inclined to listen to him as it was. At best, she'd tell him it was just a nightmare; at worst she might accuse him of attention-seeking, of maliciously trying to frighten her.

So instead, as so often in the recent course of their relationship, he chose to say nothing. The pair of them sat there in complete silence, Alex brooding over his coffee, Charlotte nibbling at her bagel and fastidiously examining her nails. He remembered the breakfasts they used to share, constantly joking and teasing, every new day together full of possibility. One time Alex had set the toaster on fire, and as she watched him flap uselessly at it with a tea towel, Charlotte had laughed until she'd given herself a headache.

And now this was all that was left. It was a total mockery of what he'd intended the weekend to be, Alex decided. Even if he hadn't seen that *thing* in the woods, they shouldn't be here. They should head back to London immediately. He just needed to say as much to Charlotte. After all, why would she care? She'd never even wanted to come in the first place.

He was about to speak when Charlotte drained her coffee mug and pushed her plate away. 'Right, I'm going for a walk in the woods,' she said.

'Charlotte, wait,' he blurted.

She gave a weary sigh and gazed across the table at him, no doubt expecting Alex to try and invite himself along.

'I don't think you should go,' he said feebly.

Her eyes rolled viciously. '*Right*. You dragged me here to relax, and now I'm meant to stay cooped up in the house with you, is that it?'

'No, no...' What the hell could he say to her? 'It...it might not be safe in the woods. There was a gang of kids messing about in there yesterday. Real little bastards.'

Charlotte snorted. 'I'm not scared of a bunch of lairy kids. Christ, Alex.'

'At least let me come with you.' As soon as the words left his mouth, Alex knew exactly how they sounded.

'*That's* what this is really all about, isn't it?' She abruptly got up from the table, before delivering her parting shot. 'Look, I meant what I said yesterday. Just *leave me alone*. I'll be perfectly fine out there. It's not like a middle-aged wreck of a man reeking of stale booze is going to frighten anyone off anyway, is it?'

Alex sat there dumbly as she strode from the room. Well, fine. He sincerely hoped Charlotte did see the little dead girl, or whatever the fuck she actually was. The shoe would squarely be on the other foot then. And if his wife did subsequently show up back at the cottage completely terrified out of her wits, maybe then he'd stubbornly insist they stayed for the remainder of the weekend. It would be worth it.

Getting up from the table, Alex stomped theatrically upstairs and shut himself in the bathroom, where he stood underneath a scalding hot shower for as long as he could stand. For good measure, he performed a spectacularly messy bowel movement in the toilet and didn't bother to clean the fecal remnants from the bowl after flushing.

Feeling a little better about everything, Alex dressed and returned downstairs, planning to enjoy another cup of coffee in relaxed seclusion now that Charlotte was safely out of the house. Whistling jauntily (*Peter, Peter, pumpkin eater…*and how did the rest of it go again?) he poured himself the coffee and turned to take his seat at the kitchen table.

In the next instant, the mug dropped from his hand, splintering into fragments against the tiled kitchen floor and splattering his bare feet with hot liquid.

Alex barely even noticed.

His attention was entirely focused upon the kitchen window, through which peered the little girl from the previous night. If Alex had perhaps thought she might appear less terrifying in the daylight, he had been swiftly disabused of that notion. There were no shadows to hide the worst of her now. The bloodless pallor of her skin seemed heightened in the warm sunshine; worse, her flesh looked sweatily putrescent, suggestive of incipient rot. Alex suddenly began to fancy that, even shut up inside the house, he could smell the vile stench of her corruption, seeping in around the window pane.

Rooted to the spot, he watched as the girl pressed her face against the glass, leaving a smear of decay on its surface. Childishly, she stuck out her tongue at him, only to reveal a blackened snarl of dead meat, crawling with eager beetles.

His vision starting to blur at the edges, Alex lurched unsteadily. Desperately shifting for balance, his foot came down on a broken shard of coffee mug, and the resultant pain finally served to snap him from his petrified fugue. Skidding on the spilled coffee, he whirled around and fled from the kitchen, pausing only to snatch up his mobile phone and car keys.

First things first, he had to get out of here.

Second, once he was a safe distance away from the cottage, as soon as there was not a dark forest or trees or even a single sapling to be seen, there was a phone call he needed to make.

He met William in an out-of-town supermarket car park. Spotting the old man waiting in the far corner, Alex nosed his car into an adjacent parking space and waited for William to climb in beside him. As soon as the old man was settled comfortably in his seat, Alex turned to face him, impatient to rid himself of the unspoken questions piling up on his tongue. Instead, he found a thermos flask thrust into his face.

'Coffee?' William asked him softly.

'No. No thanks, I'm fine,' Alex replied.

'I put brandy in it. It seemed like it might help.'

Reconsidering, Alex took the flask of coffee and poured himself a cup, while William waited patiently.

Only when Alex raised the steaming cup to his lips did the old man speak again. 'So you've seen her.'

'I've seen her *twice*,' Alex said emphatically.

'I never have,' William told him.

'But you *know* about her.'

The old man smiled sadly. 'Oh, everyone does. Sally Brown, her name was. She disappeared in the woods when I was just a small boy. I was only about six years old, too young to go off playing in there by myself. Not like her. Mind you, I don't think her folks really cared what she did.'

'What happened?'

'No one ever really knew. They never found her, you see. But people *thought* they knew.' William took a long swallow directly from the thermos, and sloshed the liquid thoughtfully around his mouth. 'There was a gang of kids that used to play in the forest. Sally was…well, back then they would have called her a bit of a simpleton. I don't know what the polite word is now. The other kids used to tease her. Sometimes they'd let her play with them, but they'd always turn on her in the end, whenever she did something stupid. Which, inevitably, she always did. So then they'd all start on her, laughing and jeering, and she'd run off through the woods crying. But one time, she never came home.'

Seeing that Alex had finished his coffee, William offered him a refill. Concentrating on pouring the hot liquid into Alex's cup, he didn't look up as he murmured, 'My older brother Mick was one of the kids.'

Tell him the truth, Mick. 'Did they do something to her?' Alex asked quietly.

'Well, that's what a lot of people *thought*,' William sighed. 'But none of them ever owned up to it, and the police never found a body, so they couldn't prove anything. It's a terrible thing to say, but no one really seemed that fussed, after a while. She was only a simpleton, after all. So that might have been the end of it, except then all the other kids disappeared too. Mick and the rest of them.'

'Jesus,' said Alex. 'They just vanished?'

'Disappeared from their beds one night. Me and Mick, we shared a room. That little second bedroom in your cottage, that was ours. Now I was only small, so I don't remember it too well, but I have a distant memory of waking up in the middle of the night and seeing Mick creeping towards the bedroom door. He turned to me and whispered, *I have to go and play with her now, Bill. If I don't, she'll never leave us alone. And I can't stand having her in my dreams anymore.* That was the last time I ever saw him.'

In the space of a few short hours, Alex realised he'd been utterly transformed. Previously, this was the sort of hoary old wives' tale he would have scoffed at, dismissed as ignorant yokel talk. But he'd seen them, hadn't he? He'd seen *her*.

'They're still out there, aren't they?' he asked William.

The old man nodded. 'Always have been. My parents knew they were there, but they wouldn't talk about it. My mum would never let me play in the woods though. But after she and my dad died and I took over the cottage, I began to hear them sometimes. Hear them calling out for Sally in the night.'

'Are they…ghosts?'

The old man wiped vigorously at his lips. 'I've often wondered about that. And you know, I don't think so. At least, in my understanding of the word. They seem as real as you or I, you know? Solid, physical. So no, I don't think they're *ghosts*. I just think they're trapped. In some kind of purgatory, if you like.'

'Because of what they did to Sally?'

The old man shrugged. 'Like I said, nothing was ever proven.' He suddenly looked very tired. 'Thing is, I didn't quite tell you the whole truth a minute ago. I did see Mick again, after many, many years. I was quite a bit older then, and was out walking in the forest one afternoon. Anyway, he just ran right out in front of me, right there on the trail. He looked just like I remembered him. I was the only one who'd changed.'

'Did he speak to you?'

'Just for a second. He said, *We haven't found her yet, Bill. But I think we're getting close.* Then he ran off into the bushes. I never said a word back to him. And the next day, I began to pack up the cottage. I'd been thinking about moving into town and renting it out anyway. I always knew Mick was out there, you realise, but actually *seeing* him? Still a young lad, after all these years? No, I couldn't face that.'

'But what about letting other people see them?' Alex said accusingly.

William bridled. 'So what? Most people would just think they're normal kids. They don't mean anyone any harm.' He paused. 'But *her*. No, I never saw her. Not once. So I don't quite know what to tell you about that.'

This was not quite the solution to the mystery Alex had been seeking. He felt a sudden wave of anger rising within him: anger at William, at Charlotte, at the whole sorry fucking mess.

'Well, what you *can* tell me is that you'll return the money for the cottage rental,' he told William flatly. 'I'm sure you understand that my wife and I can't stay there, not under these circumstances.'

The old man shrugged. 'I won't argue. But…' He tailed off, his exhausted eyes looking beseechingly at Alex.

Alex tightened his fists. 'You won't argue, *but?* What *but* could there possibly be?'

'It's just that you're the only person I know of who's ever seen Sally,' William murmured. 'It must mean something, surely. She must *want* something from you, don't you think? Maybe you can help her somehow…'

'Oh, for fuck's sake.' No one ever asked Alex what *he* wanted, but if they did, he'd say that he just wanted the old man out of his car, right now. In fact, what he *really* wanted was to be far away from here and back home in London, where the kids might have been mouthy little fuckers, but at least they were living, breathing, mouthy little fuckers.

'No, please listen,' William implored him. 'If you can help her, maybe you can put an end to it, to *all* of it. Maybe they can finally rest in peace, Sally and Mick and all the others.'

Alex stared mutely out of the car window. His view was mostly filled by a featureless concrete pillar, but still he kept on staring.

'Please tell me you'll at least think about it,' the old man pleaded.

Alex thought about it for the entire drive back to the cottage. By the time he arrived, he'd made his decision. This was absolutely nothing to do with him. Christ, he had problems enough of his own without being haunted by some dreadful little ghost girl. What if he tried to help her and she never left him alone? Perhaps she might even follow them all the way back to the city. He'd seen horror films in which things like that happened. No, he needed to wash his hands of the whole rotten business, the sooner the better.

The main issue was Charlotte. Despite never having wanted to come to the cottage in the first place, at the first sign of Alex wanting to leave it prematurely, she would resolutely dig her heels in, he was sure of it. He supposed he could threaten to go back alone, abandoning his wife and forcing her to take a train to London, but did he want to suffer the undoubtedly toxic fallout from such an act?

On the other hand, could he feasibly hope to spend another night here without completely losing his mind?

He entered the cottage and looked around for Charlotte. There was no sign of her downstairs, but upstairs he could see that the master bedroom door was open, so she hadn't shut herself away again. Moving through to the kitchen, he found the back door ajar and Charlotte sunning herself on the patio with a large gin and tonic.

He lingered in the doorway, unsure of how best to proceed. 'You're back,' was all he could finally think of to say.

Charlotte squinted up at him. 'So are you.'

'How was your walk? Did you see any kids?'

'Not a soul. It was wonderful.' *And here you are again to ruin it all*, Alex thought, mentally completing Charlotte's sentence for her.

Well, fuck it. If he was going to spoil her peace and quiet, he might as well go all in.

'Look, I need to talk to you about something,' he said, stepping down from the doorway and pulling back a chair, its metal legs scraping harshly across the brick patio.

'Yes, well,' Charlotte sighed. 'So do I, as it happens.'

He paid her little mind. 'I spoke to the old guy who owns this place, and he told me a very interesting story…'

She interrupted him. 'I'm sure it was *fascinating*, but I think what I have to tell you is rather more important, Alex.' She took a swallow of her drink before continuing. 'It's about our child. Or *my* child, to be more accurate.'

He stared at her open-mouthed, all thoughts of whatever he had been going to say next bleached from his mind, like ink in bright sunlight.

Charlotte continued: 'You see, Alex, the baby wasn't yours. I'm fairly certain of that. I never even wanted your child. But there's…someone else, you understand? I'm in love with somebody else. I have been for quite some time.'

Alex stood there helplessly, his body – no, his entire *being* – feeling impossibly thin and insubstantial. He might have been one of those paper shooting targets, his physical likeness captured on its surface for Charlotte to take deadly, unerring potshots at. 'You…'

'I should have told you long before now, I do realise that. And I *am* sorry, believe it or not. These sorts of things are never easy to navigate, and losing the baby was very hard on me, as I'm sure you realise. But I'm hoping we can both be adults about it.'

'You…' Alex's throat felt clogged, the words he longed to say lodged in his windpipe, choking him. For an instant, his mind flashed back to little dead Sally, her mouth full of grave dirt.

Charlotte sniffed. 'Do spit it out, Alex.'

'You *cunt*.'

Unblinking, she gazed back at him. Slowly, her hand moved to the patio table and picked up the sweating glass of gin and tonic. Charlotte might have been an actor in a film, her movements slowed down for directorial emphasis, the camera speed running at thirty-six frames per second, forty-eight.

'Oh, please don't be *boring*,' she finally told him.

Alex was by no means a violent man, the mere thought of it sickened him in fact, but he now understood exactly how such things happened. Crimes of passion, didn't they call them? *Crime passionnel*, a voice in his mind whispered pedantically. Trust the fucking French to have a phrase for it. He found himself struggling against an almost irresistible red tide, barely able to keep his head above the surface. He should just give in to it, stop fighting and allow himself to be swept away, take that sweet crimson water into his lungs and drown in it…

Alex moaned and staggered away from the table, lurching towards the waiting woods. He could not be here any longer. And where else was there for him to go now but the forest, where all lost things went?

Charlotte called after him. 'Oh, Alex, for Christ's *sake*…'

Pausing at the edge of the woodland trail, Alex leant heavily against a tree, before glancing back at his wife. He found that he was at last able to speak again, now they were not both trying to subsist on the same poisoned air.

'You should be dead like her,' he told Charlotte. 'You should be buried out there with her.'

Then, he turned and allowed the forest to take him.

Alex wandered through the woods for hours, pausing only to sleep for a time at the base of a large tree. He was always aware of her, constantly there by his side, lurking somewhere on the periphery of his vision. Every now and then, he would hear the little girl singing softly to herself, the gentle melody carried to him on the breeze. *Peter, Peter, pumpkin eater.* Now, he was finally reminded of the rest of the words to the rhyme. *Had a wife but couldn't keep her…*

As he walked, he began to wonder. Was it his imagination, or was Sally shepherding him? Guiding him?

It didn't matter. He was perfectly content to go wherever she wished. His earlier terror of her had almost entirely dissipated, Alex discovered. What harm could Sally do to him, after all? She was just a poor lost little dead thing. It was the living you needed to fear, not the dead.

Finally, it began to grow dark. All at once, Alex started to become uncomfortably cognisant of the sheer size of the New Forest: well over a hundred thousand acres, if he remembered correctly. And he had been wandering for hours, without any real sense of what direction he was heading in. An unfamiliar panic clutched at him. He was a creature of the city. He thrived on ozone and light pollution. What possible business did he have being out here?

Halting in his tracks, he looked around wildly, straining to catch a glimpse of Sally. But the rapidly forming gloaming made it hopeless. She seemed to be lingering in every dark shadow, concealed behind every looming tree. Alex felt as though two cold hands were closing around his lungs, crushing the breath from them. 'Where are you?' he cried desperately. 'Where are you taking me?'

In reply, he heard a sly giggle, then a burst of hurried footfalls leading away to his left. With little option but to give chase, Alex launched himself after Sally, doing his best to keep pace with the sound of her feet, the undergrowth crackling beneath her tread like kindling bursting into flame.

They ran like that for some minutes, until Alex thought that his heart might explode in his chest. *At least it'll be quick*, he thought.

The next instant, he emerged into a small clearing. Long fingers of moonlight reached down from above to part the forest canopy, allowing him to at last see clearly again.

Sally waited patiently at the base of a tall ash tree, one bare leg curled around the other. She was still singing to herself.

He put her in a pumpkin shell. And there he kept her very well.

Alex stepped forward, his eyes meeting the little girl's black stare. 'I want to help, Sally,' he told her. 'Just tell me how. Do you want me to bring you back home? Is that it?'

Another giggle. Suddenly, she started to skip around the base of the tree, quickly disappearing behind it.

Summoning the last of his stamina, Alex ran over to the tall ash, but when he peered around its trunk, Sally had vanished. He could not see or sense her anywhere. It was as though she had never even existed.

The strength suddenly flooded from his legs, and Alex collapsed to the forest floor. It was hopeless. He would have to spend the rest of the night out here, and pray that he could find his way out of the woods in the morning. He wondered whether Charlotte would notice he was missing, whether she even cared enough to bother notifying the park authorities. It might be far easier for her if Alex simply disappeared from her life, after all. She would be free, free to start again with the man she truly loved, the man who had cuckolded him. The words of Sally's nursery rhyme once again began to echo through his skull.

Had a wife and couldn't keep her…

No. He wouldn't allow himself to just roll over like that. Alex was certain he had been led out into these woods for a reason. He was determined to finish his task here, *whatever* it was, and then somehow find his way back to the cottage to take care of his outstanding business there.

And there he kept her very well…

He rolled over onto his front, scrabbling forwards across the earth. In a moment of clarity, it had now become clear to him exactly what he needed to do. *They never found her*, William had told him. Poor little Sally, lying out in these woods for decades, lost and alone. But *he'd* found her, hadn't he? After all this time. All he needed to do was take her back home.

Finding his way back to the spot where Sally had first

been standing, Alex began to claw at the earth with his bare hands. After a time, his fingernails began to throb, and he searched about for something to use as a tool, finally settling on a section of bark he prised from the nearby tree. Deeper and deeper he dug, finding nothing, but certain that Sally must be interred there, if he could only dig long and deep enough.

Eventually Alex uncovered a single small bone, browned with age and decay. Holding it up, he could barely make it out in the darkness. Was it even human? It might belong to a long-dead animal for all he knew. A fox, or even a fucking squirrel. This couldn't be it, surely? He thrust himself back into the hole, flinging aside clods of mud, but found nothing further.

Collapsing facedown into the dirt, Alex let out a bellow of maddened frustration. He didn't understand what she wanted, what *any* of them wanted. What had he ever hoped to achieve? Why had he even *come* to this godforsaken fucking place?

He lay like that for a few minutes longer. But gradually, Alex became aware that he was no longer alone in the forest. Raising his head up from the earth, he looked around to see the other children standing silently behind him, Mick and the rest.

'I don't know my way home,' Alex told them.

'We'll show you,' Mick replied.

Alex allowed them to lead him back through the forest. Even when dawn finally began to break and he could start to see clearly again, it still all looked the same to him, but the children moved through it easily and confidently. They'd had plenty of time to learn their way around, Alex supposed.

When he finally emerged from the woods, Alex had almost thought he might find himself in a different world, another time or place entirely. But no, the children had brought him back to the same thatched cottage, the same quiet back garden. He could see Charlotte's empty gin glass where she'd left it on the patio table. As they all walked up towards the cottage, the children parted ranks, allowing him to enter first. This final confrontation was intended for him, and him alone.

The cottage was completely silent, and Alex moved through it like a ghost. In a sense, he *was* a ghost, he realised. A ghost of the man he used to be. He drifted up the narrow staircase, and along the hallway to the master bedroom. The door had been left ajar, and through the crack, he could see Charlotte lying on top of the mattress.

Alex pushed the door aside and stepped into the bedroom. On the bed, his wife lay curled up into a fetal ball. She was quite naked, and her normally rosy flesh had turned mottled and grey. In places, Alex thought he could make out tiny blossoms of rot. Several wounds had opened up on Charlotte's body, from which she'd bled copiously, staining the flowered bedspread beneath her crimson.

Alex moved closer and peered down at his wife's face. She stared blankly into space, her lips softly mouthing a familiar melody.

He thought that he could see traces of grave dirt lodged between her teeth.

Suddenly appalled, Alex stumbled backwards, flailing at the thin air.

Then a small hand closed around his own, and he glanced down to see Mick gazing up at him.

'You've found her at last,' the boy told him.

—Inspired by an untitled painting by Aleksandra Waliszewska

Sibyl

Lisa Tuttle

She was desperate to get away.

Three months of lockdown in a small flat, her only (too constant for comfort) companion her landlady, Evie, had left Sibyl McAllister feeling her sanity was at stake. That she had lost her job, had no savings, and debts to pay were not good enough reasons to forgo the holiday she needed and decided to take.

The first thing was to get the car from her brother. Their father had left it to them both, but it was only Graeme who had a garage where he could keep it. He accepted her request without argument, although he was curious about her need for it.

"Going somewhere?"

"Scotland, on holiday."

"You have somewhere to stay?"

She hesitated, afraid he'd refuse if he knew she meant to sleep in the car, but he'd already guessed, and offered his camping gear.

"Won't you need it?"

"No, you're all right."

Soon the elderly Volvo was stuffed with everything a camper might require and she was driving cautiously away, tense and nervy from lack of practice, but by the time she'd navigated a dozen roundabouts, and survived the torturous crawl through congested streets, she felt ready for anything, and decided to leave that very evening and drive north through the night.

First, she would have to pack, and tell Evie. Her stomach clenched at the thought of having to explain herself, to justify her need for a holiday when she hadn't paid rent in two months, and should have been looking for another job, or signing up to some sort of retraining scheme, and she wondered if she could just wait until the other woman had gone to bed and sneak out, leaving a note behind.

But luck was against her. Evie was walking by when Sibyl turned down their road, and she stopped and watched her struggle to manoeuvre the big heavy car into a parking space. There was no chance of avoiding a confrontation.

"Your brother's car?"

"It's mine, too, really."

"I know, you said, but…" She looked puzzled and suspicious. "Why do you want it now? You know you'll have to apply for a permit if you're going to keep it here. You're not thinking of going away?"

Sibyl shifted uncomfortably. "Just for a little while. I meant to tell you."

There was a short silence as Evie waited for the explanation Sibyl was not ready to give. Then she sighed. "All right. Have you eaten? I was just going out for takeaway. Come on, my treat. Tell me while we walk."

It was, at least, a little easier to tell her without seeing her reactions. "I just need a little holiday. I need to get away for awhile, have a change. I'll camp out, so it won't cost much, just petrol and food."

"You're going camping by yourself?" Evie sounded faintly shocked. For her, the worst thing about lockdown was being unable to see her family and friends. Sibyl, on the other hand, longed for solitude – to get out of the flat, and away from Evie – but that was too harsh to say, as kind as the other woman had always been to her.

"Look," Sibyl said carefully. "It's what I need. It's so I can think about things. Clear my head and think properly about…well, about my life, and what I really want to do. When I get back I'll have a plan. I'll find a job for sure, and then I can pay you back—"

"You mustn't worry about that."

"But I do. I don't want you thinking I'm avoiding my responsibilities—"

"Of course I don't. It's—" she gave a little laugh. "It just doesn't seem like much of a holiday to me, on your own and roughing it. It sounds more like an ordeal!"

"Not to me."

Later, back in the flat, while they were eating, Evie wanted to know more about her plans. "Why Scotland?"

"Well, I've never been, and there's a lot of beautiful scenery."

"Every time I've been to Scotland it was raining. Don't mind me. I know it's your ancestral home."

Sibyl grimaced. "McAllister is a Scottish name, but my grandfather was English. His real father was called Smith, I think, but his stepfather gave him his own name." She was sure she'd explained this before.

"The Lake District is lovely, and not so far. But maybe you think it will be more crowded?"

"No." It was silly to keep her reason a secret, especially since Evie already knew about the painting – and liked it enough to suggest it should be on the wall in the sitting room, not "hidden away" in her bedroom. Sibyl had told her the story of how, at the age of thirteen, on a family holiday in Cornwall, she'd bought this little watercolour painting of a stone circle because it reflected her recently acquired fascination with ancient megaliths like Stonehenge (which they'd stopped to see on their way down), and afterwards, when she took the postcard-sized picture out of its shoddy frame, she saw that the artist had signed it: S. McAlister, and below her name was a number that was surely the year in which she had painted it: 1848. A shiver of awe ran through her. That she shared a name with the artist, and that the painting was an actual antique made her purchase seem fated, and it was at once her most precious possession.

"You remember I could never find out anything about the artist? Well, I have now. I was just…looking for something else online, and I found out that there was a woman named Sibyl – yes! – Sibyl McAlister, born in 1818, the daughter of a Scottish minister, and although she was never a professional artist – painting was a ladylike hobby in those days – four of her paintings are hanging in a museum in Campbeltown. So – I thought I could go there, and show them my painting, and find out even more."

Evie's smile was radiant; Sibyl was surprised to see anyone so happy about something that was only a big deal to *her*. "How cool is that! Where's Campbeltown?"

"On the west coast. About a hundred and thirty miles from Glasgow."

"And the stone circle? Did you find out—"

She shook her head. "The other four paintings are all local landscapes. It doesn't seem too likely that a minister's daughter would have travelled too far in those days, does it? But – I'm not sure it's a real place."

"Why wouldn't it be real?"

Sibyl got up and went to take the picture down from the wall. In greys, browns, blues and splashes of purple on heavy rag paper it depicted a circle of standing stones, seen from above.

"It's an arial view, and they didn't have airplanes in 1848."

"They had balloons – people went up in balloons," Evie protested. "Or she did several views of it, and one was how she imagined it might look from above. Artists do experiment with perspective."

Sibyl shrugged and went to put the picture back. She didn't want to talk about it anymore, the place she'd so often dreamed of but never really thought she would be able to visit. "If it's anywhere at all close to Campbeltown, I'll find it."

She drove through the night, feeling lighter, freer and happier than she had in a very long time. The sun was just rising when she reached Loch Lomond, and took the turning to Luss. Despite signs prohibiting overnight parking, the enormous carpark was well-populated with cars, campervans and caravans, and beyond the paved area, the green shores of the loch were dotted with tents, but at least there was no one stirring yet. To her dismay, the toilets were all locked shut. But there was a bit of woodland on the far side of the parking lot where she was able to do what she had to do before she went on her way again, hoping to find a less popular place to take a short nap.

This turned out to be more difficult than she had expected, as picnic areas and even lay-bys had been chained off to prevent people using them as campsites, and anywhere a van or car could safely pull off the road they had done so. In the end, she drove all the way to Campbeltown without another stop.

There she found the museum without any trouble, and parked around the corner. But when she reached the heavy wooden doors they were shut. A laminated notice declared the premises closed until further notice, in line with government regulations. There wasn't even a phone number to call for more information.

Had she come so far for nothing? Surely there was someone in this town who knew something more about the artist and her stone circle – the curator, an archivist, a librarian? She searched in vain for a tourist information office, and considered going into a shop to ask, or accosting random pedestrians, but the prospect of having to explain her own interest to people who probably knew nothing put her off, and she continued to wander the streets in search of some other suggestions…

In a little back street she found a bookshop. Like the museum and the library it was closed, but there were more hopeful signs – like one saying that face coverings must be worn, and another with the regular opening hours – that it would be open tomorrow. Her spirits rose a little. In the absence of a librarian, the manager of a bookshop might be able to answer her questions. Her spirits rose still more when she saw the books displayed in the window were mostly about local history. She took a picture of it, focused on the book in the middle, which showed a standing stone on top of a hill above the sea.

On her way back to her car she passed a café, and realized how hungry she was. There were no other customers, and it looked like they were getting ready to close, but the girl behind the counter told her she could still get a cooked meal if she ordered right away. "The specials are off, but you can have anything off the regular menu," she said, handing her a menu. "Sit wherever you like."

When the girl had taken her order to the kitchen she came back for a chat. When she asked what had brought her to Campbeltown, on an impulse, Sibyl held up her phone to show her the painting of the mysterious stone circle. "Any idea where this might be?"

A furrow appeared in the girl's smooth forehead. "Around here?"

"Could be. The lady who painted it lived in Kintyre a long time ago. The museum has some other paintings by her, but—"

"But it's closed, aye. Bet I know who would know," she said excitedly. "He knows everything – I mean about the past, people and places in Kintyre. I was at school with his daughter. He's written books and all."

Grinning, Sibyl brought up the picture of the bookshop window.

"That's him!" She met Sibyl's look. "Want to talk to him? I'll give you his number. He won't mind, honest. He gets calls from folk all the time, about their family history."

Indeed, when Sibyl phoned, no sooner had she introduced herself than he was off: "The McAllisters of Tarbert, aye? Or you're not sure? How far back can you go?"

"I'm sorry – but it's not my family. It's about another Sibyl McAlister. The one who—"

"Oh, aye, the minister's daughter. They came here from Ayr – I can't tell you much more without looking it up – but there was no male line of descent, and Sibyl, of course, never married."

"It's not the family I'm interested in; it's a painting she—"

"They're all in the museum, and it's closed for the duration – whatever that means. But you can see them on the Scottish Artists website."

She bit her lip and thought how much easier this would have been if she could have sent him an email – or even a lengthy text message. She took a deep breath. "I know. The reason I'm here is about another painting she did – it's not in the museum – I have it. I bought it a long time ago. It's a picture of a stone circle. That's really what I was hoping you could help me with. She painted a little watercolour of a stone circle, and I thought it must be local. I couldn't find anything likely on the internet, but – I thought you might know where it is, if it *is* near Campbeltown."

He made a sort of humming sound before he replied. "I know that it's not in Kintyre."

Despite what she'd said to Evie, she felt crushed. "You're sure?"

"The nearest stone circle I know of is Temple Wood, in Kilmartin Glen. There's no reason why she shouldn't have gone there to visit friends, or if her father was invited to give a sermon in the church. The church is quite near to the stones; not just the circle, but an avenue, and some chambered cairns. It's a World Heritage Site, well worth a visit. You could drive up there in a couple of hours."

As he spoke, she'd searched for images, and found Temple Wood. She remembered having seen pictures of it before.

"It's not Temple Wood. Oh, well, if you're sure it's not in Kintytre, I guess…it might be something she painted from her imagination." She sighed. "Thanks for your help."

"Wait. I've thought of something. I've never seen it for myself, but I've heard stories about a stone circle on Oa."

"On oh," she repeated blankly.

"On O-a," he said carefully. "That's a wee island out near Carradale, in Kilbrannan Sound. Haven't a clue what the name means, but there's a place with the same name over on Islay."

"Where's Kilbrannan Sound?"

"Between Kintyre and Arran."

"An island? Could Sibyl have gone there?"

He gave a dry chuckle. "More a question of *would* she, considering her father preached a sermon against it. But, then, could be that was the point."

"Why did he preach a sermon against the island? Were the people who lived there terribly wicked?"

"There weren't any folk who lived there. I don't think it was ever inhabited – bit too much trouble, I expect, without a good anchorage and no grazing, just rocks, really, although it does have fresh water."

"So what was his sermon about?"

"Superstition. Pagan beliefs, really, that still clung to the place."

She felt a tingling sense of excitement. "What kind?"

"All sorts. A surprising number of stories to be connected to such an insignificant little island. The main one I remember was about a well, or a spring, that gave water that could cure any ailment. In other stories, it was the fountain of youth, or conveyed some other desirable power. Whatever, it was a lure, but it wasn't easy to reach, because once you had made it to the island, you still had to get past the *cailleach.*"

"What's that, some kind of monster?"

"It's the Gaelic for 'old woman.' But in folklore she's not just any old woman. She's a spirit, or a pagan goddess, or maybe a witch. You find stories about her all over."

"And the stone circle?"

He gave a whistling sigh. "To be honest, I'm not absolutely sure…there are some old stones there, but I'm not sure if they're the remains of a chambered tomb, or standing stones, or what. It's not well documented; I don't recall that it's even listed in…"

"You've never been there?"

"Well, no. I don't have a boat. And I guess I've just never made the effort – it's a bit outside my usual territory. And the fishermen who usually take me out, well, they won't go near it."

She felt the tingling sensation again. "Why not?"

"Fishermen are superstitious."

She chewed her lip. "What about me? Could I go there? I mean, how can I get there, to see it for myself?"

"I don't see why not. Just don't ask a fisherman to take you." He chuckled. "Just go on down to Carradale – that's the nearest place to it, on this side of the water. There might be someone advertising tours from the harbour, but if not, try the harbour master's office, or the noticeboard in the café. I'm sure you could hire a boat. Apart from fishermen, people probably go there all the time. Or they do if there's anything to see. The only prohibitions I've ever heard is never try to take anything that belongs to the island—"

She spoke up indignantly: "Of course I wouldn't."

"—and make sure you leave before nightfall."

Two roads ran the length of the Kintyre peninsula, one along each shore. Carradale was fourteen miles from Campbeltown, on the road she had not taken, and it had a caravan site with tent pitches. She phoned the number on the website and was able to reserve one of the last remaining pitches.

"What time should we expect you this evening, Ms McAllister? The office is open until nine, but of course if you're not needing help with anything, it doesn't matter how late you arrive."

She had planned to go there immediately, to get the tent pitched and get settled in before dark, but at the last minute she didn't take the turn-off to the site, but instead drove on into Carradale. She told herself it would be good to have an arrangement in place for the morning and hoped she could get a glimpse of Oa from the harbour.

The harbour master's office was closed, and so was the

café. There was no one around; the whole harbour was eerily quiet. From the position of the sun and the balmy air it felt like late afternoon, and she was surprised to realize it was already half-past seven. She thought she was alone until a quiet voice spoke close to her ear:

"Are you looking for someone? Can I help?"

She turned and saw…a boy? Or a young woman; the smooth face might have belonged to either, and the hooded sweatsuit hid whatever clues hairstyle or body shape might have provided.

"Oh, hello! I was looking to hire a boat – and someone to take me where I want to go."

They smiled. "And where would that be?"

"It's not far. It's an island, a little island—" Turning her gaze away from the stranger, she sought in vain for any sign of it in the water beyond the sheltered curve of the harbour. Shrugging, she turned back. "I was told it's called Oa."

"You want to go to Oa?"

"Do you know it? I'd heard there might be a stone circle there – standing stones, you know?"

"I know. If that's what you want, I can take you."

She caught her breath. "That would be wonderful! What time?"

"Now." They pointed. "There's my boat, see the RIB?"

"Now? I thought – tomorrow would be better."

"Not for me. I have other plans. Sorry." The stranger turned away.

"Wait! Please…is there anyone else…someone who might take me there tomorrow?" They half-turned back but did not speak. She felt she'd been rude, like throwing a gift back in someone's face and asking where she might buy something else. "I just thought there wouldn't be enough time this evening. How long would it take to get there?"

A shrug. "Five minutes? At most."

"Really?"

Gently mocking: "Really."

"How much?"

A wince and a frown. "What? I'm not asking for money."

"I'm sorry. I didn't mean to offend. It's just that I was intending to hire someone, and it's your time, your boat – the cost of fuel."

"It's nothing. Do you want to come or not?"

She couldn't pass up the chance. "Yes, thank you. Just for a quick look; I won't keep you long."

Her guide went ahead, a short distance along the pier, swung down into the RIB, then turned to help her down. "I'm Sibyl," she said, but the other, starting the engine, may not have heard, and made no reply.

The boat began to move, slowly at first, but then as it veered away from the dock and headed out of the harbour, the wind whipped her hair in her face, and she felt exhilarated, her tiredness evaporating. As soon as they had left the harbour a small, high, rocky islet became visible, growing rapidly in size as they sped nearer. In barely five minutes, they had arrived.

The engine idled, the boat bobbing in the water beside a rocky shore. "Hop out."

"Here?" No dock, no bay, nothing, but at her bewilderment, the driver of the boat smiled encouragingly and gestured.

"See that flat rock? That post? It was put there for you to grab."

"Not for tying the boat?"

"Not this one. Look, do you want to get out or have you seen enough?"

The idea of being taken away again before she had seen the stones galvanized her. She was fit and nimble enough to swing herself out of the RIB easily. A second later she stood on the ground and looked at the person in the boat, who gave a jaunty wave. "Go on, go see your stones!"

"How long – I mean how far – I mean, how will I find them? Is there enough time?" She wished she'd discussed this question earlier and knew how long they were willing to wait.

"All the time you like. Go now. Go on, go up! You'll see them from the top."

She turned and followed the rising path. It was steep, but the way was clear. Like the post beside the flat rock, the path was evidence of regular visits to Oa, even if superstitious old fishermen stayed away.

When she got to the top, she looked back to see a small boat travelling rapidly away from the island, towards the harbour entrance. The driver was no more than a hunched grey shape, but the boat was surely the very same RIB that had brought her here. She fought down a surge of panic. There must be an explanation. They'd had to go back for some reason – why not, why bother waiting, bobbing in the water beside those possibly dangerous rocks, when the round trip would take only a few minutes? All the same, she felt a chill, and cursed herself for not exchanging phone numbers, or agreeing a definite time scale for this visit. But as long as she was here…

She turned again, this time to take in the whole of the island from above. It was like a misshapen bowl, slightly higher on this curved side than the other. At the bottom of the bowl was the circle of stones. Looking down, she recognized the view depicted in her painting, and understood. Sibyl had depicted her own first sight of the stones far below.

There was a delicious, shivery sense of the blurring of time in this revelation, knowing that she was standing in the footsteps of Sibyl McAlister. She wondered how long it would take and how hard it would be to climb down to stand among the stones. Gazing along the rim of the cliff where she was standing, she spotted a narrow, winding path leading down to the island's interior. It would have been more difficult for a woman in cumbersome Victorian dress – and hard to imagine a Scottish minister allowing his daughter to wear anything less proper. Even in her trackies and trainers she had to be careful, and sidle along with cautious steps. She kept her face to the wall and did not look down.

The descent, slow as it was, did not take anything like as long as she expected. When she got to the bottom and was able to step away from the wall and turn to look at the stone circle, her stomach plunged as she realized how she had been deceived.

These stones were not the megalithic giants she had imagined. The circle was no more than a miniature version of a lesser Stonehenge: the tallest stones came up only to her waist.

But after a few moments of standing among them her disappointment faded. Yes, they were small in stature, but the island was small, too, and there was something wonderful about their careful placement in this remote, hidden spot. She felt the thrill of discovery, amazed at her luck, to see something so few people knew about. Even the local historian had only heard of it, and there was nothing about it on the internet. She unzipped her pocket, but as her fingers closed around the slim cool slab of the phone she hesitated. To take photographs of this secret, hidden monument, even if she never shared them, felt worse than crass, almost a desecration. She remembered what the historian had said, the warning against trying to take anything away from the island.

Withdrawing her hand, she reached instead for the nearest standing stone, and lightly caressed the warm, rough surface with her fingertips. The surface of the stone was uneven, and she realized the grooves and hollows were not random even before she looked down and saw the pattern etched into the rock was a spiral maze. Her skin prickled, and the hairs lifted on the back of her neck. She traced the line with one finger, feeling how deeply it had been incised, then crouched down beside the stone. Looking at it more closely she saw that it had been decorated all over with fine lines and deeper ones, circles and straight lines and other intentional markings.

The next stone was the same, and the next. None of the markings appeared to be representational, apart from the spiral maze and one that might have been a spear or an arrow, but even those were just as likely considered as abstract designs.

Stepping back from this close inspection, she once more took in the whole circle, noticing that every stone was deliberately shaped, narrowing towards the top; so they were like fingers pointing at the sky, and the other end was buried deep in the earth. She thought of theories she had read about Stonehenge, that it had been constructed as an observatory, connected to the rising and setting of the sun or the movements of the stars with the changing seasons, that it had been built on such a grand scale to accommodate large groups of people who gathered for worship or celebration. Maybe this one had been scaled down in line with the size of the island and the number of people it could reasonably hold: a chapel rather than a cathedral.

Or were the stones bigger than they looked? She had no idea how much of them were buried beneath the earth. Maybe, thousands of years ago, twelve megaliths had been set on top of a hill, on an uninhabited offshore island, meant to be seen from a great distance, but over centuries, the centre of the island had subsided, and soil had built up around the stones, burying them deeper, hiding them from view.

She walked slowly around the circle, touching each stone and stooping to look at its markings, but only briefly – she told herself she would come back tomorrow – when her attention was snagged by something different: a row of letters. A word?

Sinking to her knees, she bent still lower, struggling to read in the gloom. She traced the letters with a finger. Five letters. She knew them well. It was her own name.

Her heart pounded wildly. The other Sibyl, of course. But this time she could not feel pleased by the connection with her namesake. *Sibyl was here.* How crude, how contemptuous of history did one have to be, to carve your name into an ancient monument, like those modern barbarians spray-painting their tags on city walls? And a minister's daughter, too…

She had been straining her eyes to see the name, but only now did she realize how dark it had grown. Her heart lurched, this time with fear. How much time had passed since she came here?

Looking up, she saw the sky above was still pale blue, but the sun had dropped below the sheltering cliffs, plunging the island's centre into darkness.

But night had not yet fallen. This far north, it would stay light until past ten o'clock, and it could not possibly be that late yet. The boat must have come back for her by now, though. Heading for the path, she reached for her phone to check the time.

It was so slow to light up that she wondered if she'd unintentionally turned it off. By then she had reached the start of the steep and narrow path upwards, and she shoved it back into her pocket before she began to climb.

When she got to the top she was reassured by how light it still was, but saw no sign of the boat. Sitting down to wait, she reminded herself of how quick the journey had been from the harbour to the island and took out her phone.

It would not come to life. She couldn't believe it was dead. She'd kept it plugged in the whole time she was driving, and it had been working perfectly well only a few hours before. It was crazy…impossible…but she could not get it to turn on.

With a lump in her throat and cold, shaking fingers, she shoved the useless thing back in her pocket. She told herself it didn't matter; she didn't need to know what time it was, and she certainly wasn't going to have to call for help. *Of course* the person who had brought her here would be back to fetch her, very soon.

But no matter how she tried to resist it, she knew the truth. Deliberately or by some accident, she had been abandoned here. Was it a cruel joke that locals played, to strand a witless tourist overnight? Of course they would expect her phone to work. Or had there been an accident?

No one else knew she was here.

Moment by moment the colour of the sky changed. Red and pink and gold splashed the clouds as the sun sank lower, and far edges turned a darker blue. She saw a star.

She stood up and shouted for help. She waved her arms and screamed.

She couldn't keep it up for long, and anyway it was pointless. The island wasn't even visible from the harbour, and she could not see lights along the shore that might indicate houses with occupants who might just happen to have a telescope pointed in her direction. But in the morning there would be holiday-makers, sailors and kayakers out on the water, and she would be able to attract attention. Someone would surely come to her rescue. She couldn't possibly swim that far, even if the water was dead still and warm.

She shivered. Her teeth were chattering. The wind had picked up and seemed to slice right through her unlined hooded top. It would be even colder in the water, and she'd have to strip down to her undies, and leave her shoes behind…

But it wouldn't come to that. Everything would look different in the morning. Someone would come for her, or she would attract their attention. She would be less tired, better able to think.

It would be full dark soon and even colder out in the wind. She would be safer sheltering on the other side of the cliff, at the bottom, among the stones. She'd better go now, while she could still see.

In the centre of the stone circle there was a mound, or perhaps it was another stone slab, or even a pile of smaller stones, thickly overgrown with moss. She expected it to be damp, but it felt soft and springy and warm to the touch, a bed so inviting that she lay down on it, and, eventually, her exhaustion was such that she fell asleep.

She woke to sunlight warm on her face and a raging thirst.

Confused, she sat up, and it all came back to her, and made her feel like crying with fear and rage. But she was too thirsty to spare any tears. She remembered there was supposed to be a well or spring of fresh water on the island, and got up to look for it.

Sunlight sparked a brilliant answering flash from the ground not far outside the stone circle. She found a silver metal cup resting on a square of slate. She lifted the slate and found a bubbling spring beneath. Bending, with trembling hands, she filled the cup and drank. The water was cold and delicious. She drank three cups.

After drinking, she felt much better. The water not only quenched her thirst, but somehow soothed her fear. She was filled with the conviction that everything was going to be all right. Judging by the light, it was still early, too soon for anyone (except some superstitious fishermen) to be out on the water, so she might as well finish exploring.

Looking past the well, she saw what she first took to be a pile of larger stones. It was sunk in shadow, beyond the reach of the early rays of the rising sun, but as she went closer she realized it was not just a pile of boulders, but something carefully constructed. Indeed, she recognized another megalithic monument from the distant past. Unlike the stone circle, it was full-sized, made of stones taller and broader than a man. Three massive standing stones supported an even bigger slab on top. She had seen something just like it in Cornwall; she remembered it was called a dolmen. Amazing engineering, her father had said; how did those primitive people do it?

The dolmen in Cornwall had stood in a sunlit field, and she had thought it looked like a summer house, a place to hold a garden party, although her father told her it was really the remains of an ancient grave. This one, too, seemed to invite her in, although it was set so deep in shadow that she could not see through, or into, it, and she stepped between the two leaning stones and walked into the darkness.

The ground dropped away beneath her feet and she fell forward onto her hands and knees. The smell of moist earth rushed up to meet her. But the drop was only a matter of inches; she was shaken, but unharmed. She stood up and waited for her breathing to calm and her eyes to adjust to the darkness and felt with sudden conviction that someone else was near, watching her.

Desperate for light, she snatched at her phone before remembering that it didn't work. She held her breath but could hear no other sound; no one else breathed or moved. Still, she felt – no, she *knew* – she was not alone.

She waited, she did not know for how long, but nothing happened until the sun had risen high enough to shine into every corner, and there was nowhere for anyone to hide. She saw something else: something glinting on the ground. She went to pick it up, and found a necklace, an oval locket on a fine gold chain. She looked around sharply, thinking that whoever had dropped such a lovely piece of jewellery would come back for it, but there was no one. For the first time since she had entered the dolmen, Sibyl felt certain she was alone beneath the heavy slab, and alone on the island: whoever had lost this locket had done so long before she arrived. Curious, she slipped a thumbnail into the crack and pried the locket open.

Instead of the picture she had expected she found a curl of wispy yellow hair.

She shut it quickly, feeling a sharp pain in her chest, and the tightness of impending tears in her throat. Surely that was a curl from a baby's head, and what she had felt was the mother's grief...

For a moment she could not move, feeling dazed, and

tried to think of what to do. Perhaps she could find a safer hiding place for it? At last she put it back on the ground where she had found it, and left.

Emerging into the strong sunshine she blinked and tried to remember what she had meant to do when the sun was high; she'd had some plan that involved climbing up to the top of the island and trying to attract attention from a passing sailor....

The thought made her inwardly flinch. Why should she want to draw attention to herself? And from strangers? Never. No, if she was to risk leaving the security of the island's core, it would only be in the late evening, when she was unlikely to be seen, and she could enjoy the feel of the wind in her hair, and a different view. For now, she was quite happy where she was, where she belonged, alone and safe among her beloved stones.

The Acolyte's Triptych

Steve Duffy

In the last days before the outbreak of the Second World War, a decision was made that the nation's most precious works of art should be removed from the galleries of London. When the war came, went the rationale, there would be massive bombing raids on the capital, and the greater part of Britain's art history might conceivably be destroyed overnight. North-West Wales, considered to be at least risk from the bombers, was chosen as the location for the temporary storage of the artistic patrimony. Stately homes such as Penrhyn and the universities of Bangor and Aberystwyth were commandeered, but alongside these there was a more secure site in a secret location. This site was known as Deep Store Number One: I visited it once, and once only, in the August of 1939.

Back then I was a night watchman at the Breden Gallery in Blackheath. It was by some way the easiest job I ever had: in my six years we never had a burglary, nor even so much as a prowler in the grounds. My nights were spent reading novels from the lending library and doing crosswords in the watchman's station, in between my hourly patrols of the gallery's long dark rooms. I carried a lantern, obviously, but the windows were tall and the skylights were wide, and on nights of the full moon I actually preferred to walk my beat by moonlight. I mention this to give you an idea of my general demeanour, back then in the days of my (relative) youth. I was not unimaginative, exactly, but I was not one to let my imagination run away with me. It seems important to explain this.

All through that summer, our most prestigious pieces

were removed one by one from display. Cards were put in the empty spaces on the walls, informing visitors that the paintings in question had been temporarily removed for renovation. In fact, they were down in the basement, encased in plywood crates, awaiting evacuation. In the second week of August, the gallery was closed to the public until further notice, and a fleet of trucks and lorries, hired from a variety of private operators, began ferrying the crates up to Wales. This impinged very little on my job, though I found the empty walls a little melancholy, somehow, on my night-time patrols. Things changed for me on the evening of the 24th, a Thursday. The eleven o'clock news on the wireless was that Parliament had just passed the Emergency Powers Act, and the rush towards war now seemed unstoppable. I was in a broody sort of mood that evening, turning the pages of my novel but not really taking in the words, when there came a tap at the door of my station.

I knew my visitor: it was Professor Geldard, one of the senior staff. I was used to seeing him in the basement rooms, burning the midnight oil over some delicate job of restoration. While most of his colleagues barely seemed to notice the low-grade staff, Professor Geldard always had a polite word for me, and I would make a point of bringing him a cup of tea when I brewed up during the night.

"Good evening, Jim," the professor said. "Hope I'm not disturbing you?"

"Not at all, prof," I assured him, setting down my book without bothering to mark my place. "Another night shift?"

"Not quite the usual thing this time," he said, smiling a little and pushing up his round horn-rimmed glasses. "Then again, what is usual these days?"

"Very true," I said. "I was just about to put the kettle on – can I interest you in a cup of cha?"

"That would be delightful," he said, "but actually it's not why I dropped by. I've got a proposition for you that would involve a nice bit of overtime, if you're interested."

This was indeed interesting, and I gave up my chair to the professor while I made the tea. "You probably know that we're going to be closed to the public for the foreseeable future," he began, "but I hope you also know that your position is secure – at least, as much as anything can be secure at the moment." This had indeed been made clear to me.

"Most of the day staff have been let go," the professor went on, "and just today young Bascombe, my assistant, handed in his notice – he's enlisting, as it happens, and good for him. But it does leave me in the lurch, a bit, for a job I've got tomorrow, and I was thinking you might be just the chap to help out."

"Always pleased to help if I can," I said. This ran counter to the only advice my father had given me when I first entered the world of work: *never volunteer for anything*. But there it was: for better or worse, I wasn't my old man.

"Good man!" Professor Geldard seemed genuinely pleased. He took the best china cup, I had the old brown mug, and we selected a Huntley & Palmer's each from the tin. The professor sipped his tea and sighed. "That's splendid, Jim. Good and strong, just the way I like it. Now, let me fill you in on the details.

"Here's the thing: Bascombe, soon to be Private Bascombe, was going to accompany me on a trip to Wales, first thing tomorrow morning. We've already removed almost all of the most valuable paintings; this consignment will be the last lot for the time being, and they're going to a new storage site which is so hush-hush that I don't even know the name of the place, just its official designation on the paperwork." He consulted a clipboard he'd been carrying. "Deep Store Number One. I'm to liaise with a chap called Bartram on-site. And that's all they've told me."

"And you need someone to lend a hand," I said. "I'm your man."

"Splendid! Now I know you'll be on duty here till seven, and the lorry is booked for eight, so this is my plan. I'll bed down on the folding bed in the basement till three, then you can wake me and get some shuteye yourself until we're ready for the off – how's that? We can probably catch forty winks on the way, you know. Then, it's just a matter of handing over at the site, a little bit of light lifting and carrying, and we can put up for the night somewhere local before heading back home the next day."

As plans went, it sounded entirely straightforward. Which tells you something about plans.

One of the things that made me suited to working night shifts was my ability to fall asleep more or less at the drop of a hat. I gave the lightly snoring Professor Geldard an extra hour in the cot, woke him at four and was up in time to make a brew before the lorry arrived.

The driver was a large moustached chap called Reg – at least I assumed it was Reg. It said "Reg Chivers Haulage of Stepney" on the door of his lorry, at any rate, and I suppose he was content to let the signage do his talking for him. When he jumped down from the cab, I saw he had a good four or five inches on me; he must have been a head taller than the professor. "Morning," I said, submitting to his bone-crusher handshake.

"Morning," he agreed. That was as far as the small talk went. I'd moved the crated artworks up from the basement during the night, using the service lift and the platform dolly, and now we hoisted them into the back of the Leyland Octopus. Professor Geldard supervised as we stuffed the space between the crates with bundles of old sacking and strapped them all into place to prevent jolting damage on the road.

Reg's bulk took up a sizable amount of the cab, but there was room enough in there for the professor and me. We set out at nine o'clock and nudged our way through the morning traffic. All around the Whitehall ministries and the landmark buildings of London, big banks of sandbags were being stacked. We stopped for a late breakfast at a transport cafe just past Watford, where all the talk was of the Crisis, capitalised. When Professor Geldard, incongruous in his three-piece Lovat tweeds, took out his copy of that morning's Times, several of the customers asked him whether there were any new developments. Pope Pius had made a radio address to the world, pleading for peace; Herr Dahlerus was imminently expected in London, carrying details of the German plan for that peace. Meanwhile, the Royal Auxiliary Air Force and Royal Air Force Volunteer Reserve had been merged into the RAF, in preparation for that war that nobody claimed to want. None of these circumstances seemed to reassure the truck drivers, particularly.

Back on the road, we made good time through Northamptonshire and Warwickshire, then ran into traffic on the outskirts of Birmingham. We took to the minor roads to bypass the conurbation, and followed our late breakfast with an even later lunch in a village pub near Cannock Chase. After the meal, Reg took a ten-minute walk to stretch his legs, and I sat with Professor Geldard on the bench outside the pub, enjoying the warm August weather and the sights and sounds of the farmland all around, loud birdsong in the spinneys and hedges, the low humming drone of bees in clover. As the church clock chimed the quarters for the unchanging English countryside, I remember thinking that we seemed to have left the threat of war behind us in London, for the time being at least.

Alongside me on the bench, the professor was chuckling to himself. He was reading from a sheaf of papers on his clipboard, and I shouldn't have thought there was anything in there to raise a laugh. He saw me looking curiously at him, and smiled.

"Nothing, Jim; nothing, really. Just a little quirk of fate. I was thinking of a professional setback I once had, that's all."

"What's that, Professor?" We had another hundred miles or so to go, and I was glad of any conversation. It wasn't as if I was going to get much out of Reg.

The professor tapped the clipboard. "I was reminded of a time, four years ago now, not long after I'd started work at the Breden. I was involved in the preliminary planning of an exhibition devoted to the Italian painter Cancelliere. Have you heard of him, at all? No, I don't suppose you have. He's a minor figure in art history, rather well thought of by students of the early neoclassicists. He spent the latter part of his life in England, where he is presumed to have died – the reference works are unusually sketchy on the actual details of his demise.

"There's never been a retrospective of his work, and I thought it would do rather well for a summer exhibition at the Breden. I sent out feelers to the other London galleries that had Cancellieres, spoke to the RSA in Edinburgh; I even wangled a trip to the Uffizi and back, which was nice. Well, it never happened: the whole thing fell through, partly because of the Wallace Collection's policy of not loaning out, and partly because the main selling point, if you will, of my scheme seemed to be cursed from the beginning."

"What was that?" I asked.

"It was to be my own little coup," the professor said mistily. "You see, the most curious example of Cancelliere's work is a thing called *Il Trittico dell'Accolito* – the Acolyte's Triptych."

"That's three paintings in one?"

"Close enough, Jim. It was commissioned by the Duke of Leman, who was a highly controversial figure in society around that time. He'd got his dukedom under circumstances that were rumoured to be less than entirely reputable; in fact, there were all sorts of stories about him at the time. Friend of Lord Wharton, friend of Sir Francis Dashwood – does the Hellfire Club ring any bells with you, Jim?"

I thought it might. "Doesn't it come up in *Three Men And A Boat*?"

"Bravo!" the professor said. "What a well-read chap you are, Jim. Shady goings-on in West Wycombe, or in Leman's case at Long Leman, his country place in Hampshire. The triptych was meant to take pride of place in a sort of temple he'd built in the grounds, and the subject matter was controversial to say the least. The three panels were painted consecutively, one after the other, under the Duke's exhaustive scrutiny. Each panel – or the first and the second panels, at least – was separately delivered to Long Leman upon completion.

"The subject matter was highly unconventional – blasphemous, in fact – a depiction of something called the Diabolical Trinity. This is a key conceit of Satanism, I believe: the Devil, the Antichrist and the False Prophet. And as if that wasn't enough, the story goes that they were *not* meant to be merely representational."

"How do you mean?"

"Well…" the professor paused; "well, there were those who said that the triptych as a whole was not just a depiction of a magical rite, it was a part of that rite – a central part, they said. It was meant to bring about a certain effect, just as a magician's conjuration is meant to bring about a concrete result."

"What effect?" I asked. Professor Geldard took his time over answering, and finally evaded the question entirely. I never got a proper answer out of him, and after what came to pass that evening I never asked for one.

"It's just a story, Jim. A story very much of its time. There was a great deal of mystification about the Duke of Leman, a great number of rumours, and I don't suppose more than a handful of them contained more than a grain of truth. In any case, the issue was rendered moot, because just at the time when the last panel was finished, the old duke popped his clogs under mysterious, not to say scandalous, circumstances, having thoughtlessly neglected to pay poor Cancelliere what he was owed for services rendered.

"Well! Our man Cancelliere stuck his heels in. He hung on to the freshly completed third panel, all the while waxing indignant in various letters to his friends and benefactors. He'd never had a more difficult job; he'd never known a more demanding patron; he'd never before placed his eternal soul in such hideous danger, as he rather colourfully put it in a lengthy screed to Giovanni Fogliani. The long and the short of it is, the triptych was never assembled. Cancelliere sold the panel he'd kept back, and the other two were split up when the duke's estate was sold off. The triptych ended up in three different pairs of private hands, and over the course of the next couple of centuries the panels gravitated to three separate galleries. One was actually down the road from us in the Dulwich Gallery, though I don't believe it was ever on public display; one was stuck in a storeroom at the Wallace, and one – can you guess, Jim?"

"And one was in the Breden?"

"Got it in one! The third panel, as it happens. We didn't have it on display either; it was a bequest in the '20s from the estate of a private collector, and the subject matter was deemed by our trustees to be altogether too indelicate. So you see, ever since it was painted, the triptych has remained broken up, and it's defied everybody's best attempts to bring it together. This was my great idea for the Cancelliere exhibition: his most notorious, his most mysterious paintings, shown as a complete work for the first time ever.

"And I couldn't swing it. Nothing doing. The Wallace were inflexible as usual, and Dulwich didn't want to know either, which was unusual for them. And here's the funny thing, Jim: it took nothing less than a war, or the threat of one at least, to bring it off."

"How do you mean, Professor?"

"I've been going through the manifest, and it seems that two-thirds of the Acolyte's Triptych – the Wallace and the Dulwich panels – have already been removed to Deep Store Number One, the best part of a month ago. And in the back of Reg's lorry there, we're carrying the third panel. As of this evening, the triptych will be complete at last."

It all put me in mind of a favourite night-time read, Dennis Wheatley. In the spirit of the author of *The Devil Rides Out*, I said, "Are you sure that's wise, Professor? Meddling in the dark arts?"

We shared a laugh. "Old Cancelliere won't be happy, I shouldn't think" he said. "Though I dare say the Duke of Leman will be pleased, when word gets down to him."

Just then Reg reappeared, stumping over to the lorry and ascending ponderously into the cab. "Ah well," the professor said, as we got up from the bench, "in for a penny and all that. I should tell you, Jim, art history is not always this lurid, or indeed this entertaining."

The last leg of our journey was the most time-consuming, as it turned out. Reg's policy of avoiding larger towns and cities left us at the prey of the minor roads, where overtaking was out of the question and the snails dictated the pace. A succession of slow-moving farm vehicles at their harvesting added hours to our drive, and we had fallen well behind schedule by the time we got on to Telford's trunk road from London to Holyhead. We passed through isolated villages by the side of the long straight Roman road, rows of tiny cottages with a bleak boxy chapel at their centre; they looked like pioneer prairie outposts in that high bare moorland south of Denbigh. Like lots of Londoners, I'm always slightly nervous of the uncultivated countryside – all that unknowable, unpopulated space, with nothing to give it boundaries or limits. Now we were approaching the mountains of Snowdonia, where the shadows were lengthening as the sun dipped into the west. The terrain became harsher, less congenial, as if it had been scraped right down to the bones of the rock below.

The professor was giving directions from his clipboard to Reg. We followed the trunk route past Cerrigydrudion and Capel Curig to the high shoulder of Snowdon itself, then turned off south on an unmarked road. A signpost had once given the traveller directions, but it had been painted out, and now a blank white finger pointed the way to nothing. I remember my ears popping as we travelled uphill, the engine of the Octopus grumbling at the steady gradient. Just as the sun was sinking in the west, we lost our view of the horizon; the road suddenly dipped and ran into a narrow gully between two sheer walls of slate. I looked at the shattered striations, close enough to touch from the window of the cab, and a distant memory from school geography class came back to me: "Slate is a friable material." I had a sudden and unwelcome vision of the exposed layers beginning to fracture, to slide loose and crash down on the track.

At the first turn of the gully the way was barred by a gate, beside which was a small sentry hut. Reg sounded his horn, but there was already a man stepping out to meet us.

He came up alongside the cab as we braked to a halt. "Permit, please," he said, in that bored yet officious manner you'll find the world over among natural jobsworths.

"Ah yes…" Professor Geldard rummaged amongst his paperwork. "Here we are. Consignment BRE-slash-23, from the Breden Gallery." He passed the form to Reg, who passed it down to the sentry. He scanned it as if we were asking him to sign away his life savings, then handed it back wordlessly and undid the padlock on the gate. "Don't crack your face, will you," I muttered as we drove through.

"Would you swap his job for yours, Jim?" the professor asked.

"Not me," I said. "This place gets on my nerves."

"Well, there might be a better job for you around the corner," he said. I remember that just then, there was a creaking noise from the back of the lorry, the squeal of wood on metal. I thought at the time that it was just because we were driving downhill, and the load had shifted accordingly. Now, I'm not so sure.

As we turned the next bend in the track, a rock face loomed ahead of us. At the foot of the cliff were a pair of massive iron doors, and on either side of these a couple of Nissen huts. Quite literally, we had arrived at the end of the road.

"Is this it, then, prof?" I asked.

"It is," he said. "Welcome to our destination: Deep Store Number One."

"You're welcome to it, alright," I said beneath my breath. "It's a grim sort of spot, isn't it, though?"

"Used to be a slate mine, obviously," the professor said. "There's a little miniature-gauge railway that ran between here and Criccieth, for carting the dressed and finished product down to the company jetty. All this" – he waved a hand at the walls of splintered slate – "is as much man's work as it is nature's."

Reg pulled up outside the Nissen huts. The professor jumped down, and I followed him. If there was anybody in the huts, I thought, they must surely have heard our approach in the echo chamber of a gully. But nobody came out to greet us.

"Are we expected, Prof?" I asked.

"Well, rather," he said, looking slightly discomfited. "Tell you what – why don't you and Reg see about getting the crates down from the back, and I'll go and raise up the welcoming committee."

Nearby, standing on a length of narrow-gauge rail that ran all the way inside the iron gates, was a large wheeled trolley that must once have been used to transport slate. Reg and I hoisted our precious cargo down one by one and set it on the trolley, 'til there was only one crate left inside the lorry. I happened to glance at the official stamp on the side of the crate. "Cancelliere, A. T. III, 1783", it read, and I knew this was the painting Professor Geldard had been talking about. I laid a hand on the crate, and even in the evening of that hot summer's day, even through the leather work gloves I was wearing, it seemed curiously warm.

Raised voices from outside caught my attention. I let the crate be for the time being and jumped down from the back of the lorry. A tall man, thin as a rake and with a prematurely balding head that would give the professor's a run for its money, was standing before the iron doors. Professor Geldard seemed to be arguing with him; there was some waving of arms, and I caught the words "have done with it before the middle of the night." Like me, the prof was thinking of that little Welsh B&B and a good night's sleep. The other man shook his head, and I could see the fraying of the professor's normally placid demeanour as he turned to Reg and me.

"Chaps, I'm awfully sorry, but there's a snag. Mr Bartram here" – he indicated the tall balding man – "tells me that there aren't any staff on site, and he says we'll have to stow the paintings away ourselves. I do apologise, I know this wasn't in our original agreement, and believe me, I'm as surprised and put out as you are. But it really does seem to be the only way we'll get away from here…?" He tailed off apologetically.

I was about to say that it wasn't a problem, when Reg spoke out. This was enough out of turn to command all our attention. "I'm not goin' in there," he said flatly, and folded his arms, as one who has spoken his piece.

"No, I quite understand," the professor said, "it wasn't what we agreed to, and I am absolutely prepared to make it worth your while in a financial—"

"Not goin' in there," Reg reiterated. And that was that as far as Reg went, which was to say, no farther.

"Jim?" The professor turned to me pleadingly. "Jim, if you wouldn't mind? I think we can get it done quite easily, really."

"Righto," I said, with an insouciance that I didn't really feel. All that slate was getting on top of me, literally it seemed. And there was something about the other man that was "off" – that was how I framed it to myself, and I can think of no better way to put it now. His thin face was fish-belly white in the gloom of the gully, almost cadaverous; he had the look of something that had lived inside that cavern for too long, and now could only come out when the twilight came and the shadows lengthened. His eyes seemed too large for those pinched and skinny features, and he was staring at us in a manner that I for one found off-putting.

"Good man," the professor said gratefully, and the warmth in his voice was its own reward. He turned back to the other. "Look here, Bartram, I was given to expect that you'd have your full staff of men ready to meet us."

"They've gone," the other man said. His voice, now I could hear what he was saying, was about as reassuring as his demeanour.

"Gone?" The professor was puzzled. "You mean they've knocked off for the evening? But look here, old chap, you knew we were coming—"

"Gone." The pitch of Mr Bartram's voice was uncertain; it rose abruptly on the word "gone", and then sank again to an indistinct muttering. "Gone for a week now. Just me."

"But—"

"They had a little meeting." Mr Bartram's smile was not an engaging sight. "It was the caverns, you see. They couldn't face it down there. Not since – well you know what since."

"I'm afraid I really don't know what you're driving at."

"Of course you know what." Mr Bartram was no longer smiling. "You of all people. You've got the third panel, haven't you?"

"But there's important work to be done – the condition of the paintings…" The professor's thoughts were all of the artworks; for the time being he let that allusion to the third panel pass him by.

"They saw the way of it, and then they were gone," Mr Bartram said. "I don't know where. One of them had already gone missing, you know. Some of them thought he'd cleared out of his own accord. Some of them thought he'd gone down there," and he jerked his head in the direction of the iron doors.

"This is all very irregular," the professor said. "I'm afraid I'm going to have to report to the board—"

"Never mind all that." When Mr Bartram spoke, it commanded the attention of us all, in the way that the sound of a far-off air raid siren commands the attention of everyone in range. "It doesn't matter. Have you got it?"

"Got what?"

"Haven't I told you, over and over? *The third panel.*" He was practically yelling now.

"We've got a full consignment, as per the manifest," Professor Geldard said, proffering the clipboard. "These fellows have loaded it all on to your trolley there."

"It's not there," Bartram said, without even looking at the trolley. "It's not one of those. But I can feel it, I can feel it near. Where is it?"

"It's still on the lorry," I said, and was surprised to find my tongue sticking to the roof of my mouth a bit as I spoke. "All the rest is in that little wagon thing there."

"All the rest" did not interest Mr Bartram in the slightest. He broke away from the professor, and absolutely ran to the lorry. Lifting aside the tarpaulin at the rear, he made a noise I can't really hope to transcribe. He sounded like the man who'd found the last lifebelt on the *Titanic*.

"You've got it. Quick, quick," he snapped his fingers at me, as though I was the waiter, "help me get it down. No!" He broke off. "No, I must open the doors. I must fetch the keys. Keys, doors, the opening of the way, and then – wait there!" Suddenly he was running off towards the Nissen huts, leaving me and the professor to stare at each other.

"What the bleeding hell?" I just didn't know what else to say.

"This is bad," Professor Geldard said, "very bad, Jim. There's supposed to be a staff of no less than four men on this site at all times, under the authority of the site manager, Bartram there. They're responsible for the upkeep of the paintings: humidity, temperature control, basic site security... why, this is just anarchy. Anarchy!"

"I don't like to cast aspersions," I said, "but your Mr Bartram seems to have gone a bit barmy."

"More than a bit," the professor agreed, but now Bartram had emerged from the hut and was over by the massive iron doors, wielding a big bunch of keys. He gave a heave, like Samson tearing down the temple, and the doors rolled aside in their metal tracks. Inside, everything was black, and a shudder went all the way through my body at the sight of it.

But Bartram was already inside and fumbling at the wall, and then a string of electric bulbs lit up the cavernous blackness for as far as the eye could see, down to where the tunnel dipped into the heart of the mountain. "Come on!" He was yelling at us, and the sound of his yelling raised deeper echoes down the length of the tunnel. It was as if there were people down there, uncountable numbers, all beckoning us to enter.

"Righto, Jim, let's get this lot inside the doors at least." The professor bent his insubstantial bulk to the wagon, which moved an inch on its iron bogeys and grated to a halt. But Bartram was yelling, "Leave that! Leave that alone! The panel!" Now he was back by the lorry, clambering up on to the flatbed. "I'd better help him," I said, and went over.

Close to, Mr Bartram was not a pleasant proposition. He looked as if he'd been sleeping rough for a week: unshaven, unwashed, and frankly he smelled. Wasn't it a chemical odour, the sort of thing I'd smelled in Professor Geldard's lab? I supposed art restoration might be part of his duties. But no, it was something else that I couldn't quite put my finger on, something I knew quite well yet couldn't seem to place. Anyway, it made his proximity in the back of the lorry weirdly disagreeable. "Give me a hand," he hissed, as he wrestled the last crate free from its strapping.

"Hang on sir, you'll need some gloves," I warned him, but he wasn't waiting for anything. The crates were rough and unplaned, and I could see that he already had scratches on his palms from the splinters. It didn't stop him, not a bit of it. He practically had the thing out of the back before I could jump down for him to lower it to me. The weight surprised me; it felt like a tea-chest full of rocks, rather than a single panel inside a plywood transit crate. I staggered a bit, and thankfully Professor Geldard was there to steady me.

Mr Bartram had with him, I now saw, a long screwdriver, and as we set the crate on the ground he was already applying the blade to its corner, levering the plywood away. "Here, stop that, Bartram," the professor said, righteously outraged. "Stop that this instant! We must get it into storage!"

He might have been speaking Greek for all the notice Mr Bartram took at first. Then he paused, as if the professor's words were coming to him on a relay, down a crackling field telephone. "Yes," he said, with disquieting eagerness. "Yes, we must get it inside. It's almost dark," and he cast a look at the sky that might have been fearful, or thrilled, I couldn't tell which. "Here, you, help me." Obediently, with a sideways look at Professor Geldard, I lifted my side of the crate. Again the queer impression of warmth struck me.

It was all I could do to keep up with Mr Bartram as we passed between the iron doors and into the tunnel. The professor trotted along beside us, raising a hand each time we missed our footing as we followed the narrow-gauge rails into the heart of the quarry. On either side of us there were brick vaults the size of car garages, clearly recent additions; the mortar scarcely looked dry, and the bricks were unsullied by dust. Their new steel doors glinted in the electric light.

"These are the storage vaults, Jim," the professor explained. "Each one is temperature-controlled and humidity-controlled, allowing for the optimum conditions for each type of artwork. All the watercolours in one, all the egg tempera in another, all the oils, all the gold leaf, well, you get the idea." I didn't like to say that I'd assumed that the paintings would all be hung up on the walls of the cavern. Anyway, I was too busy thinking that the vaults were reminding me of the Egyptian avenue at Highgate cemetery, only underground. This wasn't the comfortable dark of the Breden at night. This was something older, more elemental, and it was getting to me more than I dared admit.

Just then Mr Bartram increased his pace, and I wasn't ready for it. I tripped again, and this time I went flying. I struck my forehead painfully on the bare rock of the cavern floor, and the crate bounced and grated alongside me till Mr Bartram snatched it away.

"Jim! Are you all right?" It speaks to Professor Geldard's essential decency that his first thought was for me, and not for his prized work of art. He helped me to a kneeling position. There was blood running into my eyes, and I wiped it away with my cuff. "We'll have to get that seen to. Damn and blast that stupid man!"

He'd turned to where Mr Bartram had been standing, expecting him still to be there. But the other was off and running, dragging the crate behind him, deep into the tunnel. One end of the crate was scraping along the floor, making that same disagreeable screeching sound I'd heard earlier in the back of the lorry. At least, I think that was the source of the noise. It seemed louder than one might have expected; louder, and more complex somehow, as if it was many separate noises blended into one, and as if some of those noises – I might as well say it – as if they might not have come from inanimate objects.

"Oh lord, he's gone off his head," Professor Geldard said, horror-struck. "I'm going to have to – Jim, can you stay here a moment? I've got to stop him. Who knows what damage he might do to the paintings?"

I got to my feet, and the initial wave of dizziness passed. Though it went against every instinct I possessed, I said, "Let's catch up with him, sir."

The professor held my head steady, looked into my eyes, and I suppose he thought I'd do in a pinch. "Are you sure? Quickly, then."

Mr Bartram was already yards away down the tunnel, which seemed to grow darker the further it ran into the rock. There were still electric bulbs strung along the ceiling, but perhaps they were of a lower wattage; anyway, they gave less illumination, or so it seemed to me. Mr Bartram was already a shadow figure, and the echoes of his footsteps receded from us. Only that high screeching noise remained constant, somehow.

I wasn't quite as steady on my feet as I'd hoped, and I think I might have hindered Professor Geldard's pursuit more than helped it. But I stumbled on behind him while the light grew fainter. "Bartram!" he yelled. "*Bartram*! Come back, you bloody fool!" There came no answer; and then I became aware of a new source of light.

It was away up ahead, and it was not the weak yellow of the electric bulbs. It was a warm sort of radiance, the glow of a well-banked fire in the gloaming, and now I could see the shape of Mr Bartram silhouetted against it. "Come on, Jim," the professor urged, and I did my best to keep up.

We were past the last of the brick vaults now. This was the bare rock of the old mine, with the entrances of smaller side tunnels like unlit voids to left and right. It was from one of those dark entrances that the glow was coming, and now I saw Mr Bartram dodge inside it and vanish from our view. I was about to say "We've got him, sir," when the screeching came again.

There was no question of its origin now, in one sense at least. This was not the noise of wood or rock. It was the sound of – I was going to say a living thing, but perhaps that's to assume too much. Say instead, the sound of something that was aware of Mr Bartram's presence, or of the thing he carried with him. It stopped me dead in my tracks, and it stopped the professor as well.

"All for you!" This latest voice was Mr Bartram's, but

there was nothing of sanity left in it. It was the voice of a madman. "All for you!"

The professor and I looked at each other. It cost us both an effort to start moving forward again – walking this time, as though on eggshells, no longer running. The glow seemed to increase, and the screeching was constant now, setting up resonances in the cramped acoustic space of the tunnel, almost like a barrier against which we had to struggle. And the smell – I could place it now. It was the smell of fireworks; the reek of gunpowder, sulphur and saltpetre.

The stink made my dizziness come back in a wave. Up ahead of me Professor Geldard had drawn level with the mouth of the side tunnel. He stopped, and raised a hand to his mouth. In another time and place it might have been the comical gesture of an old aunt. Here and now, my nerve was wholly gone, and it terrified me. "What is it?" I shouted, and the professor turned to me with an arm outraised. He might have been warning me to keep quiet, or warding me away. Either way, I kept moving.

The light from inside the side tunnel was playing on the professor's face, as if he was standing at the open door of a furnace. Confusedly, I wondered what might be its cause. "Stand back, Jim," he said, as I drew level with him. But I was already staring into the side tunnel.

There was light and there was heat, but its source was nowhere to be seen. Everything was suffused with the glow, sulphur and red, flickering as if lit by invisible flames. I could sense that the tunnel went a long way back into darkness, but everything that I most urgently needed to see was within a dozen yards of the entrance.

Near the tunnel's mouth was a litter of kindling; the smashed scraps of plywood that had once formed the crate. Its contents – the third panel of the Cancelliere triptych – stood propped up with its back to us, alongside two other similar panels. We could see nothing of the paintings themselves, and for this I'm profoundly grateful still. For the first time ever, the triptych stood complete.

Facing it, and us, was Mr Bartram. The light, its source still unclear to me, seemed focussed on his face, which was a sight I shall remember as long as I live. His lips were drawn back; his eyes were open wider than seemed humanly feasible, and in them was nothing I could recognise as human. He opened his mouth as if to speak, then closed it again. From deep inside his throat came a terrible keening sort of noise, barely audible over the screeching that was now all-pervasive.

"Oh," he said at last, in a voice that barely seemed his own. "Oh masters. Oh acolytes. Oh, Adrammelech and Anammelech. Oh, Ashmedai and Amaymon. Behold." He cast his eyes around him, as if addressing an invisible multitude swarming round him in that cramped tunnel. "Behold, those who have gone before, and those who follow on their traces. It is complete."

The howling increased in intensity, so that I had to cover my ears. Helplessly, I looked at Professor Geldard. He had one arm thrown across his face to cover his eyes, and with the other he was blindly reaching out for me. I think both of us were broken in that moment, and broken irrevocably. Nothing in either of our experience had even remotely prepared us for this sudden eruption of madness, and we felt the ground dropping away beneath our feet, both spiritually and literally, I think.

I grabbed the professor's hand, and felt it fasten upon mine. "Come away from this," I said, then louder so that he could hear me. "Come away." In the end I practically dragged him back down the main tunnel, both of us running for our lives – literally for our lives, I think now. And all the time behind us, those wild piercing screams mingled with Mr Bartram's voice as it sobbed and shrieked and ranted. Soon, they drowned it out entirely.

In no time, we were at the mouth of the tunnel. The stink of sulphur hung in the cavern still, and we collapsed on the ground outside, breathing in the clean evening air of the Welsh mountains. Then from behind us there came a pummelling, deafening sound. It might have been the slamming shut of great metal doors, like the ones at the mouth of the tunnel. But by the time we had composed ourselves sufficiently to shut those doors ourselves, and to secure them with the keys left dangling in the lock, they did not make a fraction as much noise.

Neither of us had a second thought about locking those doors. Now this might sound callous at best, and at worst, given how things turned out, it might have formed the basis for a charge of manslaughter. But all I can say is, we wanted three inches of solid iron between us and whatever was inside those tunnels. As for Mr Bartram, I think we both knew that his was a hopeless case by then.

And so it turned out. For a blessing, Reg was still outside in the cab of the lorry, keeping the engine turning over. I'd had a terrible premonition, running down that tunnel, that he'd have driven away and left us to it. I don't know that I'd have blamed him if he had. As it is, he waited till we were up alongside him, then swung the lorry around and bore down on the accelerator. I didn't think about the gate until we were practically on the checkpoint, and I started to warn him, but he simply pressed down harder on the pedal, and hit it at some fifty miles an hour. The gate flew to pieces like matchwood, and Reg didn't slacken his pace till we'd put the best part of ten miles between us and the quarry. Still in all this, he never spoke a word.

We found lodgings in a small inn at the top of the Llanberis pass; at least, the professor and I did. Reg refused to budge from his cab, which I suppose was his privilege. In our chintzy room beneath the eaves, Professor Geldard and I sat on our beds and stared at the hooked rug on the floor. We couldn't bear to look at each other, I suppose. I was trying to find the words to begin to discuss what had happened; I dare say he was too. Neither of us managed it for a long time. In the course of fifteen minutes, everything we thought we knew had been shattered like those gates at the head of the quarry road; a lorry had been driven straight through them, and we were left blinking amidst the wreckage.

Eventually the professor said, "We have to go back, Jim." I nodded, because obviously we did. But when we went down and roused Reg, he was having none of it. Again, who could blame him, really? In the end, we had to wait till morning and phone for a hire car from a garage in Llanberis.

We found the guard post empty, the gate still lying in splinters from the night before. The professor and I looked glumly at each other, and wordlessly we drove on to the mine entrance. The wagon full of crated artwork stood undisturbed from the night before; the keys were where we'd left them, still in the lock. With the air of a man steeling himself to walk out and face the firing squad, Professor Geldard unlocked the iron doors, and we pushed them open, left and right.

Inside there was no light. There was shattered glass all along the tunnel's length, as if each bulb in turn had blown out. "There will probably be a torch in the Nissen huts," said the professor, and I went to look. When I came back with an electric lantern he had advanced maybe a foot inside the doors, no further. "That's better," he said, and we walked inside together.

There was the faintest residue of sulphur in the air, like the morning after bonfire night, the smell of spent fireworks in the leaf-mould. There was utter quiet; not even the rustle of vermin or the flutter of bats' wings. Everything seemed even more like a tomb, as well it might under the circumstances. We approached the side tunnel with a sort of sick anticipation of what we might find there.

I may as well say right now that we did not find the unfortunate Mr Bartram. No trace whatsoever of him remained, not in the side tunnel, not in the vaults where the rest of the artworks were stored; not for as far as we dared advance down that long passage into the belly of the earth. He remains what we reported him to be, that same day when we spoke to the local police: a missing person. Perhaps nobody was ever so missing as he was; or perhaps Cancelliere might have been, it occurs to me now. I dare say there was little enough left of him in the end that even his closest friend or family might have recognised. Whatever had taken him over had consumed him whole, and left not a trace on the altar.

There were cinders of burnt wood on the floor, that was all; a smudge of charcoal that had once been the Cancelliere triptych. So what had actually happened in the tunnel? I don't know, and I have spent a good many of the years since then doing my level best to steer clear of any answers to that question, the sort of answers that wait for the pit of a sleepless night to present themselves. By the same token, Professor Geldard and I never sat down and thrashed the thing out between us. Had everything been less sudden – if it had taken longer to play out than the time it took the sun to set on a warm summer's evening – then who knows? We might have been obliged to come up with rational explanations for an irrational occurrence, and probably driven ourselves crazy into the bargain.

Instead, it had been as if the structure of the world had suddenly inverted itself – as if the things we knew, the things we thought we knew, had turned completely inside out – and just as suddenly winked back into normality. You can ignore such a thing in the long run, or you can do your best, at any rate. What little the professor and I had to say to each other in the aftermath was surprisingly limited in scope, and pretty easy to summarise, so far as it went. Mr Bartram had been in possession of two panels of the triptych, and he had gone insane. Who could have predicted the effect of acquiring a third? What good did it do to even think about those extraneous matters that somehow lay at the absolute heart of the matter? That wouldn't bring poor Mr Bartram back. Such was the extent of our post-mortem, and neither of us was inclined to delve much deeper.

I can only repeat what Professor Geldard said to me, on the train back down to London on the day war finally broke out. "Perhaps, Jim, it was a blessing in disguise that my exhibition never came to pass." That much, at least, I think was true.

The Field Has Eyes, the Wood Has Ears

Helen Grant

He was one of the last visitors to leave the museum before they closed it for the foreseeable future. Engrossed in studying a particular work of art, he had not realised that it was nearly six. Then someone coughed close to him in the gallery, loudly and wetly, and he felt droplets land on his face. He glared at them, but they had already turned away, convulsed with hacking coughs. A woman, he saw – stout and middle aged, with outmoded bouffant hair. The sort who would not apologise; it was his fault for being there.

He became irritable, because the security guard refused to let him use the men's room before he left the building.

"I just need to wash my face," he protested, but the man shook his head.

"We are closing," he said in perfect English, shepherding David towards the doors, and there was no resisting. David found himself walking down the steps outside, scrubbing his cheek with his handkerchief.

Disgusting, he thought. He was preoccupied with his revulsion as he walked away from the museum, and it was a few minutes before his mind returned to the sketch he had been looking at when the incident occurred.

The Field has Eyes, the Wood has Ears – that was the name of it. A curious name. The picture was over five hundred years old, so it was hardly ever on display. The current exhibition rotated the sketches so that nothing would be exposed to the light for too long. If he had come a few days earlier, he wouldn't have seen it at all – it would have been *The Battle of the Birds and the Mammals* instead.

In some ways, he thought, it was a quiet picture, considering it was by Hieronymus Bosch. A simple drawing in brown ink: no lurid colours, no bustling composition. In the centre was a squat tree – a dead one, it seemed, because although the saplings behind it were covered in leaves, its own branches were bare. In the roots of the tree something was curled up – a fox, he thought – and above it, sharp-beaked birds hovered. What you noticed first, though, was the big triangular rent in the tree trunk, and the huge owl that squatted there. It was lightly sketched, the plumage merely suggested by strokes of the pen, but the eyes were shaded so that they looked out of the picture, at the viewer, in an oddly ominous way.

Where the ground stretched away from the foot of the tree, it was studded with open eyes. There was something repellent about that. The earth would be hard, thinly covered as it was with scrubby grass, and threaded through with tree roots, but the eyes would be soft and pulpy. If you walked across that field, a heel or toe might sink into one; you would feel it give under your foot.

Amongst the saplings in the background were two disembodied ears, each one poised upright on its lobe. Those, David thought, were less unpleasant than the eyes, but there was still something sinister about them. How could they hear without hammer and anvil, cochlea and vestibular nerve? Clearly they were symbolic – but symbolic of what?

He'd read extensively on Bosch. Some people believed that the grotesque things he depicted were the result of ergot poisoning, a condition which could lead to gangrene, hallucinations, and death. Others thought that they reflected a moral coding that had never been fully unpicked. A number had commented on the realism in his work which was, David thought, a little unsettling.

He considered this all the way back to his temporary lodgings, at which point Bosch was forgotten because he went onto the airline's website to try to rebook his flight back to Scotland. The woman in the gallery had decided him. It was no use staying longer. He risked being stuck here altogether if the flights stopped, and besides, it was pointless if the museums and galleries were closed. The wifi was sluggish, and while he was waiting for the website to load he looked down, out of the window. Already there seemed to be a different tone to people's behaviour. He saw one or two lugging home more shopping than they could easily carry: preparing for a siege.

He managed to rebook the flight for the day after next but then there remained the question of getting to the airport. Would everything be running as normal? It was hard to say. Nobody had been in this position before. In the end David booked a taxi, wondering whether it would turn up. Then he went through into the kitchenette and looked inside the fridge. There was food for more than two days; at some point he would have to make the decision to throw it out, to assume that he would get away safely. Come to that, he would have to leave the apartment key inside the flat, and trust that he didn't need to get back in. He began to feel stirrings of real anxiety. Unconsciously, he rubbed his cheek with his hand, scrubbing at the spot where he had felt the woman's cough.

Home, he thought, like a small boy looking for comfort. *I want to go home.*

In the event, it all went smoothly. The taxi arrived promptly, and David left the apartment for the last time. The spare food was in the *Biogut* bin in the basement, the front door key placed in the middle of the little dining table. He sat in the back of the cab and watched Berlin sliding smoothly past.

The airport was a little quieter than usual. David noticed some passengers wearing gloves and masks. On the plane, the staff were not wearing masks, but no food or drinks were to be served. When he heard *that* announcement, David frowned. He had hardly touched his breakfast because he had been so on edge about getting the flight, and now he was starving and had the beginnings of a headache. He felt irritable with himself, thinking that he should have bought something while he had the chance. He was prey to vicious migraines that filled his head with agonising thunder and lightning. It occurred to him that he had medication in his hand luggage – it was something new the doctor wanted him to try, because the triptans he had been taking were not working. David popped a tablet out of the blister pack and dry swallowed it, wincing. Then he folded his arms, turned his face to the window, and was dozing before the safety announcements had finished.

The plane took off. David's body flew, and his mind flew too. In his dreams he skimmed over a vast plain furred with short, desiccated grass. Ahead of him he saw a copse of young saplings, the slender trunks topped with cascades of silvery leaves. Beyond them, the naked and jagged branches of a tree jutted into the air. About these branches something indistinctly seen swooped and fluttered.

The ground was passing very rapidly below him. Somehow David knew what he would see if he passed over the copse and the tree beyond it. If he looked back, he would see the owl sitting in the hollow. It seemed to him that he did not want to see that; to lay eyes on it would be some kind of irrevocable step. He tried to resist whatever force carried him onwards, but it was hard to do. Travelling this way over the landscape was like travelling with a stream, or stroking in the direction of fur or quills.

He overtopped the copse and then suddenly someone was shaking him, and saying, "Sir, excuse me, sir?"

They were about to land at Glasgow. David straightened up and refastened his seat belt, nodding at the stewardess. He was conscious that the headache was still there. He had been unnerved, too, by the dream.

That bloody sketch, he said to himself. Somehow it had stuck in his head, flotsam on the tide of his thoughts. He was irritated and repelled.

Passport control seemed quieter than usual. He collected his suitcase from the baggage reclaim carousel, and then he took a bus into the city centre. The bus was only about a quarter full, and the passengers sat self-consciously apart. After they had been travelling for ten minutes, someone towards the back began to cough and heads turned, resentfully. David shrank into his corner, turning his face to the window. He did not know how seriously to take it, this disease. There was no way to avoid passing contact with people; if he hadn't taken the bus it would have to have been a taxi and—

He blinked. Then he twisted around to look back, out of the window, because he had glimpsed something fleetingly, something that had jarred in the environment of dull houses, grey streets and tired patches of faded grass. A person – yes, certainly a person – in moss green from throat to feet, but with the pink face curiously elongated, like the snout of a tapir. He stared and stared, but the figure was gone, vanished downstream as the bus forged on, or perhaps never there at all – simply the product of fatigue and stress. The headache was becoming more insistent. David put his forehead against the cool glass and exhaled slowly.

At Glasgow Queen Street he took the Edinburgh train. It took almost an hour to reach Waverley station, and he began to wish that the journey were over. It felt interminable, tedious; he was beginning to lose track of the time of day, because he seemed to have been travelling for an age.

Waverley at last. He came out onto the concourse, dragging his suitcase behind him, and started up the ramp to the street. There was a real throb in his head now, like the beating of dark wings. The ramp felt dark, the sides pushing in on him, and when he reached the top and looked towards the Scott monument he had perhaps two seconds of hideous visual disturbance: the view was reversed, like a negative, the buildings luridly bright, as though on fire, and the sky thunderously dark.

Bloody migraine, he thought. This one was working its

way up to being apocalyptic. He had not eaten nor drunk enough all day, and now his brain felt as though it was devouring itself. Sick with pain, he crept up the street, looking for a taxi. There were none – either they had all been taken or the drivers were afraid of what they might pick up along with their fare. David walked slowly home, pursued by the rumble of the wheeled suitcase, dimly wondering what the few other pedestrians thought when they looked into his face, whether they could see the agony etched into it. All that he could think about was getting home – shutting the door, collapsing onto the bed.

At his flat, it took him several attempts to open the front door; his hand shook so much that the key danced all over the face of the lock. Eventually he managed it, and he went inside, painfully hauling the wheeled bag after him. He left it in the hallway; it was too much effort to do anything else. Then he went into the bathroom and upended his hand luggage onto the surface at the end of the bath, looking for the migraine medication. He could hardly focus on the packet, let alone read the instructions. He popped a tablet out of the pack and when it was in his hand, sticking to the perspiring skin, he realised he needed something to wash it down with. David went to the kitchen, ran himself a glass of water and swallowed the tablet.

He had been away for some time, and of course there was nothing fresh in the flat. He should have stopped for groceries, or at least for milk, on the way home. Now it was too late because nothing would induce him to go out again today. David knew he ought to eat, because lack of food had caused this, but when he had torn the ringpull lid from a can of something, he looked at the wet orange contents with disgust. His stomach churned and he pushed the can to the back of the work surface, where he didn't have to look at it. A couple of crackers was all he could face. After that, he staggered through to the bedroom, took off his shoes, and fell onto the bed.

Let it go away, he thought. *Please God, let it go away.*

When David awoke, it was very early morning and there was an ominous tickle deep within his chest. He sat up, remembering the woman in the museum, her bouffant hair, the way her shoulders had shaken, but mostly the sensation of moisture landing on the side of his face. He began to cough, helplessly, and he couldn't stop it, and then the throbbing in his head started up all over again, like a violin playing over a bass drum, a symphony of pain. He coughed until his stomach muscles hurt, and then he stumbled into the bathroom, fell to his knees before the toilet and vomited.

He stayed there for a long while, his head bowed. It was easy to stay there; standing up felt like a titanic effort. But there were flecks of vomit on the crumpled shirt and trousers he had put on in Berlin and still been wearing when he fell into bed. He was sure he smelled bad too. David leaned over the bathtub and switched the taps on. Then he wriggled out of his clothes without actually getting to his feet. After that, he sat on the bath mat, naked and pimpled with gooseflesh, and succumbed to another fit of coughing.

Have I got it? he wondered, hugging his knees and shivering.

The nausea seemed to have passed, so while the water thundered into the tub he took another migraine tablet out of the packet sitting on the side of the bath, and swallowed it, scooping water from the tap to get it down. When the bath was run, he heaved himself into it and sat for a long time in the warm water. He stopped shivering, and began to feel too hot. The pain in his head became a series of sharp stabs and his vision seemed to dissolve, until the water around his knees was full of strange fish darting to and fro.

I think I'm going to pass out.

That thought provoked a twinge of fear – he was sitting in water, after all. David pulled out the plug, and while the water was draining away he made himself get out. He wrapped himself in his towelling robe and sat on the side of the bath for a while before attempting to move.

Please let these tablets work.

He curled his hands into fists, riding the agony in his skull. Eventually, he hauled himself up and tottered into the kitchen.

Fluid, he thought. *Even if I can't eat.*

He had forgotten that he had nothing fresh in, and he had opened the fridge door before he realised, thinking to find milk.

On the middle shelf, exactly at eye level, was a severed foot.

David stood there, swaying a little, his hand on the fridge door. He could see the foot very clearly. It had been severed at the ankle, and a piece of bone protruded from the ragged flesh. There was a slightly shrunken look to it, and the skin was grey.

In spite of the obvious decomposition, David could smell nothing. The fridge should have been bursting with the disgusting smell of rotten foot, and he couldn't smell a thing. He even leaned in, his stomach roiling, and *sniffed*. Nothing.

He stepped back, closed the fridge door, and leaned against it for a moment. Then he steeled himself, and opened it again.

The foot was not a foot; it was a hunk of bread, grey and furred with mould. David took hold of the plate it was subsiding onto and tipped it into the bin, where it landed in a cloud of dusty mould spores. Then he sat shakily at the kitchen table and put his head in his hands.

I have to go out, he said to himself. *I have to get food.* He thought about what that would mean: getting up, struggling into his clothes, going downstairs to street level. He would have to walk the fifty metres to the nearest convenience store; he would have to carry his shopping back with him. It was that, or eat nothing, drink nothing, until he felt better again. He kept sitting there, thinking about it.

Eventually, very much later, David forced himself to his feet, clinging to the furniture for support. He went into the bedroom, slowly, slowly, and dressed himself. Periodically he stopped to ride out another fit of coughing, but eventually it was done. Passing the bathroom on the way to the front door, he thought: *did I take another tablet or not?* The thunder inside his head made it hard to think coherently. He went into the bathroom and picked up the packet. After a moment's hesitation he popped out another tablet, put it into his mouth and washed it down with water from the tooth mug. Then he left the flat.

There was a damp cold edge to the air; it was March in Edinburgh, after all. David crept slowly down the street, walking like a man twice his age. Between buildings he glimpsed the park and it passed through his head that there were too many people thronging there, considering the situation – too many of them, and too close together. Was it a demonstration of some kind? From here they looked unclothed, but of course they couldn't be, not in this weather. He lost interest in it; a wave of heat was coming over him. His flesh was smouldering, burning him up from within.

Just get to the shop and back…

It was in sight now. For an awful moment he thought that it was closed, but then he saw the familiar row of folded newspapers hanging outside. He went into the shop, picking up a basket. There were two narrow aisles, and one of them was blocked; the girl was kneeling on the floor next to a stack of toilet rolls, restocking the shelves. David went down the other aisle to look for milk and found that there was only one bottle left: full-fat instead of the semi-skimmed he usually had. Well, he wasn't coming back any time soon if he could help it, so he put the bottle in the basket. He picked up bread, too, and butter. There were a lot of spaces on the shelves.

He went to stand by the till, and the girl got up reluctantly and came to serve him. She was skinny, blonde, uninterested. *Eilidh,* read her name badge. He couldn't imagine calling her that. He couldn't imagine her wishing him a nice day either, unless sarcastically. She rang his purchases into the till, chewing her gum intently.

It was a small shop, and the till area was cramped. If David had been less sick, he would have wondered whether he was breathing something out over Eilidh, something she didn't want. But he had to have food, at least the bare essentials, and there was nobody else to get it for him. Feeling a cough coming, he turned his head, and as he did so his gaze swept past the counter and snagged on something: Eilidh's legs, or rather, *not* Eilidh's legs, because her body, the upper half clad in a tabard with the name badge attached, terminated in a thick ribbed tail that glistened wetly. As he watched, appalled, it flexed and uncoiled, and he saw that it terminated in a barbed fork.

He grabbed the plastic bag with his shopping and stumbled out of the shop, ignoring Eilidh as she called after him, boredly asking whether he wanted his receipt. Outside, the lurid sky throbbed and flashed.

Migraine, he thought. *It can make you see things.* Visual disturbances, flashing lights, blurred vision… *Forked tails?* He shook his head, staggering on with his meagre supplies, focussed on the flat and lying down again.

Once inside, he put the butter and milk in the fridge, avoiding the shelf where the rotten loaf had been. He left the bread on the table, still in the plastic bag. Perspiration was running down him; the small of his back felt damp. His skull was full of howling demons, the pain raw and jagged. Every time he coughed it sent a spike of agony through one eye. There was an ominous tightness in his chest too. His body felt like the battleground for warring armies; he could almost *see* them in his mind's eye – tiny, faceless, armoured rabbles squaring off against each other while in the background the structures of his body blazed with fever. Plumes of fire welled up inside him, and his thoughts flew hither and thither on the smoke of burning.

When had he last taken the medication? He couldn't remember clearly. How long had he been home? One night? Two? Sometimes the sky seemed dark, and he couldn't tell whether that was night or an optical disturbance. He staggered into the bathroom. The last tablet he had taken, whenever that had been, had not touched the headache or the nausea. He pressed out another from the blister pack, his hands shaking. He drank tepid water from the tooth mug again – it was too much effort to go back into the kitchen. Then he went back to bed. He took off his shoes with difficulty, loosened the rest of his clothing and lay down.

The room was pulsing brightly around him, as though he were lying inside a lung which expanded and contracted wetly with every breath. The effect was nauseating. David closed his eyes, and dropped vertiginously into sleep.

Down he fell, down and down, until the blinding brightness above him was a fading ache in the back of his skull. Below him was a grim and ravaged landscape, brown and barren and teeming with activity. Tiny figures, naked and pale, writhed like maggots, tormented by bristly and scaly things whose skins were grey or green or scarlet. Some seemed to be being processed by some ugly machine like a mincer. Others were pierced or hung. A head bobbed in a barrel full of tar or black blood.

In spite of his delirium, David *recognised* this place. He had seen Bosch's painting of it in Vienna. But this was *real* – the tortured figures moved, the grotesque creatures sawed and stabbed, the smoke rose in clouds. The ergotamine he had taken, far too much of it, throbbed through his veins and he could hear the screams of the damned, the chugging of infernal machinery. He was falling towards Hell.

No, he thought. *No, no.*

Incorporeal, burning, he willed himself to stop falling, flexing psychic muscle he hadn't known he had. Below him, creatures howled and grumbled, tilting their knives towards him.

No.

His descent slowed, as though he were dreaming of flight and had suddenly caught the trick of it. He fell more languidly, and then he drifted, and then he stopped. David hung poised above the seething plain, as though his fate were balancing upon a decision. He fought to rise, to get away, swimming with insubstantial limbs through an atmosphere that felt as thick as treacle.

Please.

He began to rise, straining against the pull of the horrors below. Spiked and beaked things flew up from the maelstrom below, but were unable to reach him and fell back, shrieking. He was high enough now that he could see the land stretching into the distance – the tree stumps that smoked, and the ruined structures that glowed from within with a baleful light. David soared higher and higher, filled with savage relief. Escape. Now he had to make his way back to himself. He sensed that in the upper world his physical self hung between life and death; if he could make it back, he would live. It must be possible: Bosch himself had seen these things, and had returned to paint them.

Hell diminished below him; smoke drifted over the ravaged landscape, hiding its teeming hordes from his view and deadening their cries. At last he found himself moving across a vast plain, dull and colourless, as though rendered in grisaille. These, he thought, were the borderlands; he must find his way out soon. He travelled for a long time, and then he saw something up ahead.

The way shrank to a single field, and at the far side of the field stood a copse of young trees with silvery leaves. David knew this place, as Bosch had.

In front of the copse stood something that looked like a vast dead tree. Amongst its roots something grovelled; at its crown things wheeled and swooped in staccato bursts of flight. In the centre of the tree was a dark triangular rent, and in it sat something very like an owl. The owl thing radiated watchfulness and hostility; David could feel those things thrumming off it. He knew that its wingspan would be enormous, its speed unmatched. Its beak and talons were very sharp. If it caught him, it would rend him into pieces.

The Field has Eyes, the Wood has Ears. The ground was not studded with actual eyes, nor were there any ears standing grotesquely upright on their lobes in the little thicket. Nevertheless, David knew that the field watched and the wood listened. They strained and waited.

He stopped at the edge of the field. Now that he was almost back in the world, he had more substance; he could see his own body, his limbs. This place, too, seemed to be more like his own world. He sensed that it was evening, that the light by which he saw the copse and the flying creatures and the owl thing was slowly dimming.

David thought: *I have only to wait, and I can get past unseen.*

So he waited. The field was still and silent. The grass was very short and scrubby, the earth almost bald, but he could feel that strange sensation again, as though the field had bristles or spines pointing towards him; one might fly inwards very easily, but leaving would mean going against some invisible current. Bosch had done it though; he clung to that thought.

Night crept on, very slowly. Eventually the dead tree was simply a darker shape against a dark background. The creature within the tree roots ceased to struggle; the things which flew about the upper branches settled and folded their jagged wings. The owl was the last thing to sleep. For a long time its two eyes glowed in the darkness. Then they began to blink, and at last they went out altogether.

David waited a little longer. Then he set out across the field. He trod silently, carefully. He was becoming more corporeal: he could feel the hard ground under his tread, and the knotted roots that ran through it like veins. There was a soft wind that explored his skin and ruffled the leaves of the saplings. He became aware of his breathing again, and he made it silent, without so much as a sigh. A pulse throbbed in his ears and he bid that be silent too.

The Field has Eyes.

He knew that he was passing unseen before them, like an insect crawling over a closed eyelid.

The dead tree was barely visible now. He passed it without a sound. He looked into the copse and it seemed to him that he could see between the slender trunks into his own world, as though he were looking down the wrong end of a telescope. He was nearly there – so very nearly. David stepped into the copse.

The Wood has Ears.

It was becoming light again, or else the light of home from the other side was illuminating the thicket. He could see the slender saplings all about him. He saw that they were dead, the leaves desiccated. Here and there, branches had cracked and fallen.

The wind dropped. The leaves stopped rustling, and there was absolute silence.

In the silence, David put down his foot with all the weight of his solid being, and the dry stick underneath it snapped with the sound of a gunshot.

The Redeemers

Andrew Hook

Over the course of their seventeen year marriage, Bates found himself becoming increasingly divorced from Carol, to the extent that it appeared she had aged whilst he had not. He would wake each morning to a different person, each subtle accumulation of change evident in either her body or her demeanour. These changes might not have been immediately apparent to a casual observer, but Bates always considered himself to be a stickler for detail, and as such, these discrepancies were neither unavoidable in their witness nor desirable. He began to make plans to extricate.

Carol's gradual transformation was not necessarily due to traumatic events, although a gall bladder operation caused her to hang in the balance for a moment, like a drop of water timorously clinging to its point of departure from a tap, but through subtle deviations of character: the results of attempting a new recipe, a decision to take a different route on their commute to work – even when dictated to do so by roadworks – or through the effects of watching a film. Each of these *life experiences* impacted not only Carol's physical appearance, but the nature of her emotional response either increased or decreased Bates' affection towards her. In that respect, he viewed Carol as an ongoing installation, perhaps a piece of performance art, and himself in the role of observer. Of critic.

His appreciation of matter in this light wasn't restricted to Carol, but when it came to others the effect was diffused. There were nephews he only saw from year to year, whose bodily and mental changes were dramatic when such a period of time existed between viewings, and work colleagues were too remote for him to study in any depth. No, it was with Carol that the effect was ongoing, ever-present. Whereas Bates considered his mental state to have stuck around the age of twenty-one – as though in a game of pontoon, coincidentally at the age he had first met Carol – from his observation Carol had gone bust. She extrapolated extra years in a filmy gauze that gradually enveloped what she had been until she became no longer what she was.

Bates himself allowed a denial of his own physical deterioration, but instead saw a gradual hardening of his personality, of his appearance, as a form of strength. He was determined not to let himself go. Running through the streets of Liverpool each morning before his commute – and often twice at the weekends – he maintained his mental and physical capabilities to such an extent that after every run he could only view even greater changes in Carol, who had remained static whilst simultaneously declining, hunched over a piece of needlework, a hobby which she had taken up in order to emphasise her more matronly appearance, as though funnelling herself through other's expectations, a gradual peel from the core, the essence in which Bates had originally fallen in love with her.

Whilst Bates recognised similarities in relationships between their mutual friends, he was not prone to attribute such observations to the catch-all phrase *drifting apart*. If anything, such close scrutiny endeared Carol to him all the more, however he was unable to disengage from such obvious differences, so prevalent had they become in his appreciation of her. And he could only speculate as to how these subtle deformities might increase during the course of their remaining years, to the extent that some mornings upon waking he had to force back an abhorrent terror that the woman he lived with was someone he had never known.

The process came to a head on the Fourteenth of May 2009. Bates and Carol had orchestrated holiday from their respective employments in order to take in an exhibition at Tate Liverpool, their understanding being that on a Thursday the gallery would be less crowded, giving them the space to fully appreciate the artwork.

The day held a blue opacity indicative of early spring. Low sunlight glinted from metal structures. Winter coats finally shrugged free. As they walked through the Albert Dock complex, their feet interacting with the cobbles and original Yorkstone paving, Bates couldn't help but equate these period features with the modern art of the gallery, and within such an equation, compare the trajectories of himself and his wife.

Whilst Bates had been looking forward to the visit with a great deal of anticipation, his enthusiasm tempered as they viewed one piece of artwork after another, noticing a degradation in his appreciation of Carol determinant to each of her responses. Where she enthused, he disdained, and vice versa, connections between them dissolving, if they had ever even been there at all.

Whilst this was his reaction, he couldn't place himself in Carol's lovely head, couldn't observe her opinion of him. Despite their intimacy, he was a blank canvas in her mind, so there was no opportunity to document his reaction when they came across a work titled *The Redeemers*, a mixed media sculptural piece by the artist John Davies.

Later, Carol told him he had slumped to one side, that if their arms had not been interlinked he would have fallen to the floor, instead of them both staggering together like a pair of runners in a three-legged race suddenly encountering a rabbit hole. They had journeyed four or five steps to the left before one of the staff had leapt from his seat to right them, and then to lower Bates into the seat vacated. Bates remembered nothing other than the rapid increase of his heartbeat, an aberration in his vision as though kaleidoscopes had been placed – and slowly turned – before his eyes, and a cold sweat which cooled his forehead under the building's temperature controls. As his sense returned, *The Redeemers* floated back into view: static, immovable. His abiding memory being the voice of one of the curators, expressing his enthusiasm for the work before a small, huddled group of Japanese tourists. *The funny thing is*, the curator intoned, *these characters actually look like John Davies. Not* the *John Davies and probably not the John Davies you're thinking of but another John Davies.*

Two months later, Bates and Carol had separated.

Bates first encountered Krill underneath the Vyrnwy Aqueduct, a sixty-eight mile structure which carried water from Lake Vyrnwy in Wales to where it terminated at the service reservoirs north east of Prescot in Merseyside. At the Wales end, Bates had been under the opinion that the original Llanwddyn village had been submerged when the reservoir was created in the 1880s, but since came to understand that whilst the reservoir indeed covered that site, the previous village had been demolished prior to the flooding. This was possibly the final comparison he would make regarding his marriage to Carol, as through the conjuncture of time and space that arrangement had receded into an equally dim and distant past.

Krill was tall and thin, a cigarette poked at forty-five degrees from the left-hand corner of his mouth. A cigarette which Bates never saw lit. He wore a black donkey jacket and equally black drainpipe trousers. The jacket's shoulders, back and front, reinforced and protected from rain with leather panels, were polished so they resembled dark, bottomless lakes. If he hadn't been completely bald, Bates considered he might have resembled John Cooper Clarke in a parallel life, but Krill was no poet; he described himself as a producer and procurer of art, although he also described himself as an artist.

Following his encounter with *The Redeemers*, the sculpture held a fascination which Bates could only consider obsessive. Whereas the focus of his imagination had previously been on the changing relationship that had evolved with his wife, Bates no longer paid her any mind. It was as though she ceased to exist, and if Bates ever thought about her at all it was of the gentle pressure of her arm against his as she manoeuvred him across the floor of the gallery whilst trying not to lose her balance.

Bates had returned to the gallery alone on three other occasions, each visit having the same effect as before, until his behaviour had been reported to the relevant authorities, eliciting an unfathomable lifetime ban. His psychiatrist – a man who seemed to have appeared out of nowhere through a casual discussion with his GP – made mention of Stendhal syndrome, a psychosomatic condition where a person might experience rapid heartbeats, fainting, confusion and even hallucinations, allegedly after being exposed to objects, artworks, or phenomena of great beauty. *This condition*, his psychiatrist had stressed, in long low syllables, *is not listed as a recognised condition in the* Diagnostic and Statistical Manual of Mental Disorders, *but nevertheless might explain your reaction to this unusual piece.*

His psychiatrist had crossed his legs at that statement, as though emphasising the twist which occurred in Bates' mind each time he viewed the artwork. There followed a discussion where Bates confirmed he experienced nothing similar when viewing the artwork online, that it was only in the physical presence of the work that he felt such symptoms, and where the psychiatrist advised him to cease in his attempts to enter the building after dark, a memory of which Bates held no recollection but which he dimly realised formed the path followed from the artwork to his presence in the psychiatrist's office, and indeed precipitated that hitherto unsubstantiated ban.

Bates had moved from the former matrimonial home into a compact apartment affording a view of the Mersey, that view creating the illusion that his accommodation was much larger than it actually was. A sofa dominated one wall of the living room, opposite which a seventeen-inch television stood on a black lacquered stand. Adjacent to the sofa, his laptop rested on a small side table. When standing, he couldn't traverse the room without brushing against either of those items. He had assembled his bed within the bedroom with some difficulty. It filled the room to such an extent that he had reversed the opening of the bedroom door outwards, in order that he might clamber onto the bed from the doorway and slowly crawl up it to reach the pillows. The kitchen was large enough to cook within but not big enough to eat within. The bathroom, jutting out from the side of the apartment on a south-facing wall, resembled a walk-in refrigerator. There was no bath. He stood in the shower, he stood to pee, and he remained standing when performing his other ablutions.

Whilst occasional visitors might think – but never voice – dismay at his change in circumstances, Bates never entertained such an internal dialogue. He considered himself released in the confinement of this cage, and if anything the size of his apartment encouraged opportunity to examine his present circumstances under a bright, unremitting, light.

Bates had written to John Davies, the sculptor being alive and well, enquiring after the provenance of the piece, to which he had been informed it was an instinctive and improvised work created in an empty church hall which was Davies' studio for many years. When Bates pressed for meaning, Davies responded, *I have always been reluctant to explain my work as I have confidence in the onlooker to be creative, as we all are in our imagination. I liked the mystery of creating an enigma for people to puzzle over, like witnessing something on the street and not being able to stop and interview the people.*

Bates had explained this to Krill over the telephone. There was a short silence at the end, punctuated only by the sound of material ruffling, as though Krill were riffling through a large wad of paper bills. It was then that Krill had suggested the meeting beneath the aqueduct, for reasons that Bates could only assume were meant to afford a sense of mystery and dislocation.

Bates had become aware of Krill following a stunt performed by the artist outside the Liverpool Playhouse earlier that month. At the conclusion of the final performance of *The Woman in Black* on the First of February, Krill had arranged for a dozen woman-in-black look-alikes to appear within the vicinity of the venue: leaping out at unsuspecting theatregoers as they exited the Playhouse, appearing from behind trees, glimpsed in hallway mirrors, and even pulling up at the kerb driving taxis. With the heart of the play containing the mysterious presence of the woman in black who appears almost subliminally before the young actor who is being told a supernatural story by Arthur Kipps, Krill's doppelgangers created a rather disturbing and totally unofficial stir outside the venue, causing one pregnant female to faint, and others to vehemently report his *ill-considered and insensitive act* to both the authorities and the newspapers. Apocryphally, and despite clear evidence to the contrary, the fainting pregnant female had lost her baby.

Krill was of indeterminate age. The ground beneath them had frosted over a layer of snow. Bates was aware of the soles of his feet losing heat, a sensation causing his legs to cool from his ankles upwards almost in a form of paralysis. Krill carried an ebony walking stick seemingly for decorative purposes. After a brief introduction, Krill had stood face upwards, his gaze to the underside of the aqueduct as though searching for imperfections. Bates waited patiently for the conversation to begin, aware that breaking the silence might somehow dissipate the meeting, ending it before it had really begun.

Further investigation into Krill had uncovered the man's passion for *tableau vivant*, the creation of static scenes emulating works of art through living performers, a process which might have begun in the Middle Ages but which Krill had taken into the present day. According to one article, Krill had sought to surpass Jean-Luc Godard's exploration of the theme as evidenced in the French film director's 1982 film, *Passion*, where the film within the film used re-creations of classical European paintings set to classical European music, including works by Rembrandt, Goya, Delacroix and El Greco, as well as many others. Krill sought to create his own *tableaux vivant* as spontaneous performance artforms in unusual locations ranging from shopping malls to undisturbed forest where, other than through photography, the artwork could not be observed. Whilst Krill purported to work with members of the public whose participation might be orchestrated using otherwise innocuous floor markings he had prepared days before, positioning those bodies at exact moments in time for transitory emulation, in many instances he clearly had a devoted entourage who were dedicated to keeping the *tableau vivant* artform alive, many of them from Liverpool's seemingly endless living statue busker community.

And so, Krill eventually said, as though they were in the middle of their conversation, *you want me to arrange a tableau of* The Redeemers *for your personal gratification?*

Bates' mind envisioned the artwork, the two figures, both male, black-suited, one leaning a little into the other, their expressions inscrutable and all but innocuous if it wasn't for the presence of a seemingly-silk brown cape – very much like a woman's headscarf – draped over the head of the left-hand figure, fastened at the chest just below a pale tan-coloured tie. Even picturing the piece in his mind's eye caused a frisson which Bates couldn't quite replicate by any other means. Something flickered at the corners of his vision, as though a deer or a fox or some other being had disturbed the vegetation around them. Krill didn't blink.

"You make it sound distasteful, immoral somehow."

Krill shrugged. *Ours is not to reason why.*

Even in his pockets, gloved, Bates' hands were feeling the February cold. In a few months the weather would change. The air would warm, the sun would ease marginally closer, the ground would yield colour, become vibrant. Bates couldn't be trapped in the winter of his imagination. "There are certain rules," he said, finding his words flowed much simpler now. "I need an *exact* representation. No warning. No explanation. Anytime, anywhere. Martini." He laughed, then became embarrassed by his own joke, blaming his nerves. "I don't wish to see the mechanics of the...*construction*. I *can't* see them setting up, I cannot see them disengaging. I need a snapshot of existence, a moment. Additionally, I need your denial each time this happens. You understand?"

Krill pushed the end of his cane through the frosted ground until it was held there and he was able to leave it untouched, bringing the fingers of each hand together, tapping them gently. From around his cigarette he said, *to redeem is to gain or regain possession of something in exchange for payment.*

"Oh, of course I will pay," Bates enthused. Then, hesitantly, "I thought I had mentioned this in my email?"

Krill nodded. *There are always other kinds of payment*, he said.

The arrangement was such that Bates couldn't insist on a timeframe for each visitation. Krill took his payment in cash at their second meeting, in the ubiquitous *Maggie May's Café Bar* on Bold Street, where Krill attacked a steak pie whilst Bates held a cooling cup of weak tea. Sunlight warmed the window, a crack patterning a rainbow effect across the middle of the table at the exact moment when Bates pushed the money towards Krill's now empty plate. Outside, Bates was aware of a beggar watching the scene, perhaps envisaging his own tableau. Krill pocketed the money without counting it, as if depth was indicative of value.

Over the course of the next few months Bates held back an increasing, almost inexorable state of mind, which attempted to force him to contact Krill asking when the first visitation might happen. A part of him – voiced by Carol in an increasingly strangulated timbre – mocked his belief that Krill would actually deliver the goods. Bates found himself becoming increasingly jumpy commuting to work whenever anyone in a suit approached his peripheral vision. He found himself wondering if he had been too strict in his demands, whether Krill would find it impossible to entertain his request in any way that would be meaningful. As the months became a year, and then two, Bates' nervous system was close to breaking point. He left his employment and obtained work as a night porter in a medium-sized hotel. Sleeping much of the day created a sensation more conducive to seeing the artwork. Bates assumed that Krill was following his movements and the nature of employment and the paucity of pedestrians at the time of his new commute would create fewer obstacles for Krill to encounter. For despite that nagging voice of doubt, Bates couldn't allow himself to disbelieve that Krill was employing every effort possible to enable him to fulfil his part of the contract.

Eventually, one summer evening, early twilight, Bates was walking from his apartment to his employment, feeling only the vestiges of any emotion he might have held towards *The Redeemers*, when he happened to glance towards some building works which were taking place in the city. The site was dominated by a large, yellow, mechanical crane with its usual accoutrements of winder, wire rope, and sheaves, that rose from the rubbled surface and ascended towards the encroaching inky blackness of sky. Bates stopped for a moment, enthralled by the simple juxtaposition of the manmade structure against the natural background, anticipating the edifice to come, when suddenly – to his absolute incomprehension and shock – he saw, balanced on the outstretched horizontal arm of the crane at least one hundred metres above the ground's surface, two figures which even at this distance quite clearly and without doubt enacted the artwork he had so longed to see.

This revelation, tempered by a single, transitory moment of doubt, became reinforced as he found his heart rate increasing, as his vision swam with miniature tableaux of the same scene as if seen through some distorted insect-eye viewfinder, and his lunchbox left his hand, hitting the pavement only seconds before his body followed.

On his discharge from hospital – *when palpitations are due to a condition in which the upper chambers of the heart quiver instead of beating properly blood can pool and cause clots to form. Should a clot break loose, it can block a brain artery, causing a stroke* – Bates fired up his laptop and sent a message to Krill.

How did you do that?!

The reply was instantaneous, automatic.

How did I do what?

Bates paused on further communication, hesitant to receive an identical response. He wondered if Krill's mail server had been primed to despatch such a question whenever he might try to contact him. It was inconceivable that Krill would be sat at a computer, answering so swiftly. It was two o'clock in the morning.

Their agreement hadn't specified the number of incidents, but Bates considered the amount of money he had paid to cover many more. It was of little consolation to consider that if they had occurred more frequently at the beginning then they might have finished by now. Instead, he primed himself for another long wait. The hospitalisation had been worth the adrenalin rush. On his descent to the floor he had imagined a full frontal fall in orange sepia, as though being absorbed by the world from which the redeemers might be said to have come.

Time continued its twisted arc. Bates was sacked from his night porter job when he was found slumped against a mahogany side-table in the dining room, where the breakfast cereals were normally kept. He had no recollection of that journey. Over the course of the next few years there were numerous instances where he either woke or was disturbed in places that he couldn't recall travelling to: Barmouth railway station, eighty miles out of Liverpool, clutching a dog-eared copy of a novel titled *The Faceless;* Leasowe Lighthouse on the Wirral Peninsula, somehow locked in from the outside; inside the clocktower of the Liver building, halfway through a guided tour, rising from the floor with a small cut on his forehead. After each of these instances he was returned to medical facilities, but there was no indication of further strokes or mental abberation. Bates became convinced these were connected to sightings of *The Redeemers* which he could no longer recall. Frustrating in the extreme, denied the visions of his expectations, Bates increasingly confined himself to his small apartment, paid for through government benefits, his allowances providing him with just enough to get by, his freezer full of burgers constructed from mechanically-retrieved animal carcasses, which he ate accompanied by mould-spotted sesame seeded rolls.

One sultry summer night, his bedsheets discarded on one side as though the aftermath of a sexual encounter with a ghost, Bates awoke from uneasy dreams sensing a presence in his open bedroom doorway. Illumination reflected from the water of the Mersey slowly assisted his eyesight as his gaze adjusted in the gloom. Clearly, irrevocably, at the foot of his bed, two figures stood. Bates caught his breath as he listened for theirs. None was evident. The pale light seemed insufficient to induce the Stendhal effect, but he would have to move to the doorway to turn on the light, and movement was exactly what he didn't want to do. For an indeterminable length of time, Bates watched and waited, but the figures stood as still as statues. He wondered how long they could keep it up, considered whether Krill had broken his agreement and somehow made a replica of the sculpture itself, but once daylight advanced sufficiently for greater depth of vision and he saw one of the figures blink, Bates knew the truth of it and in that moment the ascending patter of his heart exponentially increased. Closing his eyes tight, upon their re-opening he saw the doorway as a glare of white against which the two figures were no more than a blur, the light illuminating wallpaper adorned with their images, replicated a hundred-fold, transferred to his bedsheets, the pillow, the pattern on his pyjamas. On the windowsill, his alarm clock was held in their plastic hands, the embroidery of a spider's web in the corner of his room mimicked their form. Bates felt himself ascend and transcend until his nose touched the ceiling. And then he dropped.

How did I do what?

From that instance in his bedroom, it subsequently proved impossible for Bates to *not* see the redeemers. At the supermarket, in the benefits office, in public toilets, on the street, in field, forest and sky. Their presence was everywhere: enigmatic and enduring. Even when Bates closed his eyes he found their image burned onto the back of his lids. Always unmoving, always perfectly rendered, always *real*. Through repetition, however, his reaction had numbed: the greater the interaction, the less of an impact. He could barely hide the comparison to other relationships, where initial mystery and expectation becomes relegated to routine and conformity. The inexplicable reaction he had first experienced at Tate Liverpool was now a dim memory, as faded as his first job, his first house, his first love.

Craving the presence of others, Bates spent as much time outdoors as he reasonably could. His presence was muted, however he soon came to realise that others viewed him at polar opposites to the way in which they might enjoy a work of art. To properly appreciate art you had to stand at the right distance, to observe, to revisit, whereas any glances foisted Bates' way were dismissive, unappreciative, people stopping for no longer than to place a few coins in the hat he had taken to placing upside-down in front of him.

On one of his sojourns in the doorway of a Debenhams department store which had recently closed and been marked for refurbishment, Bates believed he saw the redeemers placed opposite him at a distance of fifty feet. Standing beside them, not quite conversing, not quite interacting, was Krill. Bates rose unsteadily to his feet, a tattered cardboard sign falling from his lap, and stumbled over to join them. Pedestrians parted as though he were Moses, headed for the promised land. A ball of hope flourished within his chest, growing with each forward step, as if it might restore him to his former glory. When he was within ten feet, Krill appeared to notice him, and stepped back from the tableau. Bates rubbed his eyes. The image was no longer of the redeemers, but a blown-up photograph of himself and Carol, early nineties he recalled, in the first blush of love. He wore his first and only suit and Carol was dressed in a one-piece black trouser suit which he remembered she thought made her especially hip. A scarf adorned her head and shoulders, keeping her hair in place. The ball inside him fluttered and expanded, extrapolated him back to a time when life was much more complicated and yet much simpler. He could breathe, he could finally breathe again.

Carol – if she were there – wouldn't have recognised him. Bates found that he barely recognised himself.

Blind Man's Buff

Lucie McKnight Hardy

She goes through the checklist in her head as she drives. First, an estate agent to provide a valuation; then an antiques dealer to see if there's anything of interest that might be worth some money; otherwise, a house clearance to get the place empty and ready for sale. It had been the solicitor who had suggested these things, reeling them off without appearing to give them any thought, as though it was just some sort of routine for him, which Clara supposes it is. Her mother had gazed, unseeing, through the window and into the garden below during all of this exchange, her lips moving almost imperceptibly with the mantra only she could hear. Clara had held her hand, swollen veins showing through parchment skin, as the solicitor explained about her aunt's death. His tone was low, respectful, deliberately sombre, and Clara presumed that he wasn't fully aware of the circumstances of her mother's estrangement from her own sister, or that they hadn't spoken for thirty years or more.

As Clara navigates another tight bend in the road, it occurs to her that this is a peculiar place for a village to be located – in the middle of nowhere, along a dead end. They had skirted around a small town about half an hour ago, and she had noted the train station where she was due to collect her sister the following day. The roads had proceeded to get narrower and narrower after that, until the gravelled surface under them was little more than a dirt track.

She has no recollection of ever having visited this place before, although Liza had reassured her that they had occasionally come to stay with their aunt when they were little, before their parents had separated. She'd even been able to describe parts of the house.

'Dark, mostly, is what I remember,' her sister had said, as they shared a bottle of wine after Clara had put the twins to bed. 'Two bedrooms, a tiny garden out the back. Lots of paintings and photographs everywhere. And it smelt of old people – you know, boiled cabbage, mothballs.' Clara had laughed at that.

'That is such a cliché,' she'd said, leaning forward to top up their glasses. 'Old people don't smell like that. Mum's old and she smells of…' and here she trailed off. What did their mother smell of? There was her perfume, of course, the sweet floral scent she'd been wearing all her adult life. The last time Clara had visited her mother at the care home, just a couple of days before, the perfume had been an overpowering reminder of her childhood. The only other smells she'd been aware of had issued from the canteen: random meat and mashed potatoes and, yes, boiled cabbage.

A glance in the rear-view mirror tells her that the twins are still asleep, thumbs jammed into mouths. Even though it is still early in the afternoon, and the low-hanging trees that line the verges shield the car from the worst of the sun's rays, she is grateful for the air conditioning. It has been one of those summers, the sort that she has only really experienced in her childhood: the air heavy, fetid, the palpable threat of rain never being realised.

There is no sign giving the name of the village to announce their arrival, and she is only aware of having reached her destination when a farmhouse suddenly appears, and then a couple more houses rear up at the side of the road, ancient and lopsided in uniformly grey stone. These are soon replaced by smaller cottages, set back behind low walls. Soon, a terrace of houses appears that runs along the right hand side of the road, with a patch of greenery opposite, and set back from that, a small church.

The solicitor had told her to go to the middle of the village, which she would be able to identify by the church and the pub. Joan's house would be found on the opposite side of the green.

Clara parks outside what she thinks must be the pub; there is a wooden sign hanging perpendicular to the wall but whatever had been painted onto it has long since worn away. A pyramid of stainless steel beer barrels sits on the pavement outside the front door, however, glinting in the harsh sunlight, and a full ashtray is balanced on a low breeze-block wall. She engages the hand brake and shuts off the engine. She turns to the twins, and Emma gazes back at her impassively from behind long lashes. Sophie is still asleep, her thumb jammed tightly into the corner of her mouth.

'We're here!' Clara announces in a voice she hopes sounds cheerful. She had presented the trip to the six-year-olds as an adventure, a few days away on holiday with Auntie Liza. In their usual placid way they had accepted unquestioningly, so she had packed a suitcase and some food and toys and attached the keys the solicitor had given her to her key ring.

The sun is still high when she extracts herself from the car. The weather has been the subject of much attention on the news: hottest day this year, drought predicted. There isn't even the gentlest of breezes, and she has to peel her t-shirt from her body moments after leaving the air-conditioned cocoon of the car. The village appears deserted, and the only sounds are the jubilant trill of blackbirds and the lazy creak of a grasshopper. The thought stops her in her tracks. She hasn't heard a grasshopper in what... twenty, thirty years? Abruptly, the sound stops, and she wonders if she imagined it after all. She leans against the car door and sends Liza a text: *I'm here already. Will find the house and let ourselves in and unpack. Let me know what time your train gets in tomorrow. C x.* She opens the back door and Emma climbs out, keen to stretch her legs after hours of being confined. Clara opens the other door and Sophie wakes, blinking into the sunlight.

There is a dilapidated air to the village. Further along the street from where she has parked, narrow houses appear shoehorned into the terrace, a door and two windows demarcating each dwelling. The pub looms behind her, and the tiny church squats across the road, an apron of grass to the front of it, and to the sides, rows of gravestones signifying a small cemetery. The church is built of grey stone, a diminutive structure with a modest porch and plain, leaded windows. Clara's eyes follow the line of the building upwards, to where the spire stands silhouetted against the sky, and her gaze is caught by a pair of swifts darting across the blue expanse. She follows them until a sudden flash of light causes her to blink, and she looks back down again. There is a man now in the graveyard, a stocky man wearing a grubby white shirt over trousers that have seen better days. He is too far away for her to make out his face, or any expression that it might carry, and anyway, a pair of sunglasses obscure his eyes, reflecting the sun's light back at her. He is broad and solid, and his stance is impassive. She raises a hand to him but his only response is to thrust the shovel he is carrying firmly into the earth at his feet. The movement causes the sunlight to reflect from the blade again and for an instant, she is blinded.

She turns back to the car and rummages in the glove box for her sunglasses, but she must have left them at home. Instead, squinting, she takes her handbag from the passenger seat and slings it over her shoulder then locks the car and takes each of the girls by the hand. She has already spotted the house over the road. Joan's house.

It is a detached, double-fronted cottage. Like the other houses in the village, it is built of grey stone, and is long and low. It is set back behind a dry stone wall with a timber gate in its centre. The symmetry of the cottage is pleasing: four windows surround a dark blue-painted wooden-panelled door. Clara remembers when she and Liza were little, and they'd sit at the kitchen table, drawing pictures of their family: the two of them, identically dressed and holding hands, their mother and, for a while when they were very little, their father as well. They would paint a house in the background, and the houses would always look like this: solid and uniform. She wonders whether somewhere in the dark recesses of her mind she does have memories of the cottage, after all.

'Well, this is it,' she says, as much to herself as to the twins. They look up at her, silent, calm. She wonders whether she and Liza were ever this docile – certainly, when she thinks of their childhood, it is filled with noise and boisterous games. Checking her phone she sees that there is still no reply from her sister. She takes the keys from her bag, and there is only the smallest squeak of resistance before the lock yields. When she turns back to the church, there is no sign of the man with the shovel, and the last thing Clara feels as she pushes the heavy door open is the weight of the sun's heat on her shoulders.

The twins are restless that evening, the long car journey filled with too many sweets prompting question upon question.

'What time does Auntie Liza's train arrive?' asks Sophie, spearing pasta shells into her mouth.

'I don't know, sweetheart. She really should have been in touch by now. You know what Auntie Liza's like.' Despite her sister's inability – or refusal – to reply to what by now amounted to several text messages, Clara isn't really worried. Liza – the older of the two by ten minutes – had always been the less reliable, the one who'd turn up late or not at all. When they were little, it would be Liza who got into trouble for answering back, while Clara would meekly observe, and it was always Liza who blamed Clara when their toys got broken or their clothes dirty. She would also be the one to instruct their play, to assume the upper hand in their games of dolls' houses and shops, teddy bears' tea parties and tents in the garden. Clara sometimes wondered if that ten-minute head start Liza had is really all it took to make them so different.

'Who was Joan? Was she your auntie, like Auntie Liza's ours?' There is now pesto smeared around both girls' mouths, and Clara pauses to wipe it off with a piece of kitchen towel before she speaks.

'Quite right. Joan was my mum's – your Granny's – sister. They were twins as well, just like you two.'

'And like you and Auntie Liza!' Emma squeals, as though this realisation has only just occurred to her. Clara smiles.

'Yes, of course, just like me and Auntie Liza. Do you know what? Lots of people say that twins run in families, that if you're a twin, there's a good chance that when you have babies, they'll be twins as well.' The girls look at each other, wide-eyed. They are identical, if in name only. Clara thinks she must be the only one who can make out Sophie's slightly fuller lower lip, or the tiny dimple on Emma's left earlobe, or how Sophie's index finger is a couple of millimetres longer than her twin's. Clara knows them so intimately, like no other person; they are hers and hers alone.

Do you remember the games you and Liza would play when you were little? How you both inhabited your own little world and would talk in a made-up language that only you understood, a sort of pidgin English that somehow you both got the gist of, while your mother would plead with you to talk properly? You also had your favourite games which kept you amused; you had no real playmates, other than yourselves. Every time, it was Liza who was the instigator of these games, while you merely followed her instructions.

Do you remember Blind Man's Buff? It was Liza's favourite game. It was always you who was blindfolded, and Liza would take hold of your shoulders and spin you around, before twirling and shimmying out of reach, erupting into giggles as you flailed and blindly stumbled. Eventually she would allow you to catch her, once she had proven that she was too good at the game for you, and you would then have to go through the routine of running your hands over your sister's face in the charade of trying to guess who it was you had caught. You both knew it was a farce, but Liza was always very particular about the rules.

After they had arrived at the cottage, Clara had unloaded their luggage from the car and then they had cautiously explored. The front door opened into a narrow hallway, with a door to each side and a staircase reaching up in front of them. It was gloomy inside, and cooler, the thick stone walls no doubt providing some relief from the heat outside. A rust-red carpet muffled their footsteps, and the air held the combined scents of encroaching damp and, yes, mothballs. A wooden sideboard held half a dozen photographs in silver frames, their surfaces clouded by a thin layer of dust.

The girls were both timid by nature, and were reluctant to go ahead of Clara, instead waiting behind her while she went around opening doors and windows. One of the doors from the hall led into a comfortably furnished living room, a chintz-covered sofa and matching armchairs suggesting the home of an elderly spinster. Bookcases were ranked neatly along one wall, and a woodburning stove squatted in the fireplace. A magazine lay open on a side table. Everything had the look of being cared for and then abandoned, and Clara was shocked when it occurred to her that she did not know how Joan had died. She had not enquired of the solicitor about the circumstances behind her aunt's demise – had assumed it had been old age – and Clara wondered briefly if the cause had been more sudden. More malign.

A door led from the living room to the kitchen at the back of the house, and Clara was relieved to find it lit by a large window that also afforded a view onto a tiny patch of overgrown grass to the rear. Although the worktops were neat and uncluttered, and the cooker hob clean and unsullied by dirt, everything about the kitchen suggested a sudden departure. A plate and a teacup rested on the draining board, and the washing-up bowl in the sink held an inch of grey water. Against her better instincts, Clara cautiously opened one of the cupboards that flanked the window. Tea bags in canisters, a sugar bowl, jars of jam and marmalade were all ranked neatly along the shelves. The fridge yielded nothing more than a half-used pack of butter and a slimy, congealed lettuce. The date on the bottle of milk was three weeks ago.

Then Clara briefly inspected the dining room which sat opposite the living room, on the other side of the hall. Like the living room, it had a low ceiling, and the small windows allowed in little light. She doubted that Joan had used it much: a solid-looking mahogany table took up most of the floorspace, and was surrounded by eight matching chairs. The walls were decorated with paintings: landscapes and still lifes mostly, amateur things that even Clara, with her layman's appreciation of art, could tell were collected more for sentimentality than any monetary value they may have held. Highland glades; snow-capped mountains; bowls of fruit and flowers.

Turning back to the door, Clara's eye was caught by another painting. It was larger than the others – at least a metre across, and almost as tall. Even to her eye, it was clearly finer, more accomplished than the other pictures, the brushstrokes delicate, the detail more intricate.

The painting depicted two boys, their pale faces stark against the dark background. It was impossible to say how old it was: the artist had elected not to depict the boys' clothing or any other clues, choosing instead to paint only their faces emerging from the gloom. Even though their eyes were black, the irises and pupils so dark they appeared to merge into one, they still held a supercilious gaze. Both boys had tightly cropped black hair, and narrow noses that gave way to tight, unsmiling lips. The painting was hung up high, close to the ceiling, so that its subjects seemed to glare down at her, arrogant and superior. Holding their gaze, Clara felt an inexplicable sensation of shame, as though she had done something deplorable that must be corrected. Chiding herself for being silly, she turned her attention to the frame, an ornately-carved gilt object that was probably more valuable in itself than any of the other artworks in the room. Along the bottom was a flat panel, engraved with something, an inscription possibly? Clara reached out to wipe the dust from the writing, but footsteps caused her to turn towards the door. The girls had followed her in, and looked around them, wide-eyed. Clara immediately turned to usher them out again.

'Let's have something to eat, shall we?' she said, her voice loud in the silence of the room. Leading them back into the hall, she closed the door behind them.

Was it your sixth birthday party that you can remember? You haven't thought about those parties for years, but you remember your mother saying she was glad that she'd had twins, as it meant there was only one party a year to organise. That year, you and Liza had received matching pink taffeta dresses and Alice bands. You can picture the pair of you standing side by side, hand in hand, welcoming your classmates to the party. Or, at least you think you can remember it, but in your mind's eye you are an onlooker, observing your younger self and your sister in the bright glare of the July sunshine, a picnic table set out behind you with party food and a pink cake to match your dresses. Perhaps you are remembering a photograph, one from your mother's countless albums that littered your childhood and filled the cupboard in the hall?

The party had started off well enough. About a dozen of your classmates playing pass-the-parcel and musical bumps while their mothers sat around drinking tea and gossiping. Then the birthday tea: ham sandwiches and sausage rolls, cheese and pineapple on sticks and bowls of crisps. And then, when Happy Birthday *had been sung, and the cake sliced and consumed, Liza had stood on her chair and announced that they were all to play a special game. She'd even made up a song for all the children to sing, seeing as it was a special occasion. How had that gone?*

Once the girls have finished eating, Clara stacks the bowls in the sink and runs the hot tap.

'Go and put your pyjamas on. I'll be up in a minute,' she tells them, looking in the cupboard for washing-up liquid. When there is no reply she turns to where they stand, framed in the doorway, silent and dark-eyed. 'What's wrong?' Both girls are biting their bottom lips, looking at the floor. 'What's the matter?'

It's Sophie who speaks, so quietly as to barely be heard. 'You come with us, Mummy. It's dark up there.'

'Nonsense,' says Clara, drying her hands on a tea towel. 'It's not even dark outside yet and anyway, the landing light's on.'

Emma steps towards her and takes her hand.

'Mummy, please,' she pleads.

Clara sighs, but acquiesces.

'Come on then. Let's get ready for bed.'

She sends them to brush their teeth in the bathroom, while she changes the sheets in the twin room. With only two bedrooms, she and Liza will have to share the double room – the one filled with heavy, dark wood furniture that she knows without really thinking about it used to be Joan's room. She will change the bedding in there, as well.

After reading the girls a story, she tucks them in and plants a kiss on each small forehead in turn. She has forgotten to pack their nightlight, so she leaves the door ajar so they can have the light from the landing. Their exhaustion after the journey is something to be grateful for, otherwise their perpetual anxiety might make it hard for them to sleep, but after she has put clean sheets onto the double bed where she will sleep, and bundled the old ones up for disposal in the morning, the light from the landing illuminates their tiny figures tucked under the sheets, their delicate chests rising and falling steadily. She closes the door, wincing as it squeaks in the silence of the landing. At the bottom of the stairs, she makes sure the door to the dining room is firmly shut, and then heads towards the kitchen, where a bottle of wine and her phone await her.

The photographs on the sideboard cause her to stop abruptly. She hadn't paid them any attention when they had first arrived, other than to think she might pack them up and take them back for her mother, to see if any of the people they depicted might jog her memory. They did say, after all, that with her mother's sort of dementia, people tended to have a better recall of incidents from years ago than of recent events.

Now, she picks up each of the framed photographs in turn and examines them, wiping the dust away with her thumb. They appear to be arranged in date order. The one at the front, in black and white, depicts two babies, both swaddled in cloth and gazing unseeing at the camera, their dark eyes striking against the paleness of their faces and the white fabric in which they're wrapped. The next shows a pair of toddlers – two or three years old – both dressed identically in dungarees and shirts with sailor collars. Sunlight streams into their eyes, and they blink it away. A third photograph shows the same two boys – and they must be the same boys, because the resemblance has followed them through the years – sitting on a low stone wall, the one Clara recognises as being at the front of the cottage. They are not looking at the camera, but away to the side, at something out of shot, invisible. Both boys have cropped, dark hair. Their skin is pale, and unsullied by freckles or blemishes. They have identical narrow noses and thin lips, and even their cheeks have the same hollowness to them. Twins. The boys from the painting.

Further photographs show the boys at gradually incremental ages: standing in front of the little church at four or five, the ancient wooden doors forming a backdrop; a couple of years older, and standing on the village green, the pub just visible behind them. The later photographs are steeped in the faded colours of the past, the reds, oranges and browns crowding out the blues and greens. It is as though the photographs are arranged to tell a story, to relate the boys' life history. There is one final picture at the back of the sideboard, the twins crouching, looking down, their hands resting on the pair of identical teddy bears that lie at their feet. And then there are no more photographs.

Clara gathers them, one by one, not looking at their subjects, and stacks them in a pile, face down. Under her arm she still has the sheets she removed from Joan's bed, and she bundles the photographs into the folds of the fabric, wrapping them into a parcel. Then she opens the front door and places the bundle on the doorstep. She will dispose of it in the morning.

In the kitchen, she congratulates herself on remembering to bring wine with her, and pours herself a hefty measure. Her phone tells her that Liza has still not returned any of her messages or phone calls, and the voicemail messages have also gone unanswered. Clara has given up on her sister making an appearance before tomorrow, and is resigned to making a start on clearing out the cottage by herself. It had been a pleasant surprise to see how few belongings filled the house: the last thing she wanted was to have to go through years of detritus, the result of decades of hoarding, as she'd had to do when their mother had moved into the nursing home. They'd had to sell the house to pay the fees, and the process of sorting through reams of knitting patterns and hand-written recipes, half-finished tapestries and photograph albums, had been a dismal experience.

Clara pours herself another glass of wine. Darkness has fallen in the brief time since she put the girls to bed, and the window onto the little garden shows a black void. Her face is reflected, starkly white against the gloom, and she is shocked at how haggard she looks. She stands and pulls down the blind to shut out the darkness. She should go to bed soon, but the thought of Joan's bedroom – the candlewick bedspread and the plumped cushions – fills her with dismay. Perhaps just one more glass.

She wakes gasping for breath. There is something obstructing her mouth, her nostrils. Her vision is blurred; her eyes are also filled with something that clings. Clara sits upright and scratches at her face. When she manages to scrape the stuff from her eyes, she can see in the light from the landing that her hand comes away smeared with something dark, and she assumes blood. But the texture is wrong – this is something moist but congealed. Her ears, too; it's in her ears. She throws back the covers and runs to the bathroom and retches into the sink. She claws at her eyes and her nose, desperate to remove whatever it is. When the worst of it is gone and she can breathe freely again, she turns on the light.

Soil. Clumps of mud, moistened by saliva and mucus, cling to the porcelain, dark brown and sodden. And underneath, something small and pink squirms, coiled and wet against the shiny white surface: an earthworm. She turns to the toilet and retches again and again, her stomach aching with the effort. Finally, the acid taste of wine fills her mouth, replacing the gritty soil, and then there is nothing else to bring up. She sits, exhausted, on the bathroom floor, the tiles cold through her nightdress, shaking, gulping down air. Eventually, she finds the strength to stand.

The sink is empty, the white porcelain unsullied and gleaming. She looks around her, as though she might be able to find some evidence of what has just happened, but there is nothing. The bathroom is immaculate, and her face and hands are clean and dry. A dream, then. It must have been a nightmare, brought about by the long journey and the heat.

Wiping her mouth on her sleeve, she goes downstairs. In the kitchen she turns on the light, taking her empty wine glass from where she has placed it on the draining board and filling it from the tap. The water is cold and fresh and pure, and she gulps down another glassful greedily. For a few minutes, she sits at the kitchen table. She considers texting Liza one more time, or even phoning her, but the clock on the cooker tells her it's almost two in the morning. Eventually, she resigns herself to a return to bed, and the possibility of more night terrors. She climbs the stairs methodically, hand over hand on the banister, and when she reaches the top, stops to check on the girls. They are both fast asleep.

In Joan's room she turns on the small bedside lamp and it casts a pallid glow; she thinks she might sleep with the light on. She goes to tidy the bedding, where she threw it back in her confusion. On the other side of the bed the sheet lies flat, apart from two places where the fabric has been compressed into very faint indentations, as though recently two small frames have been sitting there. She wonders if the girls have come into her room while she was downstairs, but they were sleeping so soundly just now that she dismisses this thought.

Without pausing to reflect on what she is doing, she strides down the stairs and into the dining room. The overhead light is brighter than she was expecting, and throws the painting into stark relief. The boys gaze back at her. She imagines there is something new to their expression: less imperious now, more overtly hostile. The paleness of their skin renders it almost translucent, and for a moment Clara imagines the veins that run, pulsing, beneath the surface. Two identical sets of lips appear to smirk at her: thin, pursed, and sly.

She does not allow herself to consider her action, but unhooks the painting from the wall, struggling slightly under its weight. She turns it and places it on the floor, the boys now facing the wall. Then she goes upstairs, gets into bed and counts the minutes until morning.

Dawn is a time for reassessment, for thinking things through. Clara had finally managed to fall into a light doze in the early hours, a prickled, fitful sleep that thankfully yielded neither dreams nor nightmares. When she wakes, it is almost seven o'clock, and the sun is already inveigling its way past Joan's heavy velvet curtains. Drawing them back she sees that it is another cloudless day, still and oppressive. From the bedroom window, the view is that of the village green, and the church in the distance. Clara can just make out the jutting shapes of headstones in the graveyard. She recalls the man she saw there yesterday, and the metallic blade of his shovel that had temporarily blinded her. She will seek him out today, she tells herself. He is the only living person she has encountered so far in the village. She will find him and ask him about her aunt.

Clara is sitting at the kitchen table with her second cup of tea when the girls stumble in. She is reminded of how vulnerable they are, how frail, standing before her in matching pyjamas, clutching the identical teddy bears they were given by her mother on the day they were born.

'Is Auntie Liza coming today?' Sophie asks, her voice still fragile with sleep.

'I hope so,' Clara replies. 'I really hope so.'

She sets out butter and jam on the table, and slides bread into the toaster. She pours herself another cup of tea from the china teapot and adds milk. She has already found the number for an antiques dealer in the nearest town, and also a couple of house clearance companies. She'll phone them later, and try to arrange for them to visit in the next couple of days. She's already emailed a couple of estate agents with a request for a valuation, so now it's just a case of waiting.

'What are we doing today?' Emma asks.

'I thought we'd get out of the house for a bit. Explore the village. Perhaps have a look at the church.' The girls wrinkle their noses, but say nothing.

There are swifts chasing each other in the heavens when she opens the cottage door. The lucid light comes as a shock after the gloom of the cottage, and she squints and lifts a hand to shield her eyes, cursing herself for leaving her sunglasses at home. The girls shuffle out behind her, dressed identically in flowered sun dresses and liberal quantities of factor 50, and look around them, ever cautious. Clara carefully closes the door behind them, marvelling at her own sense of security in this tiny rural spot. She has only encountered one person since she's been here. Who is going to break in? Still, she gives the solid wooden door a push with her shoulder to check that it is locked. The bundle of bedding and photographs is still lying on the doorstep, and Clara picks it up and unceremoniously dumps it in the wheelie bin at the side of the house, ignoring the clatter of metal and glass. The sun's heat settles on her shoulders immediately, and she is aware of sweat prickling her scalp.

The village is arranged in a triangle around the green: the pub with the row of terraced houses along one side; the church and the cemetery on another; and Joan's house, and a few other scattered detached and semi-detached cottages along the third side. From where she is standing in front of the cottage gate she can make out the façade of the pub. Her car is still parked at the front; she will drive it round to this side of the green later, now that she has got her bearings. At first, she can't tell what's different about the scene, and then she realises that the metal beer barrels that were stacked outside the pub's front door yesterday have been removed; the village is not entirely deserted then.

She thinks she may check the pub out later when – if – Liza arrives. They might do food, and it would be a way of avoiding another otherwise inevitable meal of pasta or sandwiches.

Taking the girls by the hand, she leads them along the pavement and towards the church. The sun glares down on them. There is a lychgate set into the dry stone wall, a sparse oak structure which is in keeping with the simplicity of the church itself. The graveyard which encompasses the church is deserted, no sign of the man from yesterday. Serried ranks of graves are fitted neatly into rows, most of the headstones formed from the grey stone she has become so used to seeing in the village. Despite the uniform, grid-like layout of the cemetery, the grass is overgrown and weeds sprout around the edges of untended graves. Here and there flowers have been left in vases and jam jars, the petals brown and withered, the glass clouded. There is a despondency to the place, as though nobody really cares anymore.

And then she spots the one grave that is unlike the others. It is twice as wide, for one thing, but it is the rough-hewn gravel that covers the surface of the grave which has caught her eye. It is bright white and glistening, and twinkles where it catches the beams of the sun. Quartz, perhaps. A bunch of vivid pink flowers shrieks from a glass vase which is nestled into the gravel – carnations, she thinks – and a heavy, sticky scent reaches her nostrils as she picks her way through the other graves. The headstone is small, but there its modesty ends. It is elaborately carved from marble or some other white stone, and is evidently aged but also well maintained, the stone clean and polished. The carving depicts the faces of two boys, no older than her own daughters, and even before she inspects it more closely, she knows it will be the boys from the painting at the cottage, the twins depicted in all the photographs.

The same tapered noses, hollow cheeks and thin, pursed lips greet her, and even though rendered in white stone, she knows the cropped hair to be black and wiry. Only the eyes are changed. In the painting in her aunt's dining room, the boys' eyes are dark, oppressive. Here, carved in marble, they are blank, unseeing, the pupils and irises merging together into one stone surface. The effect is uncanny, and Clara steps backwards and stumbles slightly, her heel catching on the edge of the neighbouring grave. She rights herself and peers closer. There is an inscription under the carving of the twins, the letters hewn from the stone with precision and craftsmanship.

An eye for an eye, never turn a blind eye.

She looks around for the girls, but they are nowhere to be seen.

'Girls? Sophie? Emma!' She can hear the panic rising in her voice and forces it back down. She retraces her steps to the front of the church, scanning the churchyard, the weeds and overgrown grass clinging at her ankles. Finally, she sees them, huddled in the shade of the lychgate, and she runs to them.

'Why did you disappear?' she asks them, noting the unusual defiance that appears on their faces, and the sullenness that falls across them. 'I've told you not to wander off. Anything could have happened.' At first they do not respond, merely looking down at their feet, then they look up and share a conspiratorial glance, and a smile lands on Emma's lips, and an identical one on Sophie's. They both have their hands clutched behind their backs, and when they finally look up at her, share a petulant expression.

'It's not funny,' Clara insists, even though she knows she's being unreasonable. What possible harm could come to them here, in a churchyard in the middle of nowhere, in broad daylight?

You were used to being dominated by your sister – your twin – and had learned to live with the humiliation that came

from Liza's torments, but surely now you would be further humiliated – in front of all your classmates this time. An immense dread engulfed you, but still you meekly allowed Liza to tie the scarf around your face, shutting out the light. You were unable to protest. The children's muffled giggles as they watched you being trussed, and there, faintly in the background, the creak of a grasshopper. Then Liza's fingers on your shoulder, pressing harder than usual, as though your twin was asserting herself even more forcefully over you. And then the spinning, the rushing of air over your face, and finally slowing to a stop and standing, swaying, trying to regain your balance.

You didn't like it that Liza was always in charge, did you?

That evening the girls are even quieter than usual, eating their dinner with small bites, and occasionally throwing each other secretive smiles and dark looks from under long lashes. Their complicity grates on Clara's nerves, and at seven o'clock she announces bedtime. For once the girls go meekly up the stairs and into the bathroom, while she gathers up the toys in their bedroom. They reappear five minutes later, faces scrubbed pink and the fresh tang of toothpaste on their breath. They slip into their pyjamas silently, and when Clara asks what story they would like, both announce that they are tired and would just like to go to sleep. This behaviour is unusual, but not unheard of, so she tucks them in and kisses each one in turn. She switches off the overhead light and the room is thrown into shadow, the light from the landing barely cutting through the darkness

In the kitchen she empties the dregs from the wine bottle into a glass and takes out her phone. Once more she brings up her sister's contact page and calls her mobile and then her house phone. Still no answer. Typical. Liza was always the selfish one, always putting her own needs before those of her sister. Clara can feel the anger bubbling in her chest, and suddenly her thumbs are flying across her phone.

Don't bloody well bother, then, I'll do all this by myself as per fucking usual.

She doesn't sign off the message, but hits send before she can change her mind. The immediate effect is one of relief, a faint pleasure at having made a stand against her sister for once, but she knows it will be short-lived, and she will find herself sending another message, apologising, blaming the twins for making her stressed. In one act of reckless defiance, she goes to Liza's contact page on her phone and deletes the entry. Then she opens another bottle of wine.

The laughter was the worst thing. All around you the lilting trickle of childish laughter filling your ears, taunting you. Not just Liza now, but all of her friends, giggles and chuckles and cat-calls, and all the time your eyes and nose covered by the blindfold, your ears full of their childish taunts, flailing blindly with your arms to try to catch someone, anyone, so that this nightmare could end. And then Liza's voice, that voice you know so well, so much like your own, beginning to sing, and as though they have somehow practised, the sound of several childish voices joining in, singing in unison.

An eye for an eye, never turn a blind eye.

In a panic, you had flung out an arm and your hand landed on a bony shoulder. Liza. You knew it was Liza you had caught; even before you placed your hands on your sister's face, you recognised her thin arms and elbows, for were they not identical to your own? Your hands on your sister's face, fingers running over delicate lips, the small, button nose, exactly like yours, and then eyes beneath your fingers, your thumbs. More laughter swelling in your ears, your vision and breathing still hampered by the scarf, and then the soft give of flesh. Pressing, pressing, pushing down with all your might, feeling the jelly of your twin's eyeballs shift beneath the balls of your thumbs. Laughter becoming gasps, becoming calls for help, becoming your mother's screams and hard fingers on your arms pulling you away. The final rush of light as the blindfold was pulled from your eyes.

Clara comes slowly to consciousness, fighting sleep, but it is the squeak of the girls' bedroom door that has woken her, she is sure of that. She must rise, go to them, and she tries to push herself up, but the alcohol has made her limbs heavy, her legs and arms like lead. Then her bedroom door opens a crack, the light from the landing slicing across the bottom of the bed. She is about to sit up when she feels hands on her shoulders, gripping hard onto her collarbone, pushing her back against the mattress.

And then she hears a giggle, a light rippling chuckle that she knows is Sophie, and she manages to raise her head enough to see both girls lit dimly in the doorway, their silhouettes identical. A moment later and she feels the pressure on her ankles. She struggles to free herself, but the force is too strong, so instead she kicks her feet, but to no avail. Each of her daughters is leaning over one of her legs, their tiny hands gripping onto an ankle with impossible strength. Again, the sound of laughter bubbles from the bottom of the bed – Emma this time.

Then more hands on her shoulders, hard and cold, pushing her down, pressing her into the yielding mattress. The fingers are small and the nails are long, digging into her collarbone, relentless.

Six tiny hands now, pinning her to the table.

And then she feels the flutter of fingers on her face. Icy fingers that gently stroke and caress, brushing over her lips and her nose, her eyebrows. And then, with more force, her eyes.

The Waiting Room

Stephen Volk

Our hosts, such as they were, did not seem as subject to the cold as we did, remaining cheerful beyond requirement as they furnished us with cups of tea. We had not divulged the exact purpose for our coming, though one of them at least had experienced the phenomenon, and I could only reason that their lightness of spirit was born of the knowledge that they would soon be off to a warm bed, and we would not.

"*Au revoir.*"

"He means goodbye. Does he mean goodbye?"

"He does, my dear," said the station master. "Until the morrow morn."

The man and his doughty wife having departed, we were alone, and my companion turned down the wick of the signal man's lamp, saving it, I presumed, lest when the darkness came, we should be more needful of it. He placed a travel clock upon the table between us, assuring me that the instrument kept good time, adding the *caveat* that such instruments were prone to be affected by such – he paused… *atmosphere* as we were there to witness.

"What shall we do?" We sat with blankets over our knees and scarves wrapped around our necks, and had not yet divested ourselves of hats.

"We shall wait," said Dickens, laying down his note book and pencil beside our scant means of illumination. "This is a waiting room. We shall wait."

The first time I set eyes on him in the flesh it was with his back to me, frock coat splayed, hair salted by the limelight, proclaiming to the balcony with a theatricality befitting a Hamlet, though the words were not those of the Bard of Avon but his own. Even then, I strangely felt I already knew him, such was his fame, and such was the intimate vividness of his works. I was not alone. When an actor takes to the stage, he invariably wants the audience to love him. The extraordinary thing was, with Dickens, it was the other way around; the audience wanted *him* to love *them*.

The performance, as expected, was intoxicating. Each character sprang alive not just from his lips but from every inch of his physical being. At times, his voice boomed like a Wesleyan; at others, softened so gently as to make the audience lean forward as one. He tickled the belly of the trout like a master, and if he were any normal man I'd have wagered it would take it out of him, but he seemed forever lifted by the rapt attention of the crowd. Two thousand strong they were, that night. His adoring public, out in force, and I almost regretted I was not there to applaud him to high heaven.

Far from it.

While his words flowed like a river my own throat was dry with fear. It had taken some Dutch courage to get me to the wings, and I hoped he would not smell it on my breath. Steel was required to confront a treasure the equal of the Crown Jewels who no doubt thought himself impregnable. I had something to tell the most beloved writer in England, and I was by no means sure how he would take it.

The ghost story drew them in as it came to a close. The resolution was upon us. I knew every word – and not because I had read it in *All the Year Round*. I told myself, not for the first time, to curb any anger I felt rising. The opponents were not well matched and the one who would suffer, ultimately, if I let loose, would be me.

The final line was delivered with a flourish. Dickens' hand rolled in a wave from his breast and his fingers unpeeled from his fist as the last three words were spoken in a whisper. I saw, from behind, the merest twitch of a smile in the corner of his mouth. The house erupted, jumping to their feet, stamping for more. I marvelled at the suppleness of his spine as he took bow after extravagant bow. Three steps to the edge of the stage, three steps back. Then he strode to the wings, his visage leaving the light.

Inches away from me, he tore off his cravat and knocked back a glass of sherry with a raw egg beaten into it, which was lying in wait on a silver tray proffered by a stagehand.

"Sir—"

"At the door! At the door!"

"My name is Thomas Frank Heaphy," I said.

"Very likely. Very likely."

Cuffs askew, he returned to the standing ovation, lapping it up, delivering a swift, sentimental homily to send his public home with a warm heart – and the name of his next volume deftly placed in their ears. I was only glad we had been spared the death of Little Nell.

A glass of rum with cream awaited after his second curtain call, and a glass of champagne followed the third. The uproar gradually abated. The reading was over. He left the stage for the last time.

"Mr Dickens, sir—" I watched him walk past me. "The story, sir. The Portrait Painter's Story…" He stopped then, and turned back. I think because he was expecting a compliment on his writing, his performance, or both. I gave him neither. I gave him this: "The story is mine, sir."

"What?"

"The story you told. The story you *printed*. It happened to me."

A snarling laugh exploded from lips shiny with rum. "You are mad!"

"Would that I were."

"Would that you *were?* You *are!* There is no concept more certain! Now be off with you, and take such nonsense to the street." The dark of backstage and the darkness of the author became one. No limelight to lift the make-up on his cheeks now as he pawed away flowers from well-wishers. Nothing to disguise the furrowed brow. His rage, diluted only by an innate sense of gentlemanly decorum, resulting in – dismissal. But I was not about to be dismissed.

"I am that portrait painter."

"You are a fool, sir."

"I am not. I have no wish to give you discomfort, but you must hear me out. I shall not leave until you do."

"We shall see about that." Dickens grabbed the arm of someone in a suit I took to be the stage manager. "This man is—"

"Please! Just listen. The story happened to me. Precisely as you told it. I know it sounds preposterous. It—"

"Sir, a ghost story *cannot* be true because ghosts are *not* true. That much is quite *surely* preposterous. Now please! Leave me in peace and be on your way without further disturbance. Or I fear I shall have to – George! By all the saints in—"

"But I have *proof*," I barked, not waiting for his reply, and, lifting my voice as he showed me his back, stuck my dagger in: "Your story appeared in September, did it not? Well, by then I had already sent the manuscript of my experience to a different magazine. A rival of yours, as it happens. The editors can verify the exact date of its arrival. It is planned to appear in the Christmas issue."

Dickens went very cold very quickly, and dismissed the stage manager summarily with a fluttering gesture, after which he deigned to step closer to me, as if to keep our dialogue away from prying ears.

"Are you threatening me, young man?"

"No."

"Are you asserting foul play? That by some unknown and unbelievable method, your story fell into my hands?"

"I am only asserting," I said boldly, "what I know to be true. I was your protagonist."

"No! You are my antagonist! That much is plain!"

"Then read it and see for yourself. Here is a run of the

proof pages." I thrust against his chest a sheaf of paper I had been carrying under my arm. Dickens recoiled no less sharply than if I had drawn a pistol.

"I shall do no such thing! I shall see my lawyer and you would do well to see yours."

He spun away. It took no great observational skill to see anger and discombobulation under the bluster. Anger that his integrity was being questioned. The *originality* of his *ideas* questioned. The very lifeblood of his creativity – his *soul*. How could he have responded otherwise?

"Sir, this need not involve lawyers. Please hear me out. I am no more able to explain—" Burly figures tried to hold me back. "Mr Dickens! I can only think some supernatural agency is at work."

"I can only think you are talking utter poppycock!"

"You explain it then!" I broke away from my captors and grabbed him forcibly by one shoulder, spinning him around to face me and thrusting my manuscript firmly into his hands.

"I have no desire to. Nor shall I!" said Dickens, dropping it into a fire bucket in his close proximity, from which I had the ignominious pleasure of extracting it as I watched the door of the dressing room slam closed after him, before being unceremoniously ejected from the premises.

No curtain call. No encore. And certainly no flowers.

I am a painter, and though I have had cause to doubt the evidence of my eyes, and many will doubt what follows, I stand by every word of it, and shall not waver in my vow that it is an account of absolute veracity.

One morning in May 1858, I was seated in my studio at my usual occupation when I received an unexpected visit from a friend whose acquaintance I had made a year or two previously in Richmond Barracks, Dublin. Beholden to greet him in the hospitable manner in which he had entertained me when our roles had been reversed, I immediately offered him refreshments. Before either of us knew it, two o'clock saw us well ensconced in conversation, cigars, and a decanter of sherry. At that exact hour the bell rang. I found myself facing a well-dressed man and woman who asked for me by name. They could see I was entertaining, apologised for the intrusion, and said, in brief, that they wished, on recommendation, to commission me to paint their house in the country. Would I be free to do this in the coming autumn? I said indeed I would, and we parted, happily, with the gentleman leaving his card. Examining it later, however, I read the name JEREMIAH KIRKBECK – but no address. I subsequently tried to find evidence of the family in the Court Guide, with no success. So, frustrated, and not a little bewildered, I put the card in my writing desk and thought no more about it. It was an odd beginning to a tale that became significantly odder.

Come autumn, business took me to the north of England. It pained me to leave my wife and children even for a few nights, so when I alighted at York to paint a portrait of Lady Gertrude Delahunty it was with an inevitably heavy heart, especially as the dinner to which I was invited proved a far more substantial affair than I'd anticipated, and I was by no means a social animal. My host was already in his cups and his wife displayed considerably more of a bony chest in her low-cut Regency gown than I was prepared for. Children rattled up and down the staircase, by turns intrigued and scared, daring each other to see what the adults were up to, as if we were bogeymen. I should point out here that I have a defect in hearing which renders the effect of manifold voices as a dull, unintelligible blanket of sound, which causes me to adopt an expression of grinning stupor. However, through the din, suddenly I heard the name *"Kirkbeck"* – sharp as the cut of a knife. Compelled to interrupt the conversation I'd overheard, I asked if the family were resident in the neighbourhood, and was swiftly furnished with an address in Lincoln. Next morning I wrote to Mr Kirkbeck enquiring if the brief we had discussed in London was still open. A week later I received a letter in reply via the Post Office, York – which I had given as my return address – saying he was glad to hear from me and that, if it were agreeable, he would be delighted to accommodate my arrival the coming Saturday; furthermore, if it suited my plans, I could stay until Monday. I replied to confirm that such an arrangement would be perfect. My all too flattering portrait of the fearsome Lady Delahunty would be done by then, and I would be free.

The train from York to London was due to stop at Doncaster, then at Retford Junction, after which I would stay on the same line to Lincoln. The day was cold, wet, foggy and disagreeable – that of a typical English October. For the first part of the journey I was alone in the carriage, but at Doncaster a young woman got on. I was sitting next to the door with my back to the engine. Since this is known as the ladies' seat, I offered it to her, but she quietly declined and found the corner opposite.

I watched her settle and adjust herself, taking off her gloves, placing them on top of the rabbit-skin muff on her lap, and generally attending to matters of arrangement and plumage to which ladies are dedicated. Finally she lifted the veil from her hat to reveal a young person of perhaps no more than two- or three-and-twenty years, though if I removed her many matronly layers, perhaps two or three younger. Her hair was bright brown or auburn and I noticed she had delicately marked eyebrows, almost black. The warmth of the compartment had brought no blush to her cheeks, which remained as pale as marble, yet her expression had a depth and harmony about it that made her face, though not strictly regular, infinitely more attractive than mere perfection. Secreted in her corner, she showed what I took to be ill ease at being a lone woman in confined circumstances with a lone man. I saw no wedding ring. Nevertheless, wanting to be a gentleman rather than a boor, I found myself reluctant to inflict conversation upon a stranger who might not desire such a thing. To my surprise, it was she who initiated it.

Did I know what time the train passed through Retford? I said I wasn't sure, but I could consult my Bradshaw's, if she really wanted to know. She shook her head, thanking me almost inaudibly. Noticing the accoutrements of my trade on the luggage rack above my head, she asked what I did for a living. The smile the answer brought was soon replaced with unutterable sadness. It made me wonder if she had come from a funeral.

"Do you think you could paint my portrait?"

"Yes," I said. "I think I could, if I had the opportunity."

She looked at me, not in any peculiar or sinister fashion but one almost of simple but intense interest. "Do you think you could recall my features?"

"Yes," I laughed. "I am sure I shall never forget them."

She dropped her eyes slightly. "Of course, I might have expected you to say that; but do you think you could do me *from recollection alone?*"

This struck me as a bizarre request, almost a playful one, but I did my best to answer it. "Well, if it is necessary, I would try. But can't you give me any sittings?"

"No, it's impossible. It cannot be."

I laughed again, now thinking this a tease. "If you could grant me just one sitting, it would be better than none."

"No, I don't see that it could be."

I felt I had overstepped the mark and we both lapsed into silence. She stared out of the window at the countryside. I unfolded my newspaper. After three quarters of an hour we arrived at Retford, and she rose to get off.

"I daresay we shall meet again."

I could not, in all honestly, conceive of that eventuality, but said: "I hope we shall."

After she had departed, my thoughts strayed idly, and with some degree of shame, to a kiss I might have planted on that cold cheek, a different word spoken, a touch not made, a path not taken, to remorse and regret, if though a sweet one. The typography on the pages of *The Times* no longer held my interest and my mind wandered, returning to her strange, alluring and preposterous challenge – to remember her features. To draw her *from recollection.* Could I? *Would* I? I would.

Taking out a soft pencil and opening my sketch book, I would *try*, at least, while the freshness of our proximity still hung in the air, to catch that quality she had of a heron or swan. *Swan-like*, that was the word – not marble, but living and effortlessly graceful.

At the time I thought it no more than a way to pass the journey.

At half past five my travels ended and I disembarked in a dreary sleet at Lincoln. A pre-arranged landau drawn by a pair awaited me. Upon reaching the Kirkbeck residence, Lentney Hall, I was welcomed into a large conglomeration of family, friends, cousins, and servants, the details of which need not concern us, except to say that the gathering into which I was welcomed stood in stark contrast to the strange, quiet intimacy of my train journey.

I slept well. The business dealings were dealt with over the subsequent weekend, and I left on the Monday, pleased that my proposal as to the composition had been agreed and several preparatory drawings of the architectural detail undertaken. I am never more at ease than when concentrating on what I see and transferring that to paper. Consequently I found that the young lady in the railway compartment vanished from my thoughts almost completely.

Some weeks passed. Christmas was upon us. Eager to capture the wonder in the children's faces as they opened their presents, I opened my drawing pad accidentally to the page showing the sketch of the woman on the train, and to my surprise considered it not half bad. I'd caught her reticent posture. The arresting eyes. The layers of armour of her skirts and fur. "You should make a painting of her." My wife leaned over my shoulder. "No," I replied; "She must stay as she was, half-realised. Unfinished." I have no idea why I replied in such a way.

January saw another commission take me north once more, and on this occasion I had to switch at Retford Junction, but missed my connection. There was nothing for it, therefore, but to put up at the Swan Hotel for the night. I have a special dislike to passing an evening at a hotel in a country town. Dinner is invariably an indignity if not a punishment. Books are never to be had and local guides do not interest me. I had no inclination to learn more about the Venerable Bede, or the River Idle which once "ran foul with the blood of Englishmen". I ordered dry toast and tea, and whilst waiting for my order, it occurred to me how very peculiar it was that, on two occasions in the past six months, I had stopped at that very place. The words of my female travelling companion – her fervent belief that we would *meet again* – came as a peculiar frisson of memory. For no other reason than to dispel it, I took up my sketch book and began drawing the beer glass in front of me. The publican presently noticed my activity, and enquired if I did paid work. I answered that I did. He said a friend of his would give anything to have a painting of his daughter; it would mean the world to him. "Then I shall do it, gladly." He told me where the man lived – not many yards away, in Church Close, and asked if he could send him a note. I replied in the affirmative. The Publican left, then turned back to me. "Do not be alarmed by him. He is changed, but he is a good man." Before I could speak further, he had gone about his business.

Breakfast saw a reply begging me to postpone my current plans "as you would value the life and health of your own father". It was signed by one *Maria Lute*. Intrigued by such an entreaty, I immediately sent letters to rearrange my imminent appointments and arrived at the address, to be greeted by a fair to handsome girl of fifteen or so, clearly not a servant though she bade me sit by the fire and thrust a poker at the embers to revive it as if she were one.

I asked what kind of portrait her father envisaged. She did not know. Watercolour or oil? And what size, as that is reflected in the price? She said only "My father wants the best." At that point a tall, stooped man came downstairs, took his coat from the hook, and left.

"Will he not be joining us?" I asked.

"Oh!" She emitted a small bleat of surprise and her back straightened in the chair. "That was the doctor. My father is indisposed."

I could see that I was not going to be terribly successful in extracting more information, so opened my sketch book and box of pencils. "Then shall we start? I can do a quick study. The pose just as you are is delightfully natural. The light from the window gives the quality of a Vermeer…"

Her face fell. Her mouth hung open, then she seemed to comprehend the misunderstanding at once, and with a shuddering intake of breath both laughed and seemed on the edge of tears.

"Mr Heaphy, the portrait is not to be of me. It is to be of my sister Caroline, who died four months ago. On September 13th, to be exact. My father was devotedly attached to her and, cruelly, has no record of her likeness." I quickly learned that it had been his one thought ever since the tragedy, and she hoped, if something of the kind could be done, it would improve his health, which was suffering abominably. Every day the pain of loss grew deeper and she feared that sooner or later he would sink beyond the doctor's reach. "He speaks only of wanting to end his life, so that he can be with her."

Sympathetic though I was, I was also perplexed. "But how can I draw a face I have never seen?"

"You must try."

Maria held back more tears, tilting her head towards her lap, and suddenly that sadness, that expression, made me think of another face I had encountered before.

"Miss Lute. Maria…" I was almost afraid to ask. "How did your sister die?"

I was told she had perished in a train crash, just outside the station at Retford Junction. I cannot describe sufficiently the hollow feeling I felt in the pit of my stomach, yet somehow I retained my capacities enough to show her the sketch in the front of my pad. The one I had made in the railway carriage back in October.

As she shot to her feet, I feared she would faint. I rose to grasp her by the elbow lest she did, but shortly her steadiness was assured and her gaze fixed on the drawing I held out in front of her.

"Let me take it to Papa."

Before long I heard a thin cry from upstairs. When she returned, Lute was on her arm, dishevelled, but glowing. How could this be? he asked. A minute's preparation had been enough for me to provide him a *half*-truth – that I had drawn his daughter months ago, by incredible coincidence, when we happened to be in the same train compartment. I did not say when. I did not say *after her death*. The words refused to come to my lips. Nor did I want them to. I was only happy that what I said placated their mystification.

A painting was commissioned. I executed it in London. Once it was completed, I returned north. Upon seeing it, father and daughter embraced each other tightly. "Uncanny," was the hushed verdict. They had no idea just how *uncanny* the true derivation of the artwork had been. Whilst I was applying the final lacquer, the spindly doctor came again to examine Simeon Lute, and pronounced his health remarkably, and permanently, restored. "Your arrival here was an act of God." How could I say it was not the act of God but the act of another that had guided me?

At the doorstep Maria declared it was all her father wanted; something to remember her by. "Caroline has given him that, through you."

I said: "It was what she wanted, also." But I said no more.

The portrait now hangs in his bedroom, with the following words engraved on a small frame plaque below it: *"C.L. - 13 September 1858, aged twenty-two."*

I returned home from St James's Hall, Piccadilly, feeling desolate, annoyed and foolish for not having anticipated Dickens' reaction. I suppose we hold our heroes in high esteem, so when they disappoint us as people, or treat us with contempt, the hurt is more than a blow one might feel from a mere stranger. But I was no idiot. I knew fame held the upper hand, and what was I? Nothing but a struggling nonentity. I had little hope of taking on the rich and powerful, even though I knew my tale was true. *Absolutely* true. Yet – how could it be? When it had come from Dickens' pen?

Waking with a thick head from wallowing in too many brandies the night before, I decided I had nothing to lose by taking the author's own caustic advice, and posted my manuscript to his business representative, John Forster.

Days passed. I received no reply. I expected to hear nothing, but the reality of doing so poured salt on the wound. To be dismissed was one thing, but to be *ignored?* Too distracted to work, I snapped at Eliza and the children, and the matter tortured me; not least the notion that I might be denied a solution to the confounded puzzle.

Then, one night, the bell rang. The gas lighting of the street gave my visitor's silhouette a halo which I might have rendered on canvas as a yellow line. In shadow, his face possessed an alarmingly grey pallor. My wife had opened the door wordlessly. When he saw the children clustered in night shirts at the foot of the stairs, he said: "I am Ebenezer Scrooge. I have come on the business of ghosts." He smiled broadly as he saw them run away giggling, but his eyes hardened to ice as he looked at me.

Without further introduction Dickens requested privacy. I took him to my studio while Eliza absented herself to the drawing room. I asked if I could take his coat. He did not answer.

"This strangeness. I appreciate…"

He cut me off. "You accuse me of plagiarism."

"That is far from my thoughts. I never said that."

Sitting down at my drawing board, he produced a leather-bound cheque book from his overcoat pocket and laid it flat. I saw the name of Messrs. Coutts & Compy, and his signature already made out with multiple underscores. My name was written in the space between *Pay to* and *or bearer* but the amount on the next line had not been filled in. He snatched a pen from a broken cup and dipped it in the ink pot next to it before looking up at me. "Well?"

I frowned.

"You have a price in mind."

"No."

"What do you make in a year?"

I was affronted. "A gentleman would never ask such a thing."

"I am not a gentleman," Dickens said tensely, rolling the pen in his fingers.

"I am not interested," I said. "Nor, I think, are you."

"You know nothing of me."

"I know what I see."

Which was a man who looked considerably older than his forty-nine years, whose visage was known to every household in the country. And if they could see him now, they would see the same as me – a man afraid.

"Name your price. Please name your price and we shall have done."

"I will not, and you do me a disservice to think otherwise." I snatched the pen from his hand. "The only thing I want from you is the truth, so that I can pack this away in the dusty attic of my mind and forget about it. You think I enjoyed skulking around a theatre backstage waiting to pounce on you?"

"I have no idea what you enjoy. Human beings and their enjoyments are a continent of which exploration has revealed only a mere fraction."

"Very clever. Then let me put it like this. How do

you think two stories written by perfect strangers can be identical?"

"They cannot."

"Do you think I must have read your mind? Read your thoughts before you had them? And then lied that those ideas were my own? The accusation, sir, is yours."

Bristling, Dickens walked away from me. Dickens prowled. Perhaps nobody had rounded on him quite like I had done. But I was at the end of my tether.

"I seek only an explanation," I said.

"And I do not?"

With his back to me he stared at an unfinished portrait of my wife. I could not tell whether he found it of merit or considered it ghastly. I saw only his clasped hands twitching at the small of his back.

He said he had talked to his lawyer and manager. I was uncertain whether he meant one man or two. He admitted he had been riled, horribly. "Inexcusably." Then *gave* an excuse – which was that similar slings and arrows had been outrageously flung in his direction before. "When you are young and published in piffling numbers, nobody says you stole their ideas. Oh no! But as soon as you are rich and reviewed and *fêted*, all manner of snakes crawl from under the rocks with their *Davy Copperheads* or *Olivia Twists!* You take so many to court you begin to wonder, head against your pillow, if you ever had a thought of your own in your entire life. Half the time they want to hang on your shirt tails, the other half you spend as Prometheus on the rock having your liver pecked out. Not a bad theme for a painting, if I may say so."

"It's been done," I said laconically. "Rubens, amongst others."

"I'm sure you could make it your own."

I wasn't sure if he was serious.

Dickens rested himself on the stool I kept for models, a weary lion resigned to lick his wounds. His coat over-spilled onto the paint-stained floorboards, looking like black wax from a night-long candle. Head downturned, his beard was hard to separate from his Elysian beaver collar. With his duck egg blue cravat loosely knotted he retained the semblance, under the air of respectability, of a dissolute fop.

It transpired his lawyer had examined both versions, and had found them "similar, *very* similar... very *extraordinary...*" – even down to the date, the very *date* I had used at the end of my own narrative: *September 13th*.

Dickens had settled into a state of perplexed wonder, and it somewhat perplexed me, as did his gentler, almost fragile, tone of voice. "You see, when I came to revise my *own* story in the proof for the press, the need of a *precise* date was so clear to me, that I inserted in the margin, *September 13th*. The exact same date as mentioned in your account." The wet of his frightened eyes glistened. "How can that be?"

The smell of oils hung unpalatably in the air between us.

"I am profoundly unable to say."

"I mean, could I have heard it from another source? Whom have you told?"

"Not a soul."

"Then have *I* read *your* mind?"

"How is that possible?"

He knew as well as I did that it was not. He prowled some more, picking up my encrusted palette then tossing it down. Lifting my magnifying lens then disregarding it just as sharply.

"I have racked my brains. How I came by it. How it burst the surface. How it flowed from the quill. I remember the delight with which it formed on paper, as it always does. No differently. *No differently*, I say." He peered at me for reassurance, but I could give him none. He saw that and looked away. Moonlight fell on him from the skylight. "It has kept me awake. I sleep like a log. A forest of logs. So what is it? An undesirable bit of beef, a blot of mustard, a crumb of cheese? More of gravy than the grave…?" I recognised the passage he had quoted, but the pun rang a discordant note. More a funeral knell than a chime of Christmas cheer. I knew then that not only did Dickens have no explanation, but this whole affair had shaken him to his core. He was used to being in control at all times, fastidiously so, obsessively so – but this?

He was adamant. "The Portrait Painter's Story came from inside my head – I swear it's the truth."

"And mine no less so."

I slid open the top drawer of my plans chest and took out one of the engravings I had made from the drawing in my sketch book. The cross hatching suited the subject of the young woman in repose in the railway compartment. Eliza always urged me not to limit her to a pencil sketch. I peeled back the covering from the print. Dickens let out a cry. The back of his hand attempted to stifle it.

"Dear Christ. It is the same woman I saw in my mind's eye," he said, hushed, as if confiding the most horrible sin. "She was my clay."

"She is not fiction. She was real."

"Real, but not alive."

The writer turned away, shaking his shaggy locks. Looking for escape but finding none, he had no recourse but to turn back to me. "What conjoins us?"

"Madness? I don't wish to contemplate the fact, but I can think of no other."

"There *must* be other! What is the connection between us? We have never met. No two souls could be more different. But there must be a link. There *must* be!" Dickens twisted his head as my wife entered without a knock, asking if we wished for sustenance of any kind. "Tea. Tea is the refresher, the brandisher of swords, the furnace of the spirit. Tea conquers the waves. Tea, my dear, if you please." He was a gunpowder man. Pearl.

"Brandy. Thank you."

When she had gone – "Dead, you say?"

I nodded.

Dickens gave the thinnest of laughs, almost a shudder. "I have always enjoyed the eerie tale. The spectre in the churchyard. The malign influence of the unquiet spirit. The power of the penny dreadful to mesmerise and instruct... I am not enjoying it now." He stared down at his outstretched, trembling hand. "I am as scared as a child. One of the perils of an active imagination." I admired his honesty. We heard the banging of footsteps in the children's bedroom above our heads. We both looked up. "It is past their bed-time."

"I'm sure they have been told so."

"I could go and tell them a story. They tell me I have a knack for such things."

"You'll scare them to death, or have them in tears."

"No. I only reduce adults to tears. When I want to."

The brandy and tea arrived, and Dickens effusively praised my wife in an attempt to make up for his earlier rudeness. A pattern I imagined not to be a rare one. He then pored over the engraving of Caroline Lute as he sipped, and his mood grew more contemplative, if darker, as the moon drifted behind a cloud.

"My concern is this. She visited you to enable you to give her father a likeness of her... but why did she visit *me?* Am I to be tormented like Scrooge until my tormentor gets their way? Am I to be shown some error of my ways? If so, what is it, in the name of God? What can I put right? What is the spectral message I must hear?"

"I do not know." I sighed. "But there are those who converse with the dead. If—"

"I will not go to those people!" Dickens' face contorted in repulsion. "The spirit racket and their ludicrous shenanigans..."

"Where else can you turn?"

"To you," he said, as if visited by a sudden revelation. "You are a seer. Seeing is your profession, after all. You have proven as much, and you will recognise her if we see her again."

"What?"

Revived with the most explosive animation, he shot to his feet and said we must catch a train. Too late now, clearly. He would not travel back to Gad's Hill, but stay at his residence in London overnight. We would meet at noon. No, a quarter past. No – half past one. We could luncheon together, to discuss plans.

"I was intending to have a haircut."

"Then *unintend* it."

He disappeared in a whirl of overcoat, a sense of excitement having replaced his former dread – or what I took to be dread. I hurried to accompany him to the front door but he was already through it. Needles of sleet glinted in the air. The temperature had dropped radically and I heard my teeth chatter.

"Your babes are a-slumber." He noted the silence as he pulled on his gloves, flexing the fingers. "Do you look in and kiss their warm cheeks while they sleep?"

"Always."

Dickens smiled and shook my hand vigorously, holding my eyes as he did so. "Your ghost is mine."

"And yours mine," I said, long before he let go.

Some persons, attracted by the lowness of the fare, have an inclination to ride third class, destined to pass the next few hours of their existence tightly compressed between two rough specimens of humanity, but for all his public declamations for social justice, these were not the tickets Dickens acquired. He strode ahead. I had difficulty keeping up. We leapt from platform to locomotive – me breathless, he not – embarking from King's Cross (the old Maiden Lane terminal, as was), steaming up the East Coast route to Retford, via Peterborough. My travelling companion wore an Inverness cape and cheviot trousers, and had hardly compressed his gibus and placed it on the luggage rack before a fellow traveller had identified him, quipping an introductory "God bless us, every one!" before affording himself a self-congratulatory chortle. I had already realised from the many stares we had garnered that Dickens was recognised everywhere – such was the unenviable result of a life lived in the public eye – and for his part, played the role of national figure well, returning a smile and cocked eyebrow in good grace. The man, whose tartan waistcoat was in bitter conflict with its buttons, took this as a signal for conversation, and we were soon regaled with every cherubic charm of his offspring, whose Christmas, it need hardly be added, was made whole and wondrous by the author in whose presence he now found himself. The seat was vacant at Stevenage and Dickens remarked that for all the man's feelings for his own brood, his cufflinks alone would have fed a workhouse boy for a month.

The subject was never far from his thoughts. Children, cruelty, the damage created in our formative years. The roads we are set on. People think of his books as full of mudlarks and pickpockets, snuff-sniffers and chirruping old maids, but the blood that pumped in them at their best was his crusading zeal against inequality; against harm. I think that is why he kept moving. If he stayed still he might see in full the real horror around him.

No sooner had we sat than he had his head down, correcting proofs laid out on his lap. Only as an afterthought did he say he had work to do, and would appreciate quiet in as far as such a thing were possible. I said it was. I looked out of the window as we passed a gang of navvies working on a cutting. One waved his cap, revealing a pink scalp above a brown face. Dickens never looked up.

I took out a pencil and the penny farthing notebook I kept in my inside pocket. A poor likeness, but something of the brooding intensity made it from lead to paper. His was a life of the mind, but he was energised by intellectual curiosity. I had seen how his mental train changed tracks when he saw how to tackle our problem. His security was threatened by things he could not understand, and he meant to put that right. As a painter, on the other hand, I was used to living with abstractions.

Retford is not a busy station. Those who disembark there do so to get somewhere else, not to stop there *per se*. We were therefore the exception. Dickens introduced himself to the station master, one Erasmus Egg, a rotund man with mutton chop whiskers, who straightened his spine as if addressing a commanding officer. His wife, a wren in an eye patch who kept the ticket desk spotless with home comforts, sank to a curtsey. Dickens thanked her but he was not the Prince Consort. She tumbled rather than scurried to the samovar, plying us with digestive biscuits, damson jam, scones, Devon cream, and freshly baked muffins.

"We shall starve," I said.

"He jests. Does he jest?"

"He jests, my dear," said the station master.

Given his surname was Egg I could only pray her Christian name was not Henrietta; the reduction of which to its first syllable would have been a rare affliction. If I were to draw her, I thought at the time, I would have only needed circles.

Dickens wasted no time in saying he was there to investigate details of the disaster that had occurred on 13th September '58. The station master shifted his feet and toyed with a frown.

"For a story?"

"For a story, of sorts," Dickens replied, throwing me a slight sideways glance. "The back issue of *The Times* gives scant account of it."

I noticed the man's wife take out a handkerchief and apply it to her face, scuttling away. Egg apprised us that she had been there, in the thick of it. "Being a former nurse, like. Seeing all sorts, like. Didn't like to, you know, remember, like." The man wiped his palms on the hem of his jacket. I don't know why our faces were anathema, but he chose to look anywhere else. "Eat. Eat! She goes to that much trouble. Too much trouble, I tell her. 'Woman,' I say. 'People need feeding,' she says. Look at me!" He patted his waist. We weren't interested, and neither was he.

"Ahem! Ahem!" He plopped into a chair. A drop of sweat congealed on his upper lip as he told us of the day the goods train hopped the rail. How the passenger train was taking the curve, how the impact took the wheels off the metal. How the carriages tipped and rolled. How the engine itself was a topsy-turvy furnace, coughing coke and fireflies. How the bodies were crushed and scattered. Not bodies. Not all. Not whole.

"We did what we could," he breathed.

"I have no doubt of it," said Dickens, placing a hand on his shoulder.

"I have carried the dead and the dying. I have been at their ear when a priest, by right, should have been."

"That they were not alone in their final moments is a testament to you, not an indictment," said Dickens.

"Excuse me. Did you ever see this woman?" I took the engraved print from the back of my sketch book. He blinked and strangely settled into a mode of resignation, nodding.

"I have seen her since."

"*Since?*"

"So have others. Not clearly. Never clearly. But…" He looked back at the print through sad rather than troubled eyes. "Yes. Her. Often at night. Pale… so very pale. They tease the young apprentices about it. They call her The Lady of the Lines."

An unbecoming part of my anatomy prickled.

Dickens took the picture away, in fear it might upset the poor man further. "How did she die?"

The station master shrugged. "Their faces were covered. Did I tell you? It was all we could do to bring them in from the embankment where they were strewn. We pushed back the furniture. Cleared the floor. They were laid out, in rows," he said, gesturing with a feeble hand to the floorboards we stood on. "Here. In the waiting room."

The building having no supply of gas, we were given plentiful candles which we lit and placed upon the table-tops in cups and saucers to light our vigil. I set the filter of the signalling lamp to clear glass – "no danger" – more in vain hope than solid conviction. The night proved foggy and frosty; the windows seemed whitewashed on the outside. Ever restless, Dickens paced past the GNR timetables, back and forth, back and forth. I wondered at times if he sought a misprint or that a wall of type gave him comfort.

"Wainscoting," he said, gazing at the floor then at the ceiling. "Finial… Finial O'Flynn. Phineas Fripp from Frinton-on-Sea. Merchant of alliteration." He walked to the door and back again. "I can't help it. Words buzz around me like flies. I cannot rest till I prise them out of me. Yesterday it was 'irascible'. 'Irascible!'" He adjusted his scarf and his wispy fringe in the mirror. "What a blessing it must be to be simpleminded."

He saw that I was sketching him.

"It pays the bills?"

"I could ask you the same." I smiled.

"Touché," he acknowledged. "Your career, though. I never asked."

No, he hadn't. I told him briefly of my early paintings. Historical. Biblical. That I had learned generally at the knee of my father. That he was an R.A. and expected no less effort than he had applied to his craft. The hours he gave me were hours of failure, by and large. Yet he gave me my trade, whether I wanted it or not.

"Fathers have a lot to answer for." After a few moments he ventured to show another sliver of curiosity. "Your charming wife."

"Eliza."

"And tumbling, tow-headed children. How many?"

"Just the two."

"Tsk! You've barely started. Fill the house with them."

"Our house is full already. With noise, anyway."

"The best noise in the world."

He displayed no obvious sadness on the surface, but I knew, as everyone did from the newspapers, that he was separated from his wife, and though he had custody of his children, under the guardianship of Georgina, their aunt, his eldest had chosen to live with his mother.

"I too have a son named Charlie," I said.

Dickens looked at me with a deeper gratitude than the statement warranted.

"She had become mad, you see. I had no choice. Five hundred pounds a year is no pittance. Did she want my blood? In exchange for what? Her child-bearing years? Was my cheque book not enough?" I thought very probably not. His expression became clouded, perhaps with guilt, perhaps with self-pity. Why he sought to justify himself to me I had no idea. "Her presence had become a distraction. From the work. You see?" I could not say that I did. What work was more important than being a father and husband? But perhaps I thought that because I was incapable of being a Great Man. If so, I was happy with that.

Dickens took out a Dutch pipe and filled it with dark leaf Syrian latakia.

"Thomas…"

"My wife calls me Frank."

"Then Frank it is," he said, striking a match and soon as swathed in smoke as any locomotive. And what followed, to my astonishment, was the approximation of an apology. "You wrote under your own name from your own address. There was no doubt in you being a responsible gentleman; it became my duty to read your communication attentively and without delay. I regret any injustice my suspicious mind and manner may have conveyed."

"We are who we are."

"Indeed." He scanned the room, its mahogany lightened

by flower vases only adding to the impression of a funeral parlour. The grand clock ticked its wagging finger. "As a child my nanny scared me with bugaboo tales. Savages. Torture. Pirates…"

"Like the station master's wife?"

Recalling the eye patch Dickens laughed, expelling a grey, bulbous cloud. "I imbibed *The Terrific Register*, with its catalogue of cannibalism, death, murder, and above all—"

"Ghosts."

"It led, unforgivably – or forgivably – to a hankering for, and interest in, all things supernatural."

"Yet you ridicule the séance room."

He drummed the table top with his knuckles. "Two knocks for yes. Three knocks for no. Five knocks for how's your father. Bark if you recognise Uncle Tom. Where was Moses when the lights went out? Ringing a bell or blowing a horn? Do the clowns not ask for it?"

"The grief-stricken are not clowns."

His pipe stem stabbed at the air between us. "And there you have my repugnance in a nutshell." He leaned back in the upholstered creak of the chair, an ethereal swirl of tobacco rising, enveloping, as he sucked. "But for the strong restraining power of common sense, I might have fallen into a belief in such follies. As it was, the fanciful side of my nature stopped short at such superstitions as luck and fortuitous dreams, and marvels such as coincidence and earthbound spirits." The irony escaped neither of us. "No man was ever readier to apply sharp tests to a story of a ghost or haunted house, even as I demanded absolute credence when I told them."

"A contradiction?"

"Not at all. An author is not bound by legal contract to believe what he writes. We would all be the poorer if he were. Therein lies the task, as I see it. To make the downright impossible feel, if for but a minute, for a page – for a *book* – more real than the world at the reader's elbow."

"So you hold no fear of ghosts?"

"I hold no *fear*—"The great lion, chin on chest, listened to the brittle hush of the stove and considered his response carefully: "Let us say… I prefer my lost souls shackled to the printed page."

"Tonight I don't think we have a choice."

An hour later it was me doing the pacing. I said something about feeling uncomfortable walking over the spot where those who had been killed had been lain out. Without looking up, Dickens said we tread on memories every day. I said, nevertheless, it felt like sacrilege. He asked would it be less so, had we not been told? He recalled he had walked many a church aisle and seldom thought of those buried beneath – though on occasion, as a child, had taken charcoal rubbings of their names and dates. His first gateways to other lives. Lives imagined. "Their secrets and injustices, their hopes and prayers. A mother and son. A man and wife. I'd pick up my copy book and put flesh on the bones."

I stared at the mopped and bleached floorboards. I felt my skin was bleached too. I scratched my cheek, continuing my perambulations.

The clock struck twelve.

I spotted a pack of cards, either provided for the entertainment of journeyers whiling their time at this inauspicious interchange, or else left behind by one of the aforementioned themselves.

I sat, shuffled, and dealt for a game of Beat the Knave Out o' Doors, the only card game that Pip knew how to play in *Great Expectations*, Dickens' big success of the summer just past. Eliza had consumed it voraciously. I enjoyed more seeing the delight in her face as she turned each page.

"We crave them," he mused. "They appear. Why do they appear? Is it their longing, or ours?

"The public itch to be spooked, and you oblige them. Does that make you better than a medium? You take money for your ghosts too."

"I never espouse that they are real."

"And now?"

"Now is the perfect end to a chapter," he said.

"If only. But here we sit. The chapter is not over. Nor the tale."

I shuffled the cards again and dealt a second time.

The windows grew more densely opaque. As natural darkness, at close of day, bathes the earth in an ever deeper black, so, in a peculiar and unsettling manner, an ever thickening *whiteness* seemed to surround us that night.

Strip Jack Naked is not a game of tremendous skill. Even so, Dickens' mind was not on it. Distracted, and now bored, he scraped at the embers in his pipe with a sterling silver cleaner, but they would not relight. The shoulders sagged, weighty with yesteryear. The pipe hung from the hand, which hung from his knee.

"I once attended a séance in Berkeley Square. The lamp was turned low and I heard a female voice. I recognised my sweet, dead sister – Fanny. Dear Fan…" An unmistakable scar of memory flickered across the writer's features, tempered by a feather-touch of joy. "It was even a song she sang. The dark was never so filled with prettiness, nor my eyes so gushing in thanks. Then a sergeant's hand shot out and grabbed the wrist of a whippersnapper cursing to the four winds. The gas came up on the most dissolute exposure. A boy in silk, his wig half off. A rapping machine attached to the underside of the table. Cheesecloth hidden in orifices it does not care to specify." He placed the Dutch pipe next to the signalling lantern and picked strands of leaf from his fingers. "I was enraged. I so *wanted* it, you see. And there they have you. The hook of the *want*. Not even the strongest pike can escape it."

"But is there more than this?" By which I meant the material world around us. "Surely a perfectly legitimate question?"

"Not if answered by tricksters and criminals."

"One of my greatest joys is painting the impression of

light. Sometimes I think to myself, we are the paint, but we are not the light. We are simply the rendering."

Dickens said nothing. At least he did not grunt, though I am not saying he wasn't tempted. I took the print from the back of my sketch book, and placed it on the table between us.

"She needed your artist's eye. Our unwanted muse. If anyone can answer our questions, it is she."

"Will it bring her?"

"I have no idea," he said.

"Shall we join hands?"

"I think not."

Mine were in prayer and I blew into them. They had become icy, wrapped up though we were. I had trod on the Cairngorms in the thick of winter and the weather had been more temperate. I dug in my pocket and took out a hip flask. The malt would warm us at least. Dickens partook of it eagerly. It robbed him of breath. He said, not inaccurately, it had "more of the thistle than the heather."

A minute later his thoughts turned back to matters ghostly.

"Once a spiritualist said my creative talent was akin to psychic ability, if I but knew it." He laughed, loudly and scornfully. "They'd love to get me in their tribe!"

"Perhaps that is not as ludicrous as it sounds." I upended the hip flask and took a second mouthful, which burned my gums but sharpened my brain. "You said yourself how the image of her burst the surface unbidden. How it flowed onto the page with you as its… well, yes – *medium*. What if you were to put yourself into the same enraptured, *entranced* state you experience when writing?"

"Will it help us see her?"

"It helped you see her before."

He could not deny that was a fact. He reached out to me – I thought, ridiculously, for my hand, but in fact it was for the hip flask. Pattison's Morning Dew did its job. The Scotch hit the back of his throat.

"*Talitha cumi*," he whispered. "Quickly—" Though why *quickly* I do not know; the dead, in as far as I know, do not keep a strict timetable of appearances.

He bade me fetch the blackboard hung near the door to the platform, used by the station master to habitually scrawl messages such as the one it still displayed: YORK TRAIN DELAYED: COW ON TRACKS. At his instruction, I laid it across his lap like a breakfast tray, resting it on the arms of the chair. I understood then what he was doing; we had to recreate the circumstances of his daily occupation. It was a substitute for his writing desk.

He opened his carpet bag and extracted a travelling ink set, which included a Bohemian threaded glass ink well in a leather case with rounded edges, and a three-section mother of pearl dipping pen with four nibs. These he assembled and arranged with the precision of a surgeon, though he said it was sorely inadequate to reproduce his writing habits with precise exactitude; his usual paper was not to hand, nor his goose quill, nor the surrounding beds and sofas – which had to be all placed in every detail according to the author's meticulous eye. The sturdy iron stove was poor imitation of his home fire back in Kent, but still – as he rolled back his shirt cuffs and unscrewed a bottle of Blackwood & Co. writing fluid – it would have to do.

For some reason I was minded to turn the filter in the signalling lantern to red; something to do with mediums operating all the better in dim light. I had done it before I questioned it, and by the time I had, my companion's nib was hovering over the blank sheet I'd torn from my sketch pad and placed on what amounted to his makeshift drawing board, next to the print of the young woman from the railway carriage.

"Caroline… sweet child," said he, scribbling down her name then shutting his eyes. "Caroline *Lute*. The most plaintive of instruments. Such beauty. Such sorrow. May we hear your music this night, Miss Lute?"

I said nothing as he took several very deep breaths, holding them on the intake.

The pen did not lift from the paper, but remained held there, making only the most miniscule movements – a tiny scratch here, a twitch there, the angle of its mast adjusting – as if waiting to be compelled to do so.

"You are a mystery. And every writer has to know the answer to the mystery before he begins." Dickens took two more breaths, deeper than the first. The red light shone like blood on one side of his face. His eyebrows arched. His thinking almost visible… "What were you doing on the train, my dear? Why were you alone? A young lady travelling with no husband, no chaperone? Where were you going – and why? That is your story. What were you fleeing from… or to?" He tilted his head, waiting for the reply to come on the metaphorical or actual ether. As perhaps he did when composing his characters. "Had you loved? Or been loved?"

Answer came there none.

I could not see how there could, but in another way I prayed that we would get… something. That tiny movement of her head as she left the train came back to me.

We shall meet again.

I thought then: *How? How can we? How are such things possible?*

I was terrified I would soon find out.

Meanwhile Dickens listened to the silence. I saw no fragment of impatience in his face. He had sunk into another realm; I think even become another Dickens. The bodily one had left him. The pen-smith was all, now.

"Why would a woman travel alone?" His frown disappeared. "Ah, but you were not alone. There was another with you." A smile slowly came to his lips. "That's it. I see it now. My friend told me how you kept your fur on your lap. How you were covered in layers. Was it to prevent a lump being noticed? The life you carried inside? Ah, yes! *Yes!* He said you wore no wedding ring. Of course! You are on your way to tell the baby's father. He doesn't know yet, does he, on that September 13th? The man who might embrace you and marry you or refuse to even see you? *No!* A man who has a wife and children already. Is that it? A man of whom your father would never approve. A man about whom you can never tell him. And so you sit on the train, facing a future that terrifies you – that you hardly know how to face. The loss of your family, the loss of your reputation, the shame, the rejection, and then—*THEN—*"

Dickens turned to stone, his limbs stiffening.

I took away the board and placed it on the floor, half on top of his bag.

His hand did not falter. It held the pen in mid-air.

"Go on. Go on."

I watched as a ghastly pallor drained his features. His breath quickened with alarm and he convulsed, no less than if he were being stabbed by unseen spears.

He suddenly stood up, poker-straight, eyes remaining shut – but now as if he was willing them to fight against their natural instinct to spring open.

"Did you not hear it? The piercing shriek of the wheels torn from the rail! The awful silence before the endless thrashing of mangled metal! Then, dear Lord above, the sickening hissing of the slaughtered engine, the roar reduced not even to a purr… and *now,* like the most base insult to humanity, rising, there come the cries – not *screams,* but more pitiable *by far* than that – the *moans,* the powerless wails of unimaginable pain. Guttural calls in the dark of night to their invisible Maker. Isolated voices as stars in the heavens… each one pleading from throats clogged with blood for help as shallow life ebbs away – Do you hear them? *Do you hear them now?*" Dickens dropped the pen and reached out with both hands to find my lapels. "Tell me you do! *In the name of God, tell me you do!*"

"I hear nothing. There is nothing!"

Terrified by the look on his face, I shook him hard, but he would not wake, which terrified me all the more.

He rocked, as I have only seen Quakers do when the spirit moves them.

Still with his eyes closed, he said: "I see her!"

Only then did he open them.

"I see her!" he said again, unblinking – his gaze fixed at something over my left shoulder.

I turned, bending to lift the signal man's lamp from the table as I did so, though what I saw did not require the light to fall upon it. In fact, no light did. It was content in its own shadowy reality, untouched, and could not be touched any more than the figure in a Daguerrotype could be – even by light. The most fundamental component of the physical, and so beloved of my art school tutors – *light and shade.*

Framed by the glazed double-doors behind her, with the roiling mist beyond, she stood, looking exactly as she had done when I first saw her in the railway compartment. The same furs, dress, ankle-length coat. The button-up shoes buffed to a shine. The hat with a veil – which, as she had before, she lifted away from her pale countenance with coy but exquisite reluctance. This time, however, I read in her troubled, downcast eyes the narrative that Dickens had intuited. She smiled only, I felt, to remind me of her unearthly promise.

We shall meet again.

It had been amusing, odd, strange – but now was fulfilled. I felt a blockage in my throat.

She looked down at the rabbit-skin muff she held against her stomach. I saw now that it was not a muff at all but rather a swaddling blanket, and that nestling within it slept a newborn babe.

A sharp bang made me turn away. The Dutch pipe had rolled off the table and lay on the floor. The tiny embers it spilled glowed brightly then faded almost at once. I looked up into Dickens' face and beheld a man in the grip of shock.

I looked back at the phantom.

The woman said with unparalleled sorrow: "Could you not touch me, Papa?"

Now it was the sound of a sob that made me turn. I could not believe that it had come from Dickens, but it had. I do not think his critics often thought him either mute or powerless but those two qualities overwhelmed him then. For the first time I saw in him the boy in the boot blacking factory. Hopeless, frightened, small.

Withered, he walked – no, staggered – past me, like a man in a dream.

The young woman's smile did not waver as he neared her. She merely looked down gently as Dickens placed his hand on the baby's head, the great meat of life on a perfect, pink skull that had seen none of it. He leaned over and kissed the child's forehead.

Behind me the door to the platform sprang open as some devilish behemoth howled and my blood turned to ice. Smoke or steam or mist rolled in as a locomotive clattered through the station at high speed without stopping, its horn blaring. The sudden displacement of air must have nudged the door off its latch. The draught caught the angled board upon which Dickens had been writing, and his ink well slid off it onto the floorboards, making a puddle which resembled a splash of blood.

I quickly looked back.

Dickens had turned towards the sound, sallow eyed, and towards me. The cold air from the door raked through his stray locks.

The figures of the young woman and the child were both gone. So too, in the next instant, was the rattling of the milk train, leaving us nothing but its whirling, slicing echo, and thereafter only a welcome but all-consuming quietude.

The large clock mounted on the wall showed half past five. My pocket watch was slow, or it was fast. Not that it mattered. I turned the signalling lamp to "clear" and turned up the wick. The stain on the floor looked a lot less like blood when it was seen to be blue. I picked up the mother of pearl pen, dismantled it and packed it away in the travelling case.

Dickens sat with his elbows on his knees, a lifeless effigy after Guy Fawkes Night, shoulders hunched, head slumped, uncharacteristically void of conversation, or even action. Little as I knew him, he worried me in such a state. With few weapons in my arsenal, I offered the hip flask again.

He waved it away with a flicker of disdain.

"The travel clock shows half past nine," I said, holding said object, for the sake of something to say. "The time of the crash was half past nine. Maria Lute told me. I didn't put in it my account. You said it kept good time."

Dickens did not answer. Nor did he look at me.

"You do not beckon love," he said, apropos of nothing. "Love beckons you. It seizes your heart, or grows there. There can be no will to resist it. It is a truth that can only be denied, and to deny it is a betrayal of our nature." He now seemed to want to shrink away from me. "She was an actress. Is no longer. We had to be discreet, you see. Of necessity. I was a married man. I had a reputation. Children. Many who would by hurt by the knowledge of such a person… such a thing. It could not be seen, but it had to continue. We could not resist the pull of it."

"Sir—"

I did not want to hear what was clearly agonizing to get out, but his eyes narrowed and his firmness told me he wanted his say.

"It died, you see. That child. On that summer's eve. Two days it lived and breathed. I tell you, more did it suffer in those forty-eight hours on earth than in my forty-nine years. And when it lay in its cot, cold and still… I could not touch it." Now – *now* he looked at me. "Not a living soul could know such a thing. None but a dead one." His voice quivered. His lip twisted. "That is why those charlatans who pretend they can…"

I could say nothing.

"Perhaps we should have gone to one," he continued. "She wanted to. I said no. 'Death is death, the child is gone. It is not to be endured. *Life* is to be endured.' She said: 'You pretend he was nothing, but he was our son.'" Here he broke, and his body shook with the pain he had held inside for so long. "Why could I not touch him? *Why could I not?* And why do we need the dead to instruct us?"

I did not know.

I did not know the answer to any of it. Just as I could not know the extent of his shame or his guilt. All I did know, now, was that the ghost had visited Dickens, as it had visited me, for a reason. And though I saw tears rolling down his cheeks and falling onto those floorboards where the dead had been given their last resting place, I somehow knew a weight had been lifted. A great weight, lifted by something as unsubstantial as a feather, a quill, as air, as a memory, as a prayer.

The mist lifted and the day arrived like scenery sailed in from the wings. Dickens was revived in spirit, or seemed to be. We had not slept, but soon after dawn had taken ourselves for breakfast at the Swan Hotel. It was no time to regale Dickens with my misgivings about provincial fare and, in fairness, the cooking did not poison us. He indulged in more boiled eggs than seemed wise for the human constitution and I hoped he had taken into account the probable effects of a long journey on his digestive tract. For one in a sedentary profession, he devoured food in a way that made me wonder why he didn't have a belly the size of Mr Pickwick, but I think his energy burned it away with the ferocity of a forest fire.

We reached the station to find Mr and Mrs Egg in their allotted roles. Too many *eggs* for one morning, I thought to myself. The samovar bubbled. We partook of more tea. There was always space for more tea; we were

Englishmen, after all. The station master asked if anything had happened during the night. "Anything – *ghostly*, like."
Before I could answer, Dickens, lifting his carpet bag, said that there had not.

"Well. Oh, well. We shall keep you posted if we see the lassie again."

"Do. If you address your envelope to *Dickens, London* it usually gets to me. Thank you for the candles. And thank you for the tea. Both were efficacious."

The two of us made our way to the platform to await the train from York to London. I couldn't help considering what the events that had occurred might mean to my companion in the future. "A woman on a train, travelling alone to tell the father of her child that she is expecting. That's a story for you."

"No, that's *her* story," Dickens said, tugging on his gloves. "It is enough that we know it. Perhaps, with God's blessing, that will be her release." He craned forward, staring towards the end of the track, the better to spot our train approaching. Perhaps he was eager to rejoin the metropolitan throng. I could not read his thoughts. Such territory belonged to mystics and clairvoyants. Though it was a territory we had ventured into ourselves, if only for a passing overnight visit. I should not wish to live there.

"The public do not need to know the mistakes and wounds of fallible men," he said without meeting my eyes. "Enough for them to enjoy from me a tall tale or two."

I understood he wanted me to keep his secret. Of the mistress. Of their love. Of the child they had lost. And I would. Until now, when all those who might have been hurt by it are gone, and can be hurt no more.

Before long we were joined by others, the platform filling with a steady stream of passengers, all with their little voyages to make, be it the trudge to factory or office, a visit to an ailing relative or needy child. All had their stories. All stood preoccupied with them, oblivious to the invisible world around them, a world beyond the foibles and unfairnesses of Man, where spirits remind us of our flaws or ask our help even as they plague and terrify us. Perhaps we deserve no less. I was made no happier by having those thoughts in my mind, and envied those who didn't. I want to paint every glorious, ignorant one of them.

Once we had found our compartment, Dickens immersed himself in his papers, dragging the page proofs onto his knees once more, head down, blind to my presence as I knew he would be.

At one point, though, he looked up, after a few moments of thought, and said: "The ghost has done her duty."

"She has."

"I think she is at peace now."

"I think so too," I said.

I was tempted to draw him, and if I had, I think I would have drawn a different Dickens on my return journey than I had on the way up. I chose not to, and instead closed my eyes and let sleep's balm engulf me. It was sorely needed and my lids were heavy. But with slumber came a picture in my mind's eye. That of Dickens, kneeling to place flowers on a tiny, unmarked grave. It brought to mind an inscription on a headstone I had once seen when flitting through a churchyard as a boy: THOSE WHO HAVE BEEN LOVED, THEY SHALL NOT DIE.

Those who have been loved, they shall not die.

I opened my eyes, looked at Dickens and smiled.

"Go back to sleep," he said. "I'm working."

Afterword

Incredibly, "The Waiting Room" was inspired by a true ghost story involving Charles Dickens. His tale "A Portrait Painter's Story" first appeared in a journal he edited, All the Year Round, *in September 1861. Immediately after publication, Thomas Frank Heaphy, an artist, wrote to the author claiming that the protagonist, who encountered a ghostly woman on a train had been, in fact, himself. Furthermore, he could prove it, because he had sent an exact account of his preternatural experience to a rival magazine.*

Dickens was shocked by the bizarre coincidence. He called the episode "so very original, so very extraordinary, so very far beyond the version I have published that all stories turn pale before it." In the absence of any rational explanation, the two men eventually reached an agreement; Heaphy's MS appeared in the October issue of Dickens' All the Year Round. *It was later reprinted, alongside the correspondence between painter and author, as "A Wonderful Ghost Story Being Mr H's Own Narrative" (price one shilling).*

Four years later, in 1865, Dickens was involved in the Staplehurst train crash, during which several carriages plummeted into the Beult River. Many say it was the inspiration for his story "The Signal Man" – one of the most revered ghost stories in the English language. Five years after it, Dickens himself was dead, and his son said in his eulogy that his father had never fully recovered from the trauma of the accident. So perhaps the cries he heard in the waiting room at Retford Junction were not an echo of the past – but of the future? An ill portent of Tragedy Yet To Come?

One thing is true. That the events surrounding "A Portrait Painter's Story" did nothing to diminish Victorian England's most celebrated wordsmith's interest in the supernatural. A year later, The Ghost Club was founded in London, and Dickens became one of its most pre-eminent and active members.

SV
Christmas Eve, 2020

Brian Evenson
www.brianevenson.com

Helen Grant
www. helengrantbooks.com

Muriel Gray
www.twitter.com/artybagger

Sean Hogan
www. seanhoganstuff.wordpress.com

Andrew Hook
www. andrew-hook.com

Sarah Lotz
www.sarahlotz.com

Lucie McKnight Hardy
www. lmcknighthardy.com

Teika Marija Smits
www. teikamarijasmits.com

Lisa Tuttle
www. facebook.com/lisatuttlewriter

Stephen Volk
www. stephenvolk.net

www.blackshuckbooks.co.uk

Also available:

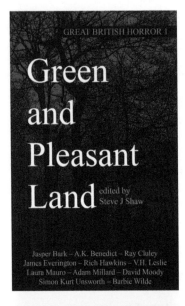

GREAT BRITISH HORROR 1:
GREEN AND PLEASANT LAND

FEATURING STORIES BY

JASPER BARK

A.K. BENEDICT

RAY CLULEY

JAMES EVERINGTON

RICH HAWKINS

V.H. LESLIE

LAURA MAURO

ADAM MILLARD

DAVID MOODY

SIMON KURT UNSWORTH

BARBIE WILDE

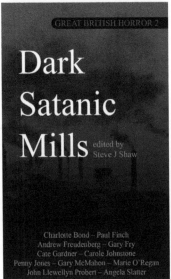

GREAT BRITISH HORROR 2:
DARK SATANIC MILLS

FEATURING STORIES BY

CHARLOTTE BOND

PAUL FINCH

ANDREW FREUDENBERG

GARY FRY

CATE GARDNER

CAROLE JOHNSTONE

PENNY JONES

GARY McMAHON

MARIE O'REGAN

JOHN LLEWELLYN PROBERT

ANGELA SLATTER

Also available:

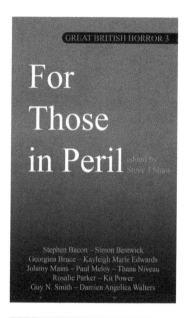

**GREAT BRITISH HORROR 3:
FOR THOSE IN PERIL**

FEATURING STORIES BY

STEPHEN BACON
SIMON BESTWICK
GEORGINA BRUCE
KAYLEIGH MARIE EDWARDS
JOHNNY MAINS
PAUL MELOY
THANA NIVEAU
ROSALIE PARKER
KIT POWER
GUY N. SMITH
DAMIEN ANGELICA WALTERS

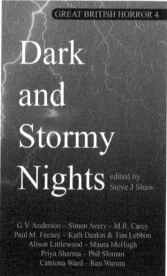

**GREAT BRITISH HORROR 4:
DARK AND STORMY NIGHTS**

FEATURING STORIES BY

G.V. ANDERSON
SIMON AVERY
M.R. CAREY
PUAL M. FEENEY
KATH DEAKIN & TIM LEBBON
ALISON LITTLEWOOD
MAURA MCHUGH
PRIYA SHARMA
PHIL SLOMAN
CATRIONA WARD
REN WAROM

Also available:

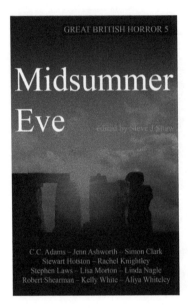

GREAT BRITISH HORROR 5:
MIDSUMMER EVE

FEATURING STORIES BY

C.C. ADAMS

JENN ASHWORTH

SIMON CLARK

STEWART HOTSTON

RACHEL KNIGHTLEY

STEPHEN LAWS

LISA MORTON

LINDA NAGLE

ROBERT SHEARMAN

KELLY WHITE

ALIYA WHITELEY

Lightning Source UK Ltd.
Milton Keynes UK
UKHW011259120921
390444UK00001B/25